THE

# *Brain*

STARLING KEY BOOK 1

# JANUARY JAMES

*For Sarah.*
*Because if 40 years of friendship doesn't get you a dedication*
*in a book, I don't know what does.*

# PROLOGUE

awny

I COULD HARDLY SEE the nurse through the thick veil of shock. It seemed to shroud everything in sight.

"I'm sorry, how is that possible?" I said, my voice sounding so far away it could have been in the next county.

She took my small, sixteen-year-old hands into her own warm, plump ones and squeezed them lightly.

"It's just something that happens to some people," she said. "Proteins attack the nerve cells, and it creates a kind of debris that spreads and damages the brain. It usually happens to people when they're much older. But sometimes, for a very unlucky few, it sets in at a younger age." She waited while I pretended to process what she'd just said. Then she seemed to realize I hadn't understood a word. I'd hardly even heard her.

"You know what? There's still so much we don't know about Alzheimer's, especially when it sets in this early. Do you know what I think? I think that when your daddy died of a heart attack two years ago, your mom's heart broke so deep, part of her brain shut down so that she wouldn't remember. It's protecting her."

"Protecting her from what?"

"From the pain of carrying on without your father."

"But, what about me? How am I supposed to carry on?"

She gripped my fingers tighter. "Our bodies work in strange ways," she said, kindly. "They will do things to stop us from hurting, without realizing it's hurting other parts of itself or other people."

"How quickly will it happen?" My voice had become a whisper, acknowledging the inevitable.

It had crept up on us—Mom's forgetfulness. At first, it would only be the day of the week she forgot, which I guessed was quite normal for anyone as busy as she was. But then I noticed she was asking me the same questions over and over, even though I know she heard my replies. It wasn't long after that she lost her job. It was just a part time gig helping out at the local wildlife center but she loved it there. Mom wouldn't tell me what had happened so I called Bob, the general manager. He told me he'd given Mom repeated warnings because she'd been misplacing medicines, feeding animals the wrong foods, leaving cage doors open. Then one day, Mom forgot which pen she'd taken a Cottontail rabbit out of, and accidentally put it in with the coyotes. It didn't end well. Mom couldn't give Bob any explanation other than she just couldn't remember doing any of those things, so he had no choice but to let her go.

The nurse closed her eyes and slowly opened them again, her expression almost as sad as I felt. "She's at stage four right now, so her symptoms are moderate. When she reaches the next stage, the decline can happen quite quickly."

"How many stages are there?"

"Seven. Stage seven is when she may no longer be able to walk or communicate. It's the last stage of the disease."

My head started to throb.

"It takes about five to six years to reach that stage," she added. "But it really depends on the individual."

Five or six years? I felt a sudden rush of gratitude. I wasn't going to lose her for a while yet. But before I could feel too optimistic, the nurse spoke again.

"But honey, don't imagine she's going to be like the mom you have now," she warned. "It won't be long before she has trouble remembering where she is and who people are, including you. She'll need help to get dressed, go to the toilet, clean up after herself." She sighed, as though the words were weighing her down. "I want you to know what to expect. It's only fair, so you can be prepared. But you don't have to take this on alone. There are places she can go to stay, people who can help…"

"I'm not interested," I said, firmly. "She's my mom. She's staying at home, and I'm staying with her. I'll look after her." Even as I said the words, I knew it was going to be the hardest thing I'd ever do, but I couldn't consider any other option. She was my mom.

The nurse smiled, sympathetically. "You will need to think about getting help at some point. You can't miss school. You have your own life and your own future to think about."

"I can go to school any time," I said, hearing the conviction loud and clear in my voice. "But I won't always have my mom."

———

I CAN STILL SEE the nurse's expression as I turn off the highway onto the ramp. I wish I couldn't. I want to take in the view instead—the golden sands of Starling Key, the place I'm to make my home for at least the next few months. But I can't, because all I can see is the nurse's face. A large tear escapes her eye and rolls down her cheek, then I feel dampness on my face and realize the tear came from my own eye.

"Tawny! Look out!" Millie's shriek yanks me back to the present moment. My eyes suddenly focus on a raccoon ambling across the ramp right in front of me. I'm driving too fast to stop before I reach it, so I pull the wheel over to the right, missing the animal by a whisker.

"Tawny!"

Now I'm barreling towards the opposite side of the ramp, so I drag the wheel back to the left and am immediately stunned to see a giant wall coming at us at forty miles per hour. I slam my foot on the brakes and we slow a little but it makes zero difference. I reach out and grab Millie's hand, then I close my eyes and wait for the screeching wail of crunching metal, as we slide straight on into the bricks.

# CHAPTER ONE

THE FIRST TIME I see Connor Johnson is not the only time he turns his back to me and growls expletives under his breath, but it is the only time I deserve it.

"Tawny, are you listening?"

"Yes, Aunt Millie," I reply. "I'm listening."

I'm not though; every single one of my senses is trained on the man crouched on the dusty ground about ten feet away. He has his back to me, having just made it clear in no uncertain terms, I am not welcome at Starling Key—as an employee or otherwise.

I can't drag my eyes away. He's bare from the waist up, his back thick with muscle that moves beneath his skin, and glistening with pearls of sweat. A prey bird is tattooed across it, from one shoulder blade to the other, it's back and tail reaching down his spine. Every time he moves, the bird looks as though it's taking flight.

I was surprised when I first saw the tattoo; he didn't strike me as being that sort of guy. When he first approached, he was wearing a smart shirt and immaculate dark jeans—he looked almost clean cut. Only his narrowed eyes, deep angry frown and clenched jaw suggested he was the head of Starling Key Security, and the man I'd just made an enemy out of by driving my car head on into the perimeter wall. That's the reason for the rippling muscles. Having flung his shirt to the ground with gritted teeth, he is now rebuilding the wall, brick by brick, in the blistering Florida heat, by hand, because of me.

My punishment is being made to stand and watch as he does so, because he apparently has the key to my new digs and he isn't giving it to me until he's fixed the damage I've caused. And it's punishment indeed. I'm melting, and not just because of the sun.

"Don't even think about driving that thing until it's fixed, do you understand?" Millie says.

"It ain't going anywhere," I assure her, admiring the skyward angle of the hood and the partially crushed engine beneath. I've never crashed a car before in my life, and I'd managed to drive me and Millie all the way to the Florida Keys from New Jersey without getting so much as a scratch. Then, right as we arrive, I try to save a damn racoon crossing the ramp and… BAM. I'm stuck on an island I didn't particularly want to come to, and now I have no way of getting back off.

"You're not listening to me," she says, and I feel two hands spin me around. "We can't take this to just any old mechanic, ok? I'm not made of money. I've found one cheap, who can get here tomorrow. He'll tow it and bring it back when it's fixed. You'll just have to stay on the resort 'til then."

"Great," I mutter, although I don't expect to go anywhere else anyway; I'm due to start work here in the morning, providing I don't melt completely before then.

I wipe away the sweat that has started to seep into my eyes, and turn to sneak another glance at the 'back'. Just as my head turns, so does his, and our eyes meet. He is still clearly unhappy about the damage I've caused, but that doesn't stop my chest thumping. Perhaps it's the fact I haven't been within arm's reach of a boy since I dropped out of high school, but something inside me is flapping about like a butterfly on steroids. I now know what people mean when they say that something—or someone—takes their breath away. All it took was one timid and guilty glance at his perfectly chiseled, clean-shaven face, crowned with the silkiest mop of dirty blonde hair, and I can honestly say I forgot how to breathe. Like, I really had to give it some thought.

He is beautiful—movie star beautiful—and equally as intimidating. Ok, so I've become a little institutionalized, having spent most of the last six years in a small house in the company of one adult woman—my mom—who most of the time didn't know me from Adam. I've almost forgotten how to be around people. So, the reason for my strong chemical reaction to this man could simply boil down to culture shock. My world has been pretty small up to now. Maybe it's not that uncommon for grown men to be so jaw-droppingly gorgeous. I mean, even through the angry squint, his eyes are striking. A little blue peeking through long, dark blonde lashes, peppered with dust from the bricks. They zero in on me like lasers, reiterating his annoyance with one glance. Then they are gone.

It was Millie who arranged my move to Starling Key. I suppose, in theory, it's for the best. I lost all my friends when

I dropped out of school and there's no Mom keeping me in Monmouth County anymore, so why not come and live somewhere sunny for a while? The owner himself was apparently keen to have someone like me join the resort staff. The fact I'd been a full-time caregiver since the age of sixteen meant I might be good with people—specifically, the kind of rich and famous people that supposedly visit this island.

A little part of me is excited by the prospect of spending a season in the Florida Keys. I've read Hemingway, I adore F Scott Fitzgerald, I've watched Bloodline... but from what I've seen of the island so far—a great expanse of green which I assume is the famous golf course, and the unending stretch of pale blue ocean reaching up to the horizon—none of it prepared me for the physical reality of this paradise.

My thoughts are broken by the sound of a truck circling to a stop at the other side of the gate. Heavy feet land on the gravel drive and seconds later, two men appear. Again, I have to think twice about the mechanics of my lungs. If I thought blonde guy was well-built, I hadn't seen anything yet. The two new guys are built like the truck they just got out of and, although for different reasons, they are just as handsome as the guy my chest is flip-flopping over. The slightly taller one has long, wavy hair to his shoulders. At one point it would have been chestnut, but I'm guessing with the extremity of this heat, the sun has bleached it somewhat, and now he has highlights a woman would pay good money for. He also has week-old stubble around his jaw and *the* most ridiculously long eyelashes, which are hard to look away from.

The first thing I notice about the other guy is how pristine he looks. They're both wearing the same scuffed combat shorts and black t-shirt with an SKS logo on it, but where long-haired guy looks like he just rolled off a dumpster, the other guy looks almost smart enough to work in an office. His jet black hair is close cut and even his facial features seem neat and tidy—no rebelliously long eyelashes that I can see. But he's just as good-looking.

"Hey, boss, why didn't you call me? We can do this," says the long-haired one.

"I got it," the blonde guy hisses at him before dragging an arm across his forehead. He flicks his eyes towards me. So, he doesn't need to do this—there are obviously others around who can rebuild a wall. He just wants to make me feel guilty for putting a Chevy-sized dent in his day.

The two new arrivals follow his gaze and they both size me up. The shorter haired one grins at me, then promptly whips out his phone, unmoved by the scene. Maybe clumsy and inept girls like me are constantly driving into the perimeter wall. The other one eyes me suspiciously. Even though he turns his head away, his eyes remain glued to me until the last second, then they flick back to Boss Guy who is dropping the final layer of bricks into place.

"Where's she staying?" Long Hair says to Boss Guy.

"Don't worry about it. I'll take her," he replies, bashing the last brick into place with his fist.

"You sure? I know how busy you are."

"I'm sure."

Long Hair looks back at me again, this time with something resembling sympathy, then turns his attention back to Boss Guy. "You still coming to the bar tonight?"

"No man, I'm not in the mood." Another fling of the daggers in my direction. "And I've got a lot of paperwork to catch up on."

"Anything we can help with?" asks Short Hair.

Boss Guy sticks his hands in his jeans and eyes them both.

"Sure. Isaac, can you send me the latest update on the

casino build? Starling needs an update first thing and I know he's keen to see where the restaurant is going to be situated." He jerks his head towards my truck. "Carter, can you deal with this heap of scrap? Knowing my luck today, if I attempt to move it, every single fucking panel will fall off."

"A mechanic is on his way," Millie butts in.

"Great." Boss Guy says, unsmiling, then to Long Hair—Carter: "Just stick it behind the wall."

"No problem. Sounds like you're having a tough day, huh?" Carter asks.

"Wasn't so bad 'til an hour ago." He gives me another venomous glance. "I *was* on track."

Carter nods, knowingly. "Well, shit happens. You can't control everything; I keep telling you."

"I need the keys to 8A," Boss Guy says, ignoring Carter's last point. "Is Maggie in the hole?"

I silently wonder who this poor Maggie is, and who on earth would put her in a hole.

"Yeah, I just passed her," Isaac replies. "We've got two more newbies coming this afternoon; she'll be there a while. Told me to go grab her some conch fritters from Arnauld. I told her to take a hike."

Carter snorts. "That's mean, bro'."

"Hey, I'm doing her a favor. She's on a goddamn diet; won't shut up about it. The woman's boredom-eating."

"You know she'll just have got someone else to get them for her," Carter says.

"I don't care. At least I won't be responsible for those extra pounds."

"You're just a lazy fucker," Boss Guy adds. "Go get me those plans."

"Sure Connor. See you later," Isaac flicks two fingers

from his head in a mock salute and turns to head back down the drive.

Connor. Nice name. Not befitting of those poisonous stares. At all.

"Can I get a ride back to Miami?" Millie asks, making me jump; I'd almost forgotten she was there.

"A ride?" Connor turns to her, his eyes the widest I've seen them, which still isn't particularly wide. It's like he was born with a glare. "Are you serious? It's an eight hour round trip."

"It was agreed with Mr. Starling," she replies.

"Right. In that case, of course. I'll see who's headed out that way," Connor sighs heavily. If sighs could talk, that one would have said, 'You're dropping Charlie fucking Chaplin on my doorstep; you can damn well get yourself back to Miami.'

"I'll go check," Carter says and I look over to where he's now standing—on the other side of the gate with my car behind him. How the hell has he moved it without even making so much as a grunt?

"Thanks, man."

"Thank you, sir," Millie replies. "I'll wait. We can say our goodbyes here."

"Sure," Connor says, walking through the gate, presumably to give me and Aunt Millie some privacy.

"How are you doing, kiddo?"

I feel tears start to prick at my eyes. I knew this moment would come eventually and I hadn't dared think about it. Maybe if I had, I'd be better prepared. This is it. I'm saying goodbye to the last person I know.

"I'm ok. I'll be ok." I repeat it in my head.

"You will be ok, honey," she says, kindly. She tucks a strand of auburn hair behind my ear, the way they do in the

movies, and looks me right in the eyes. "What you did for the
last six years was incredible. You took such good care of your
Mom. But this is your time now."

I nod, keeping my lips pursed so a sob can't escape them.

"I wish someone had sent me to a luxury hotel resort to
carve out a new life." She straightens up and looks around.
"You're going to have such an amazing time here. You can go
down to the beach, swim round the reefs, learn to dive...
You'll make friends, maybe even meet a guy... I mean, those
three were pretty hot," she grins. I raise my eyebrows at her.
As much as I agree, I'm not in the mood to think too hard
about guys right now.

"Seriously," she says, her tone changing again. "It may
take some time to adjust, but hang in there. Work hard but
remember to enjoy the party. If you don't like it after the
season, we can look at something else, but give the place a
try. At the very least, you'll get some experience to put on
your resume."

"I will. I'll give it a try, I promise."

Millie puts her arms around me and I feel a tear roll down
my cheek. Heavy boots crunching across the gravel pull us
apart and I look to see another obscenely large and unfeasibly
handsome man—this time heavily tattooed with long, curly
hair that flows down his back as though he's in some sort of
hair commercial—walking towards us.

"Aunt Millie?" he asks.

"That's me."

"I'm Hudson, ma'am. I'll give you a ride."

Millie leans forward and presses her lips to my cheek.

"Go get your new life," she whispers into my ear, then
she turns and walks away.

Connor appears from around the corner. "Let's go," he
says, sharply.

I watch as he bends to grab his dirt-covered shirt then shoves it into a back pocket of his jeans.

"This way."

A truck's engine grumbles to life and I see Millie sitting in the passenger seat looking surprisingly small next to the huge hunk of man that is Hudson. I watch and wave as my past drives back the way she came, then turn back to see my present so far ahead I have to run to catch up.

# CHAPTER TWO

onnor

I MAKE a point of walking quickly so she has to jog to keep up. I know I'm being an ass but I can't help it. There's something about this new girl that makes me feel things I really don't need to be feeling.

I saw it happen. My office is lined with CCTV cameras and nothing too interesting tends to happen at two pm on a Sunday. So, when one screen shows an archaic black truck flying down the ramp, then swerving to avoid some rodent or other, and smashing unceremoniously into my wall, I fucking notice it.

I zoomed in to get a closer look at whoever the obscenely bad driver was. An older woman with blondish hair tied up in a bun was the first to climb out. She walked round to the front of the truck, took in the damage to the hood and the wall, and clapped a hand over her mouth. Then the driver's door opened and out of it emerged a young woman, pale-skinned, with darker hair—which I now know is red—also tied back, wearing the tiniest pair of denim shorts. Even through the grainy screen I could see her large eyes, smooth cheekbones and bee-stung lips. That was when my stomach clenched, squeezing some of the air out of my lungs.

We have a lot of pretty girls and beautiful women here on the island every damn day, but most of them have paid for their looks—not including staff, who can't afford it—and it shows. I could tell instantly this girl was all natural. No amount of money could buy eyes like that. And looking at the age of the car—early nineties—she was unlikely to be a guest here. They all rock up either by helicopter, boat, or these days the latest Tesla. Which meant only one thing. She was probably staff, so she was probably sticking around.

I tried to think of the current job openings we have. I am normally across everything on this resort—in the absence of much interest from the owner himself, I pretty much run the place—but the development of a brand new casino on the island is dominating most of my brain. There's a vacancy on the events desk just outside the security offices. Knowing my luck, she'll be that person, and that could be a problem. That would mean I'd have to look at those eyes and those lips and those legs every damn day, and I can't afford to be distracted.

My work on Starling Key has only just got started. Five years I've spent making this island home to the best beach resort in the Florida Keys, and five years I've spent honing a very profitable sideline too. The way I operate—shrewd, calculated and focused to the exclusion of all else—is what has got me and my team this far. We've made a name for ourselves, not only in security, but in luxury tourism. And we're making money for the people who need it, not just to line Starling's pockets. In order to keep all the balls in the air, distraction is not something I need. Not right now. Not ever.

"I'm really sorry about the wall," she says, jogging to keep up.

"Don't sweat it. It's fixed." *For now*. I'll need to send someone over to do it properly, but I'm not telling her that.

"Yeah, I know but, it sounds like you're real busy and you had to take time out of your day to do that, and I… I'm really sorry."

"I said don't sweat it."

Thankfully, she falls quiet again. I don't want to get into a conversation with her, because that could lead down roads I don't want to travel. If she's anything like the other girls who land fresh on this island, she'll attempt to 'get to know' me. One minute she'll be asking how long I've worked here, the next she'll be asking how many exes I've got, and that's nobody's business but mine. But for the record, it's only the one. That doesn't count one night stands—I've had plenty of those since I've been in the Keys. But nothing goes past one night, and for good reason.

"So, how long have you worked here?" She asks. I roll my eyes knowing she can't see me.

"Five years."

"Is that the golf course over there?"

I don't even look. "Yes."

"And what's over there, straight ahead?"

"That's the reception building."

"Oh right. So, that's where guests go when they arrive?"

"Yes."

I hope my short answers convey that I am not interested in talking, but she doesn't get the hint.

"And what's beyond that? Is there a beach?"

"Yes, there's a beach," I snap, mentally kicking myself for being unnecessarily short with her.

"I can't wait to see it."

I don't answer. Instead, I turn off the driveway and lead her down a dirt path to the northeast wall. The northeast wall is where all the supplies are kept, where all the action takes place that Starling doesn't want guests to see, like recycling and laundry. And it also happens to be where most of the staff live and, after a tiresome week—which is most weeks—party. Hard.

"Where are we going?"

"To the dorms."

"Dorms?"

"It's what we call the staff accommodation."

We reach the steel security gate and I punch in the code.

"It looks like a prison."

Part of me is quite pleased about that. The wall and the gate are meant to be fairly imposing. They're designed to keep guests and VIPs out, and the staff and the noise of the parties in. The gate unlocks and I step backwards to open it, and that's when I collide with her.

"Owww!"

I turn quickly and see her clutching her nose.

"What the hell are you made of? Titanium?"

I see blood trickling out of her nose through her fingers, so it would be inappropriate to smile at her comment. I spend a lot of time building muscle to ensure I'm as close to titanium as I can be. No fucker is going to blow me up anytime soon.

"Hey, I'm sorry, I didn't realize you were standing so close." I move her hand away from her face so I can get a better look at the damage I've just caused.

"Shit." It's pretty bad. "Tip your head back."

I pull my shirt out of my jeans pocket and press it carefully to her nostrils. I guess this is my punishment for being rude to her. Just wait 'til she gets to her dorm. I almost feel bad about that, too. But I made the decision and texted Maggie to get a key ready as soon as I saw the state of the wall. The fact the perpetrator was standing by looking indecently cute and chewing coyly on a fingernail didn't do anything to dissuade me either.

"Hold this to your nose and keep your head back, ok?"

She nods, eagerly.

"That's not keeping your head back."

Without thinking, I smile, and she flicks her eyes down and catches it. *Damn.*

Seeing as she now has to stare at the sky, I take hold of her free hand. "I'll lead you, ok?"

She lets me take her hand and I guide her slowly round various patches of grass and bushes, through an alleyway between two of the accommodation blocks, and across the yard to Maggie's hole in the wall. It's not really a hole in a wall, it's a proper office, but the door is inside one of the blocks and she prefers to do business out the window overlooking the yard.

"Hey Maggie," I say, pulling the girl up behind me.

"Hey Connor, who've you got there?"

I actually have no idea what the girl's name is so I give her a gentle nudge.

"Oh, sorry. Um, it's Tawny. Tawny Graham," she says, still staring at the sky.

*Tawny.* I roll the name silently over my tongue.

"Okaaay," Maggie says, as she runs a finger down the list of new employees.

"She's in 8A," I remind her, before she can find keys for another room.

Maggie does a double take then mouths, "Are you sure?" at me.

I nod. Just one night. She needs to know she can't go

driving into walls and thinking her looks are going to get her off the hook. I've met way too many girls like her; I know exactly how they operate.

"Ok, here you go," Maggie passes me the keys. "Welcome to Starling Key!"

I lead Tawny away towards Block 8.

"Thanks!" she calls back to Maggie, brightly, and I instantly regret what I'm about to do. I stop short and turn back, but Maggie's gone. Damn. Well, it's just one night, I remind myself.

We walk back across the yard and through another set of buildings, then we reach Block 8. I push open the door and realize I have to get the girl up two flights of stairs.

"Ok. We have steps," I say, reaching an arm around her back to guide her towards them. My palm nestles comfortably into the dip of her waist and I unintentionally brush the skin between the waistband of her shorts and the cotton fabric of her shirt. She jumps a little.

"Is this ok?" I ask.

"Yeah... um, it's fine." Her voice breaks.

I shuffle her forward until her toes touch the first step, then I wait patiently as she finds the edge with her foot. She could probably do this on her own, but she seems fragile somehow. I don't want to let her go for fear she'll career off into something else and break it.

With each step she takes, her shirt moves, allowing my fingers another taste of the soft skin beneath; I have to use every ounce of my willpower to focus on getting her to the top of the stairs. We reach the last step and I pull the key out of my jeans. I unlock the door to 8A and brace myself. No one has been in this dorm, that I'm aware of, for *months*. It's the dorm we put people in when we want to punish them on the sly, when we want to have them sit somewhere and metaphorically 'think about what they've done'. A slight whiff of stale air hits my nostrils and I silently hope the blood congealing in Tawny's nose masks the smell. Seeing the room again, seeing how small and poky it is, sends a fresh current of guilt through my veins, but it's too late now. We're here.

"This is it," I say, as she lowers her chin to look. "Do you have any bags?"

"Ah man," she sighs. "One. I left it in the car."

"Ok, I'll have someone bring it over." It's the least I can do after this. She's holding my shirt in front of her chest. It is pretty drenched in bright red blood.

"Oh God, I'm sorry," she says, spotting it. "I'll have it cleaned…"

"Nah. Throw it out when you're done."

"I really am sorry," she says again, then she looks around while I hold my breath. "So these are my digs, huh?"

She's no doubt noticed the narrow bed, small sink, chipped and broken dresser and the door leading to the world's smallest toilet cubicle.

"Yup," I say, quickly. "There are showers at the end of the corridor and lockers in block 4 if you need to store extra stuff."

She nods slowly and looks out of the window.

"Where do I go tomorrow?" She says. "I'm starting a new assistant job but I don't have any paperwork. All I know is I have to ask for Rhonda."

"Right. Just go to the main reception building tomorrow morning at eight and ask for Rhonda there. She works in resourcing. She'll tell you where you need to go."

"Ok, um, what… what should I wear?"

Before I can stop them, my eyes drop to her shirt and shorts. I'm at least a foot taller than her, and looking down I can see the peaks of her nipples poking through the cotton. I swallow.

"Maybe something like... I don't know, a dress? Shirt and pants? Just not too casual, ok?"

"Are you sure I shouldn't go get my bag?"

"No, it's fine. I'll get one of the guys to bring it over. I'll leave you to settle in," I say, and take a step back. "I'm sorry about... you know..." I nod towards her face.

"It's ok." She smiles, giving me a glimpse of her slightly buck, terribly cute teeth.

"Great. Well, see you around Tawny," I say, practically running out the door.

I'm already down the stairs before I hear her door close and despite what I said, I hope to God I don't see her around. Because I already know, in my bones, she could become the one distraction I really don't need.

# CHAPTER THREE

awny

I LEAN BACK against the door and stare into a space that just might suck the oxygen out of me. Now I know why all the other windows I saw, as I held my head back and allowed Connor to lead me through the blocks, contained so many damn plants.

I have nothing to unpack so I sit down on the unsurprisingly squeaky, lumpy bed and look out of the window. The yard is right below and I can see Maggie's window, although she doesn't appear to be sitting in it anymore. I can also now see some makeshift stools and plastic chairs stacked in the corner, and gaslights hanging on the wall of the building opposite. My window overlooks something of an atrium so my only view is that of other buildings and the yard. I was hoping for an ocean view but I can see now that was way too optimistic. So, with not the most welcoming of welcomes, and a dorm the size of Harry Potter's bedroom under the stairs, all I can do now is hope my job is mildly enjoyable, otherwise I doubt this will be the fresh, happy new start Millie thinks it is.

I don't know how long I've been sitting here for when there's a knock at the door. I open it and come face-to-face with Carter, the long-haired guy who'd looked at me suspiciously earlier.

"Hey," he says, jerking his head the way guys do to other guys when they want to seem cool. Instead, he seems awkward. "Here."

Ah, another man of many words. He holds out a small bag. I take it and peer inside.

"Ice pack," he says.

Then his other hand holds out the bag from my trunk, which I take, gratefully.

"Thanks."

His eyes scan the room quickly, while mine scan him. He has a kind face with a small dimple in his chin, and there are those long eyelashes again. I'm tempted to ask him if they're fake.

"I didn't think we put people in this dorm anymore," he mutters, almost to himself.

"Aren't all the dorms like this?" I ask.

"Well, most people bunk in pairs, so the other rooms are bigger," he says, quickly.

"Right," I reply, slowly figuring out what's going on here. "So, this isn't the box you put people in 'cos you've taken an instant dislike to them, 'cos they just drove through your wall?"

I was joking, partly, but Carter is staring at me like he's been caught stealing GI Joes from the local toy store.

"Don't take it personally," he says quickly. "It's just the way he is."

"Who, Connor?"

"Yeah. He's, um, a perfectionist. He's busy and… you know, it takes a lot of time to rebuild a wall, and…" He shrugs as though he's exhausted with keeping up appearances. "Actually, he's fucking anal and hates shit messing up his day. But he's a great guy if you stay on his good side."

"I didn't drive into the wall on purpose."

"Yeah, I know." His eyes soften and I can see he's being genuine. "But it doesn't matter. Connor likes having everything under control. He gives himself a lot of things to do and not much time to do it in, so if anyone messes with his schedule, he gets pissed. But…" he sighs again. "He's a good guy and a fucking genius. This island wouldn't be the place it is without him, so…" he runs a hand through his long, slightly damp waves and doesn't finish his sentence.

"He sounds like a bully," I suggest. Even extremely hot guys can be bullies so it isn't beyond the realm of possibility.

Carter's eyes narrow on me. "He's not a bully. Me and Connor… we go back a heck of a long way. We were in the Marines together. He's the most loyal, considerate and kind-hearted guy I will ever be lucky enough to work for."

I cross my arms defensively.

"He just likes things done a certain way is all. And if that way means we make a few more guests happy, we make the Starlings happy, we make a few more bucks for ourselves and everyone else who works here, then I'm happy to do it his fucking way, ok?"

"Ok, ok," I say, holding my hands up. I've clearly touched on a delicate subject. Either that or Carter has genuine love for the guy who stuck me in this room apparently out of spite.

"If you want to stick around here, you'd do well to give Connor a little more respect."

Now *that* annoys me. "I didn't say I don't respect the guy. I don't even know him." I jam my hands onto my hips. "But it's going to take more than your word for me to look past the dead eye stares he's given me so far, and the irritated huffs, and the one word sentences to convince me he's worthy of my respect."

Carter's shoulders relax a little and he breathes out.

"Fair enough. Just don't take it personally…"

He's said that twice now. "I'm not. Why should I?"

"No reason," Carter says. "Just… I know him."

"Ok, well, thanks for my bag and the ice pack," I say, cocking my head to one side in a way I hope communicates that I want to be left alone now. I'm tired. I seem to be pissing people off every which way today, and I need to acclimate—to the heat and this 'exciting' new life I'm supposed to be creating for myself. Note the sarcasm.

"No problem." A small smile curls the corners of his mouth. "Catch you later, Tawny."

"Yeah. I'll look forward to it," I mutter.

He lets out a quiet chuckle as I close the door.

I pull out the ice pack and notice something fall to the floor. I pick it up and see it's a business card. Connor's business card. Against my much better judgement, my heart rate doubles and I turn it over. Above the printed cell numbers and email address is a handwritten note in black ballpoint pen.

*For emergencies only.*

I fling the card onto the dresser and flop down onto the bed, placing the ice pack over my nose. If I close my eyes, maybe when I open them again I'll be back home and none of this will have happened. I won't have driven my truck into the perimeter wall of a luxury resort; I won't have been forced to watch the most beautiful back in the world rebuild the result of my clumsiness; and I won't have experienced an immediate, breathtaking attraction to a man who clearly can't stand me.

---

I'M WOKEN up by the guitar riffs and dulcet tones of Linkin Park, along with lots of loud voices trying to communicate over the top of it. I can feel something cold and heavy weighing down my face. I pull the ice pack off and stare at the ceiling, and it all comes back to me like a kick in the stomach. I live here now. This tiny, lumpy hovel with walls and windows made of paper is my new home. I wasn't entirely convinced this was going to work when Millie told me the plan. I was even less convinced on the road trip down here, the further away I got from the only home I've ever known. Surprise, surprise I was not at all convinced when I drove my car into the freaking wall, and now? Now, I am pretty positive this was the worst idea in the world.

A loud bass kicks in outside and thumps against my window. *For fuck's sake.* I peel myself off the lumpy mattress and lean over to the window. Everything in my dorm is within leaning distance. Below me, the small yard I spotted earlier is nowhere to be seen. Instead, all I can see is bodies— tons of them, all crowded into the little space beneath my window. The gas lamps are lit and a makeshift bar has been set up by some Latino guys juggling bottles around as though they're auditioning for a role in Cocktail. I notice a group of women, still wearing what look like housekeeping uniforms, sitting on a circle of upturned bottle crates, deep in conversation and occasionally howling with laughter.

I notice another group of guys, all blonde and tan, wearing beach shorts. There's one girl with them, also blonde, super pretty, holding her own against guys doing shots and fist-pumping. Then my gaze travels to another group of guys and I recognize one of them. No, wait, two of them. Carter's hair is tied back showing off a serpent tattoo snaking around his neck, and Isaac stands opposite him, shirtless and glistening. I guess sourcing plans for a casino is sweaty work. Or maybe it's because it's as hot out there as it is in here. I push open the window and immediately regret it—the noise is deafening and there's no way I'm going to be able to sleep through that, or the heat. I lean further to see who else is standing there. I remember Connor saying something about not coming to a bar tonight so I figure this is what he meant. My eyes search the crowd for him anyway.

Another two guys are standing with Carter and Isaac—a surfer-type guy with blonde hair to his shoulders and a dark-skinned guy with a shaved head. From up here, I can see a long scar down the right side of his crown. Every single one of them looks like they live in the gym; they have muscles literally bursting out of every limb.

I allow myself a few seconds to take them in, knowing I'd never get away with such voyeurism in broad daylight, then a figure comes into my peripheral vision. He looks like he's heading for Carter and Isaac but it's slow progress. Everyone he passes seems to want to talk to him. I can't hear anything over the din of the music and the chattering but he makes time for every single person who stops him, then he reaches the guys below me and my suspicion is confirmed: it's definitely Connor.

I settle my elbows on the window sill, readying myself for a few moments of secret spying, but I'm busted. Within seconds, his head tilts upwards and his eyes glide from the bottom of the building up to my window, where they land on mine. Someone shoves a bottle into his hand but he doesn't look away. His gaze is locked on mine and I can't escape it; I can only stare back.

An eternity passes. I try to smile but my face hurts and the dried sweat seems to have solidified my expression into one of permanent pissed-ness. He looks away, finally, and I can breathe.

I realize now, I am not just screwed; I am double screwed. I'm stuck in supposed paradise without a friend to my name. Not only that, I realize I'm attracted to a man who's made no secret of the fact I'm a big fat inconvenience. And not just any man—the Head of Starling Key Security himself.

# CHAPTER FOUR

 onnor

MISSION *SORT OF* ACCOMPLISHED.

She knows I put her in there on purpose because I was pissed. Pissed that my day got totally hijacked by some ditsy redhead driving into my wall. I mean, the gate was right there. Only a complete and utter dufus could have missed it. She needed to realize, you don't cause serious damage to a resort that I am responsible for, before you've even entered the property, and get away with it. Doesn't matter how pretty you are.

But who am I kidding? She isn't ditsy; she can see right through me. She knows she's being holed up in the room where we put people we want to punish, and she knows why. Carter told me about their little conversation. I know she doesn't respect me yet, and she doesn't have to. She just needs to stay out of my way.

I could have stuck her in that room feeling nothing if I

hadn't gone and busted the girl's nose. That made me feel like a prize prick. She didn't even get mad. She didn't cry, she didn't swear at me. And worst, she trusted me to take her to her dorm. She just let me lead her by the hand. And it felt so small inside mine. I barely held onto it for fear it might break. It's been years since I last held a woman's hand and it brought back the very feelings I've been on a mission to repel ever since.

I can't look up again, as much as I want to. I can't head up there and pull her across the corridor to the room she was supposed to be staying in, as much as I want to. *Just one night*, I tell myself again. *She needs to know who she can and can't mess with around here.* I take a swig of beer instead. I check the label first. Bud Zero. Good. Carter knows it's a rare moment when I can stand to be even mildly intoxicated.

"Heard from Hud?" I ask Jaxon.

"Yeah, he's on his way back now. I told him to grab some lobster and grits, so that's breakfast."

"Nice. Who's on shift at the marina?"

"One of the temps. It's pretty quiet out there though. Only four boats in this week."

Jaxon runs his palm over his head. It's a habit he has, as if he's trying to erase the fact he ever had a brain injury, like it's something to be ashamed of. I try to ignore it.

"So," he starts. "How are things looking for the next few weeks?"

"All good so far," I reply, leaning in. This is not a conversation I want to have overheard. "Couple deliveries coming in —one by boat, two by truck from Key West. Shipment to Miami a few days later."

"What's the score with Starling?"

He's talking about Eric Starling, the owner of not just the resort but the island on which it sits. All money but no idea.

He bought the island as a place for his family to live, then realized he could actually make more money off of what used to be a rundown resort. The place had been battered by one too many storms and had run into partial ruin. To his credit, Starling managed to get the basic structures fixed—mainly the golf course and some guest villas—but it wasn't until he hired me, Carter and Isaac to keep an eye out for rafters, smugglers and squatters, that Starling Key became the luxury destination it now is.

It didn't take long for us to polish up the place. I won Starling's trust early on by dealing with a couple of migrant boats and a handful of smugglers. Shortly afterwards, I was recommending stuff he could do to improve the resort. I made connections and I got to know people in the business. I was able to help Starling develop the resort for less money and in less time than most of our competitors, which meant he was raking in the dollars fast. Eventually, he just handed over his credit card. It's amazing how quickly you can get shit done with money. Money talks, and thanks to me, Starling is now raking it in. It's now time for us to get our small slice of that very large Key Lime Pie. And smuggling firearms for less-than-legitimate associates is the way I'm making it. Ironic, huh?

"Most of the activity is during the day. The majority of the goods will be buried amongst kosher deliveries—nothing suspicious. The Grand House is so far over the other side of the island, Starling's hardly likely to see the trucks, and anyway, he spends all day on the golf course. The only delivery I'm concerned about is the one coming in from Mexico."

"By boat?"

"That's the one."

"We'll clear the marina. Leave it with me, Connor. I'll figure something out."

"Thanks Isaac." I know I can trust my left hand guy. While Carter—my right hand—makes sure no one comes at me with a physical weapon when I'm turned the other way, Isaac fights with numbers and a level of mathematical and intellectual genius I haven't seen anywhere else in all my years, including the ten I spent in the armed forces.

I chat with the guys until my bottle is empty, then I fling it into the trash can by the bar. I nod to Ché who's creating some high percentage Cuban concoction, then slap Carter on the shoulder.

"I'm gonna hit the sack, bro'. Early start tomorrow."

"Sure thing. We've got a new camera system being installed in the diving club late morning but I'll see you in the office first thing."

"Great, thanks Carter."

"Anything else I need to do with Little Miss Ice Pack up there?" Carter arches an eyebrow. He knows exactly why I've reacted the way I have to Tawny Graham, but he knows better than to say it out loud.

"No. Let her sweat."

"Oh," he makes a hollow laugh. "She will up there. Without a doubt."

I push my fingers through my damp hair.

"I'll deal with it tomorrow."

"Ok, bro'. See you in the morning."

I turn to leave and without thinking, I glance up again at her window. Something floods my chest when I see she isn't there.

It takes me twenty minutes and a cold shower before I realize what it is. Disappointment.

# CHAPTER FIVE

"HONEY… Are you ok? Can I get you something? Some water?"

I can feel someone rocking me lightly on a very hard but thankfully cool surface, but I don't want to open my eyes; I'm exhausted. And I've remembered where I am and I don't want to face it.

"Honey, you're worrying me now. Do I need to get someone?"

My eyes shoot open and land on a kind face peering down at me. She looks like a housekeeper.

"No, no…" I say, pushing myself up to sitting. My back is killing me. "I'm ok. Don't get anyone." I have a feeling who she might get and I don't want to give him the satisfaction of knowing I slept in the corridor last night.

"What time is it?"

"Five thirty. Did you come from…" her face contorts into a grimace, "8A?"

"Yeah," I reply, my voice croaky from lack of sleep. I rub my eyes which feel as though they're coated in grit. Not the best start to the day.

"Lordy, girl. Who did you piss off?"

"It doesn't matter," I grumble, clambering to my feet. I walk back towards my hovel.

"Oh no, no, no," she says, grabbing my shoulder. "You take my bed for a couple hours."

She steers me in the opposite direction and opens another door. To a much bigger room. Man, Connor really does have an axe to grind. She pushes me onto a bed. I notice there's another bed over the other side of the room with someone asleep on it. I look up as the woman bends at her knees to bring her face level with mine.

"Sleep here as long as you need to," she whispers. "Shell over there was on a late shift so she won't wake up 'til around midday."

I rub my eyes again. "I start work at eight," I groan.

She sucks in a breath. "Ah, jeez. Where?"

"No idea. I have to go see someone called Rhonda in main reception."

She chews her lip for a moment, thinking.

"Ok, you know what? I'm working there all morning. I'll meet you at the front desk at eight. My name's Esme. I'm going to ask her to go easy on you, and move you to another room. You can't stay there; it's practically in the bar."

"The bar?" I look at her warily. A party—a one-off—I can handle, but a regular bar right outside my window, I cannot.

"Yeah, it's there most nights during the season. It's where most of us go to hang out after work, away from the guests and stuff. Ché and Camiro make a mean daiquiri. I'm thanking the Lord right now I stayed away from it last night."

I sink my head into my hands. "Where in God's name am I?" I mutter to myself.

I feel an arm around my shoulder.

"Doll, welcome to the northeast wall. The best freakin' place in the Keys."

---

I HANG up the four dresses I brought with me and select the one with the fewest creases. I feel marginally better after sneaking a shower in Esme's room. I will be forever grateful to her for letting me have an extra two hours' sleep on something that isn't made of concrete. I scrape my wet hair into a bun and promise myself I'll deal with it later, then I head out of the building and miraculously find my way to the gate. When I reach it, I realize I don't know the code, so I try to find my way to the hole in the wall where Maggie gave Connor the key to my joke of a dorm.

I get there and the window is closed with no-one to be seen anywhere.

*Shit.*

I'm due to start this new job in ten minutes and I'm locked inside a prison of buildings I've no idea how to get out of.

Cursing, I make my way back to the gate. I have no option but to scale the damn thing. I stand back and appraise it. It's about eight feet high with bars across each quarter— totally doable. I tut loudly. The security team didn't quite think that one through, did they? I back up and tuck my dress into my panties so it won't rip—I have no money right now, I do not need to be one dress down. I take a little run and jump up to catch the upper bars. This is when I realize just how unfit and inflexible I am. I scrape my feet against the vertical bars, trying to gain some traction until finally—*finally*—they land on a horizontal one and I can push myself up to standing.

As I look down, I feel dizzy. I'm up pretty high and still not able to swing my leg over the top. At least I get a good view though. Yesterday, I could see the ocean in the distance. Today, I can see a long line of villas *in* the sea, connected by some sort of walkway. I can see more buildings to my left, a block that looks as though it might be more accommodation, and I can see an immaculate white beach peppered with life-guards. It is stunning.

I stand for a few minutes on the bars of the gate just taking it all in. I've never seen anywhere so beautiful. I've never really seen luxury before, but I'm pretty sure this is it. I also have no idea what amount of money people pay to stay here but I'm quite certain it's more than the cost of my mom's whole house. For the first time since I left New Jersey, I feel something resembling excitement in my belly. It will never come close to the comfort, love and security of home, but it might go some way towards compensating for the fact I don't have anything to go back for anymore.

I grip the top of the gate with both hands and peg my foot onto the highest bar. Trembling slightly, I push myself up and hover at the top. I'm bent double, knowing that all it'll take is a slight breeze and I'll topple over the edge. I hold my breath and swing a leg over the top, bringing it down to the bar at the other side. Then the sound of an electronic klaxon deafens me.

Lights shine on me from every angle and if I'm not so damn petrified at falling off the gate, I could laugh out loud at how dramatic it all is.

I hear a gun cock, stilling the breath in my throat.

"Freeze!" Comes a voice from the resort side of the wall. I would lift my hands up in surrender but I know I'll be in a pile on the floor if I let go.

"Tawny?" Comes the same voice.

I look down through the glare of the floodlights and see who I think might be Carter.

"Yeah?" I grimace.

"What the fuck?"

"I don't know the code," I say. It's a perfectly good explanation as to why I'm balancing on the top of a thin slice of iron, wobbling with fear.

"Why didn't you call Connor?" Carter shouts, over the whine of the alarm.

*Is he going to get me the fuck down?*

"That's why he left you his card."

"I don't have a cell!" I yell back at him.

"W—are you kidding me?"

"Carter, help me!" I squeal, feeling the iron gate shift slightly. I don't know who's moving it; I can't see a damn thing.

"Woah, wait," I hear Carter say, but it doesn't stop whoever is opening the gate. I fall backwards the way I came, grabbing at the bars, but it's too late. The wind rushes past my ears, almost as loud as the alarm, and I can sense the ground hurtling up towards me. I squeeze my eyes closed and pray.

Apparently the Lord is standing right there with open arms. I feel myself being curled into a chest, the breath knocked out of my lungs. I dare not open my eyes. I know who's caught me and I don't want to give him the satisfaction of knowing I'm so grateful I could cry.

"You ok?" His voice is soft and its tendrils alone draw my eyelids open. I feel as though my pulse can be felt throughout my body as his blue eyes burrow into me. I can't help but stare up at him. My insides have melted and the parts of my body that are touching his are on fire.

"Um, yeah," I mutter.

He lowers my feet to the floor and I step back to brush myself down. I dare not look up in case I'm paralyzed to the spot, so I look behind me to see Carter staring at Connor curiously. Only then do I realize the floodlights have disappeared, the alarm has stopped and there's an uncomfortable silence surrounding us.

"You don't have a cell?" Carter repeats.

I shake my head. "I need to get a new one".

"The code is 9914," Connor says, curtly. "You should memorize it."

"Sure," I say, turning to face him. Gone is the softness of his eyes and back is the glare I am more familiar with. "Thank you. And I will do that, now that I *know what it is*."

He watches me as though I'm a cat about to pounce, but I turn and walk back to the gate which has closed again of its own accord. I punch in the numbers and wait for the buzzer, then I open the gate and strut through it, defiantly.

"I'm late," I say to Carter as I pass, leaving them both staring as I walk away, not realizing my dress is still tucked into my underwear.

# CHAPTER SIX

onnor

"What was that about?" Carter says as I close the gate behind me. "She would have got over the gate fine and I was going to help her. You didn't have to frighten the crap out of the poor girl."

"Carter," I say, my voice low. "She missed the goddamn entrance yesterday and left a Chevy shaped hole in the outer wall. Do you really think she'd have got over that gate fine? She's a constant accident waiting to happen."

Carter kicks at the gravel. He knows I'm right.

"Ok, fine. But you seemed pretty keen to help," he says, raising an eyebrow.

"What is that supposed to mean?"

"Maybe you like her? It's ok, I won't tell a soul." He crosses his heart with his fingers and bats his eyes at me.

"C'mon Carter. We both know nothing would come of it, even if I did."

"So, you *do* like her?" He feigns shock and I elbow him in the ribs.

"So what if I do?" I'm toying with him. Kind of. His face turns serious all of a sudden.

"Connor, I don't think she's like the others. She doesn't strike me as being a party girl type. I think her heart could get broken."

I shove my hands in my pockets and start walking. "Well, it won't be by me, I can assure you."

"You know, you don't need to be with a girl to break her heart."

"I'm not following."

"I know you're not," he replies, jogging a little to catch up. "You're racing off ahead. Careful there Connor, anyone might think you were running away from something."

I spin around and glare at him.

"What are you getting at Carter? Just spit it out."

"I know chemistry when I see it, and when you two looked at each other back there? That was it. Even if you don't do anything about it, that girl is halfway hooked."

I stop fighting the conversation and sigh heavily.

"So, what? I just avoid her? Because that's what I'm planning to do."

"Or, maybe you… I don't know… go there?"

"What, start a thing with her?"

"Well, why not? New season, new start?"

I turn around and start walking again.

"She's exactly your type."

"Because she has red hair?"

"Well, yeah. And freckles. And curves."

"So have a lot of girls and you haven't seen me get caught up with those, have you?"

"No, but I think you might actually like this one. She isn't pawing at you; she's different. And… I haven't seen you be this mean to a girl before."

"I'm not being mean."

"You put her in 8A."

"I've put other people in there too."

"Like who?"

I can't think of anyone off the top of my head so I just shrug and walk a little faster.

"Are you going to move her out of there?"

"I'll think about it." I know I am. And I'll do it today, but I don't want to give Carter the satisfaction of knowing that.

We walk the remaining two hundred yards in silence then arrive at the reception building and push open the doors. Immediately, I see Tawny standing at the reception desk talking to Rhonda, and Esme from the housekeeping team. Tawny turns and flashes her eyes at me then looks away quickly. A blush floods her cheeks and I recall the way she walked through the gate in a huff with her ass cheeks on full display. She probably didn't realize until one of these girls told her. I bite the inside of my cheeks to stop a grin forming at the memory. It's a shame I can't do the same to my cock, which also seems to fondly remember the sight of her butt walking away.

"I'm going to do some paperwork and then go down to the diving center. See you there later?" Carter asks.

"Yeah, sure. I'm meeting Eric this morning but I'll head on over after that."

I walk towards the reception desk; I have to, seeing as our security offices are behind it.

"Yeah, I found her out in the corridor," I hear Esme say. "On the concrete floor. The poor girl had slept there all night." My ears prick up. Does she mean Tawny? Tawny slept in the corridor? Guilt hits me like a slap in the face.

"Is that right?" Rhonda says.

I feel Tawny's eyes follow me but I don't hear a reply.

"I'm putting you in a different dorm," Rhonda says, the apology clear in her voice. "That's unacceptable. I don't understand why you were put in there."

I slope behind the reception area into my office and lean back against the closed door. She slept in the corridor. What kind of a monster am I? I should have stuck around to find Maggie the second I had doubts. I was pissed about Tawny crashing into the wall, but putting her in that room was shitty. And worse, Rhonda will know I'm the one who assigned it. I can sense some sort of penance coming my way. I might be senior to our head of resourcing but she can certainly hold her own when it comes to fairness.

I sit at my desk and try to focus. I'm meeting with Eric in ten minutes. My suspicions that Tawny Graham would be trouble have been resolutely confirmed. She hasn't been here even a day and already I'm being caught off-guard, I'm behind schedule and I can't seem to concentrate on anything. This isn't good. I can't afford to be distracted by anything, least of all by someone who has managed to smash up a car, knock down a wall and set off a million alarms in less than twenty-four hours. Setting up this new casino is the biggest gig I've had so far, and our sideline hustle is growing nicely. I know I've taken on way more than I can handle but it keeps my mind off my past. I'm determined to be a fully functioning civilian if it kills me.

---

I SETTLE into the swing seat on the porch of the Grand House, cradling a papaya juice freshly made by Maria, Eric's wife. I'm not used to seeing Maria around; Mrs. Starling is usually enjoying a spa treatment or an early morning dive class with Jonas, her own personal cabana boy. Eric is showering, apparently.

I take the opportunity to look out across the family's private beach and take note of anything we can do to improve the view. A happy Starling means a happy Connor. Not that the Starlings are ever unhappy; I don't give them a chance to be. I want this resort to run like clockwork—to be the most successful beach resort this side of Miami. Because that way, my team will have jobs for life, which means everything to them.

I stare at the crystal clear water; it never gets old. Growing up in downtown Detroit I didn't see the sea until I flew to Iraq the first time. And even then it was at a distance and I had very different things on my mind. Now, I count my blessings every day: I can sit by that sea, swim in that sea, and dive in that sea as much as I want. I rarely do, but I can, and that's what counts. I make a mental note to get the grounds men to position a hammock between two of the older palms just before I hear Eric's booming voice echo behind me.

"Connor! My friend! How are you?"

I stand and let him embrace me, which I tolerate, barely. My dad was never a tactile man, and growing up in the armed forces, I was more used to slapping backs and pumping fists; we didn't hug. But I have my eye on a prize. Letting Eric Starling wrap his doughy arms around me is a means to an end.

"I'm fantastic, sir," I say, sitting back down opposite him. Eric Starling is pink and portly, as they would probably say in England, which is where he's from originally. From a family of old money, he and his parents moved to the States forty years ago, meaning Eric displayed none of the stoic Englishness one might expect of that breed of Brit, and instead had embraced the more effusive and outgoing mannerisms of a born and bred American.

As far as I've researched, Eric worked on Wall Street for a few years but math was never really his forte so he left to live off his family money. Then, thanks to the death of his father, leaving him with even more money than he knew how to handle, Eric decided to buy an island and name it after himself. The rest, as they say, is history. And now, here I am, sitting on his porch.

"Are you ready for the snowbirds?" He beams, rubbing his hands together. We have one month to go before the main tourist season begins and the island is fully booked from October right through to May—usually with people escaping a freezing winter to soak up the Florida sun.

"We are," I smile. "It's a good thing we've had no major storms this year. As a result, the casino is on track for a grand holiday opening."

"Excellent," Eric says, lighting a cigar. "We'll need to double up on our identification processes. We don't want any dirty player scandals hitting the Key. Keep it clean."

"Of course," I say. "Isaac is on the case and you know he's ex-CIA."

"Ah yes," Eric waves his cigar around, as though this information is beneath him. "I knew one of them was. Isaac. Right. The blonde surfer dude."

"Yes," I reply. Actually, no. Isaac is the dark-haired, Italian American dude, but I've lost count of the number of times I've corrected Starling on this.

"How far are we on the building work?"

"We're pretty much there. Just some final snagging to do. Decorating supplies arriving this week then we'll have the decorators in."

"And what about the good stuff? The tables, the chips?"

He grins, rubbing his hands together again.

"Within the month. Along with slot machines..."

"I hate those things."

"Me too. But every big casino has them and we don't want to disappoint."

"Plans for the opening night?"

"We're working with your PR team on that, sir. I can have our events manager send you a proposal when they get settled."

"Of course, I forgot Anna went back to Canada," he says, startling me with his recollection of the young woman who'd assisted us with events for the last year and a half. He looks almost wistful. Had the sly fucker been cheating on his wife? Not that I should be surprised about their extra-curricular activities. Not only does Maria have her cabana boy, me and the guys have witnessed several other of their indiscretions during our time on the Key.

"We'll get something to you soon."

With that out of the way, no further questions asked, I update him on the usual security activities: How many eyes I've put on the marina and beaches, to look out for any smugglers and rafters coming in from Cuba and the South Americas; what security detail will be on the casino and bars, as well as the front gate, the jewelry store in the main building and some of the guest accommodation, depending on who the guests are. We're often called upon to carry out personal security work for guests on site and nearby—we know the area and the risks—and we sometimes do private work for clients, be it investigative or interrogative.

"Well, son," he says, despite being only a decade or so older than me, "everything sounds good. I need to run. Got a caddy waiting for me outside."

"Of course, sir," I say, unsurprised. Eric lives on the golf course. When he's not getting down and dirty with event managers that is.

I say goodbye and head back to the offices. It's a long walk so I usually jump into one of the Key buggies. Today, for some reason, I need the fresh air. I need to rid my head of the events of the last twenty-four hours and focus. The casino build alone is on a tight schedule. If we go over it by even half a day, we will lose money. And not just little handfuls of the stuff. A casino can make hundreds of thousands of dollars a day. That's how much we stand to lose every day the launch is delayed. And that won't be happening. Not on my watch.

I arrive back at base and just as I push open the doors, I walk head on into Carter.

"Hey, man." He looks like I've just caught him bunking off school.

"What are you doing back here? I thought you were at the diving club."

"Yeah, I had to come back. Rhonda called."

"What did she want?" I push past him and feel him tense as I look up.

He speaks slowly, because he suspects I already know the answer. "For me to train up our new event manager."

Tawny Graham is sitting behind the events desk, her back straight, looking intently at the screen in front of her.

"I tried to talk Rhonda out of it; I didn't think you'd be happy," Carter says. "But she was adamant."

I nod. Rhonda knows full well the event manager role falls under our security team remit. It's a little unusual, I admit, but nothing about this resort is usual, especially when it is practically run by the head of security. Rhonda has done this on purpose.

"It's fine," I say, finally. I'm a professional. I can't let on that this is the worst—*worst*—thing that Rhonda could have done. Not only is Calamity Jane now responsible for the events that we sustain an impeccable reputation on, but she's going to be living right outside my damn office. And doesn't she own a dress that isn't so short I can see the entire length of her thighs? The sooner Rhonda gets her in a proper uniform, the better.

"You look like you need a beer," Carter says, and that's saying something; he knows I rarely drink.

"Coffee," I almost choke out.

"Coming right up." Carter makes a run for it, no doubt chuckling about this in his head. He's made no secret of the fact he wants me to find someone, if only to prove I can actually love someone else and not get hurt. But because he's single too, I just turn the topic onto him. He hates it; he shuts up. I dread the day he meets someone he really likes—I won't be able to tease him back.

I don't realize I'm still standing just inside the doorway, staring at Tawny, until she looks up and her eyes land on mine. She offers me a slightly nervous smile; she's clearly feeling awkward about this situation too. A normal person would have smiled back, maybe walked over to welcome her to the team, maybe offered to get her a drink. But I'm not normal. Instead, I drop my head, stuff my hands into my pockets and stalk right past her to my office.

# CHAPTER SEVEN

 awny

I TRY to ignore the sinking feeling in my chest as Connor passes without any acknowledgment that I'm his new event manager, and I focus again on the company website. Carter suggested I get to know as much as I can about the resort because I'll be selling it to our guests—the diving courses, the taster dinners, reef tours, excursions to neighboring Keys.

Despite our first meeting being slightly tense and defensive, I've decided I like Carter. He's the polar opposite of Connor. He's funny, softly spoken, has way more patience and is actually pleasant to be around. Maybe that's why they work together so well, because opposites after all, do attract.

After Carter had shown me around the website and then given me links to where all the brochures were saved, I ventured the one question that had been on my lips ever since I arrived and overheard their conversation about casino plans.

"What exactly does the security team do? It seems to be a lot more than just security."

Carter sits back on his chair and crosses one leg over his knee. I'm surprised he can manage it with the size of his thigh muscle straining against his combat shorts.

"Well, you're right there. We do more than 'just' security…"

"I'm sorry, I didn't mean it like that. No offense."

He laughs. "No, it's ok. We do a lot of things. We look after the staff here, manage all the development and maintenance. It's a little odd, I know, but it's all down to Connor really. Before Starling Key became the big, luxury resort it is now, Connor used to help Starling out with some of the building works. You know, he found decent suppliers to improve the golf course and the sports center. He had great ideas and Starling went along with them." He leans forward and says in a whisper, "Starling doesn't have a clue what he's doing, and he doesn't care either. Only about the money." He leans back again. "But this resort… it saved Connor in a way."

"Saved him?" I feel some of the wind knocked out of me.

"Yeah." He looks a little uncomfortable so I don't push any further. "It gave him something to focus on. He realized he was pretty good at the business side, and Starling did too. So, over the years, Starling has just given him more and more responsibility. It's been great for us, too. We all get to do stuff we wouldn't normally do anywhere else. I mean, we're getting to help build a casino of all things. We love a bit of poker, so to create a whole casino from a scrap of land is the stuff of dreams."

He smiles and his face lights up. It's infectious and I smile too.

"Actually…" He's grinning to himself as though an

extremely amusing thought has just popped into his head. "Maybe you should come to our next game…"

"Oh no, I have no idea how to play."

"You don't need to. I can teach you."

"Don't I need money to play poker? I don't have any."

"It's ok, I can sub you. You'll have a great time. Think of it as our way of welcoming you to Starling Key."

"Who do you mean by 'our'?"

"The security team, of course. We play every second Wednesday. It'll be fun to have a guest for once. Some fresh blood. I can introduce you to the rest of the guys."

This doesn't sound like fun to me, I am worried and I'm not even there yet. "Won't Connor mind?"

"Nah," he says, waving his hand. "Well, he'll get over it."

"I'm not sure…" I say, but I don't think he's heard me.

"Yeah, that's what we'll do. We'll let you play poker with us."

"Ok, but I'm telling you…"

He's definitely not listening. He's wringing his hands, gleefully.

"I'll let you know the details. Just… don't tell anyone yet, let's keep it a surprise for now, ok? It's going to be perfect."

I attempt to say 'sure' and 'thanks', but he's got up from his seat and is walking away as though he's in some sort of a trance. I shake my head and look back at the screen. I have to learn about beaches and trips and sun-filled fun, and although it feels premature to admit it, I think this might actually be quite enjoyable.

As MUCH AS my day has picked up, I'm relieved when six pm arrives and I can go to meet Esme out the front of the building.

"How was your first day?" She asks, looping her arm through mine.

"Well, after a weird start, it actually turned out ok," I said, walking with her to the buggies parked up in a tidy little line. "Where are we going?"

"For a ride," she grins. "I'm going to give you the grand tour. I doubt your boss will have had the time to do that yet."

"I doubt he will ever have the time," I say. "I don't think he's too pleased I got this job. He hasn't said a word to me all day."

"Really?" She frowns, climbing into the driver's seat. "That's unlike Connor. He's normally the nicest guy on the island. Anally efficient, yes; obsessively perfectionist, absolutely; but unpleasant? Never."

"Then why did he put me in that awful room last night? That doesn't sound like something a pleasant person would do if there were other options available." I climb into the buggy next to her.

"Yeah, um, I'm still trying to figure that one out. I don't know, maybe you did really tick him off by crashing into the wall. It's unlike him to hold a grudge though." She puts the buggy in reverse and backs out of the line-up, then drives forward onto the gravel road.

"You heard about that, huh?"

"*Everyone* heard about that, girl," she grins. "This is the smallest non-town you'll ever come across. Everyone knows everyone's business around here. I put money on it even the old boys in the retirement village knew about it before you stepped foot out of the car."

"A retirement village? Here, on the resort?"

Esme laughs as she turns a corner and drives around the edge of the northeast wall.

"That's what we call it. Its official name is Reef Street; it's a community of villas Connor had built for people who want to stay for longer than your average guest. So, they have kitchens and other facilities. We also offer onsite round-the-clock care. Some of them come down here for the season; others stay a lot longer. Some of them have stayed ever since they moved in, and honestly, I don't see them ever leaving."

"Are they made of money?"

"You know, I think some of them actually are. Some of them are so paper-thin, I do worry they might blow away in the wind," she replies.

I look ahead as we turn south from the wall and make our way towards a collection of small villas enclosed by a white picket fence and carefully placed palms. To my left is an expanse of sand.

"Wow, look at that beach."

"I know. If you look backwards a little, you'll see ours—the staff beach. It's right behind the dorms. There's a little fence that separates it from the guest beach but no one really comes up this far."

"What about Reef Street?" I ask, as I can see that's what we're heading towards.

"Oh they have their own beach. With their own specially designed ergonomic loungers, and walkways created for those who are less able. As I said, it's basically a retirement village."

"Is that where we're going?"

"Yeah. I try to pop by a couple times a week. You should meet some of the residents—they're fun. They're really good to us too. They tip us extra nice at the holidays."

Esme pulls the buggy up alongside a few others and we

hop out. She opens the small gate and I walk through it, my mouth falling open at just how pretty the place is.

"Did Connor design this?" I can't help myself.

"Not personally. He had the vision then got a buddy to design it."

"A buddy?"

"Yeah, he has a lot of those. Like I said, he's a really nice guy."

I sigh, inwardly.

We walk past the front of the villas. Each one faces the ocean and is raised up on pale struts with wooden steps and ramps leading up to spacious porches. Each one has a track around the outer edge serving as a curtain rail, so that residents can pull the drapes around for some privacy. It is quiet enough that I can hear small waves lapping against the sand but I can also hear voices chatting from inside some of the villas. The sun is getting lower in the sky and some of the residents are cradling iced tea and rum cocktails as they admire the view. If this is what retirement looks like, I think, bring it on.

"Here we are," Esme says, as we reach the steps of number 20.

"We're going inside?"

"Oh, sure. They'll be expecting us."

"They?"

I have no idea who she's talking about but I follow anyway. I'm curious to see what these villas look like inside. We reach the top of the steps and see the doors to the villa opened fully, the curtains shifting slightly in the soft breeze. It looks like a picture from an expensive catalog.

"Esme, darling!"

I narrow my eyes to see a small woman who looks to be in her seventies, dressed head to toe in the most extravagant kaftan I've ever seen. She's gliding towards us in a cloud of purple and gold, carrying a cigarette perched inside one of those cigarette holders from the fifties. In her other hand is a crystal tumbler with something clear bubbling inside it. The ice cubes tinkle against the walls of the glass as she gets closer.

"Come in, my sweetheart. How are you?"

Esme bends down to receive an air kiss on both cheeks, then the woman spots me looking on curiously.

"You brought a friend! How wonderful! Darling, darling, come here, let me see you!"

I step forward so she can take a good look, then I feel her wrists clamp against the side of my arms and I'm pulled forward for two air kisses of my own.

"You," she says, pointing her cigarette at me, "are adorable."

I feel my cheeks flush. Whoever this woman is, I love her already.

"What's your name?"

"Tawny," I smile.

"Tawny," she repeats. "Adorable. Just adorable. I'm Barbara, my love. But you can call me Barbie—everyone else does. Now come on in. Fitz is going to love you. You're exactly his type. He's a sucker for redheads and freckles."

I catch Esme giggling as I follow them both inside. If I thought the outside of the villas were stunning, the interior is something else. The floors and walls are of the same pale wood, and the furnishings are in various subtle shades of white and cream. Fans whir discreetly overhead, while the early evening light filters through every strategically positioned window. It is as though the villa has been designed to receive the sun wherever it is.

"This is beautiful," I gasp, as we pass through the living space into an open kitchen.

"Isn't it, darling?" Barbie trills, spinning around as she talks. She stops then and sidles up to me like a naughty schoolgirl, then whispers in my ear.

"Mr. Starling and Mr. Johnson thought I was only coming for one season. But I've been here for three and I don't plan on going anywhere." She pulls back, giggling, and I catch Esme arching an 'I told you' eyebrow.

Barbie opens her arms as she walks away and calls out, "Fitz! Darling! There's a new girl here. She's adorable, darling, You're going to love her!"

I'm starting to feel slightly nervous. Not only because I feel like I might be being set up with a man four times my age, but because Barbie is building me up to be something I really am not. No one has ever called me adorable before in my life.

I hear footsteps and into the kitchen walks Fitz. He's fairly small too, like Barbie, but far more conservatively dressed. In fact, he looks a little bit like Fred Astaire. Actually, scratch that. He looks a *lot* like Fred Astaire. He sees me and stops, then he lets out a long whistle. I stand there wishing the ground would open up and swallow me, because I have never been subjected to attention like this. Probably because I spent most of my days indoors with just my mom for company and I missed all those things most kids experience, like proms and fresher parties and first dates. I still consider myself lucky that, thanks to some misguided ambition, I decided to lose my virginity to a guy who lived on our street just before Mom was diagnosed. But after that, well, let's just say I have totally forgotten what male attention feels like.

"What did I tell you?" Barbie trills, clapping her wrists

together because she's still gripping her cigarette and her drink.

Fitz's pursed lips break into a broad smile and his whole face softens as he walks towards me.

"Ignore Barbie. She's always trying to fix me up," he says, as he reaches me and holds out his hand.

I sigh with relief and reach out to take it. I expect a hand-shake but instead he lifts the back of my hand to his lips and kisses it.

"I'm old enough to be your great grandpa," he says, in a wonderfully deep New York accent, shrugging his shoulders.

"Oh, Fitz." Barbie sighs, exasperated. "Fitz, meet Tawny. Tawny, meet Fitz."

"Tawny? What an adorable name!"

I cock my head slightly. Why aren't these two together? They are clearly as thick as thieves and speak *exactly* the same language.

"Come on girls, let's sit outside. I want to hear about your day!"

Esme shakes her head. "You really don't. Our days are boring, you know that. We want to hear your stories. They're fascinating!" She gives me a nudge as we walk back out to the porch which is rapidly becoming bathed in a sheet of gold thanks to the setting sun. "Barbie is the widow of a Holly-wood studio owner, and Fitz here was a child star in the fifties, weren't you, Fitz? Didn't you film alongside the greats —Gene Kelly, Rock Hudson, Sinatra?"

I turn back to see him waving a hand.

"Tawny, that's all she ever wants to hear about. I'm betting young Esme here is a frustrated thespian."

"C'mon Fitz, you've had like, the most glamorous life. He once snogged Marilyn Monroe," she whispers in my ear, just loud enough that Fitz can hear.

"It was no snog, young lady, it was a peck. I was eight years old."

"Peck, schmeck," Esme laughs. "You kissed Marilyn Monroe, dude!"

We all settle onto the swing seats on the porch—Barbie and Fitz on one, me and Esme on the other.

"Oh, my days. I haven't fixed you drinks!" Barbie springs up from the seat as if she were twenty, not seventy. "Fitz, can I get you anything?"

"Hell, no," he replies. "You know I don't need the fuzzy stuff. I get the same effect just from standing up."

Barbie rolls her eyes. "Girls?"

"No, Barbie, we're fine," Esme says. "We can't stay. I just wanted to introduce you to Tawny. She's new here. Day two isn't it?"

"Yes."

"Well, my dear, you couldn't have come to a more fabulous place," Barbie gushes, sitting back down. "This really is paradise on earth." She looks out wistfully at the sea. "You know, my late husband left me very comfortable. I could retire to any place I want to, places that cost ten times this place, but I chose Starling Key."

"Why is it so special to you?" I ask.

Barbie sighs and looks at me. I notice her hair is just pink enough to be rebellious and her lips still hold dramatic red lipstick incredibly well. "It's the people if I'm honest."

I notice Fitz squeezes her leg.

"Mr. Starling is a doll, although I don't see him around too much. He's generally glued to that damn golf course. But then there's Mr. Johnson and his team. They definitely make Starling Key everything it is. It's safe, it's fun, it's well-kept, it's always developing. I don't feel like I've come here to decay, you know? I like to see things moving. When you get to my age, you can't turn the clock back, but you can wind it up. Isn't that right, Fitz?"

Fitz opens his mouth to speak but Barbie railroads him.

"The casino, for example, I'm so excited about it. My late husband co-owned one in Vegas for a while. He could not get me away from the blackjack table. Left me there all night once. You know, there's no timekeeping in those places!"

I can't help but chuckle.

"You are impossible, Barbie," Fitz says, shaking his head.

"What about you Fitz?" I ask. "What brings you to Starling Key?"

He looks almost surprised that I've asked, as though he's grown quite comfortable with Barbie always being the one to ask and be asked questions.

"Oh, well, I journeyed south following a crush. It didn't work out how I'd hoped but it's so beautiful here and, like Barbie says, the team is so amazing I never got around to leaving."

"I'm sorry to hear about your crush," I say. "At least you guys have found each other. I hope I have friends like you someday."

I notice Fitz blinking up at Barbie with a hint of sadness in his eyes. Barbie on the other hand launches into another spiel.

"Oh, darling, you have friends in us, and Esme. Once you've become a part of this team, you'll have friends and family for life. It's rare that anyone leaves Starling Key, isn't that right, Esme?"

"It really is," she says. "A lot of people have made this place their home."

We chat some more about how beautiful the island is and I promise Barbie and Fitz I'll go back and visit them regularly. I find myself genuinely looking forward to it. We say our goodbyes and head back out to the little street that winds alongside the villas.

"What's the story with those two?" I ask Esme as we get back into the buggy.

"What do you mean?"

"What Fitz was saying about following his crush. It wasn't Barbie was it?"

"Hey, you catch on fast, don't you? Yeah, it's Barbie. He's loved her forever, but back in the seventies, before she got married, he made his move and she didn't bite. He's always loved her but she won't see him as anything more than a friend."

"That's so sad. They're perfect together."

"I know. But listen, don't try saying anything to Barbie about it, and don't let the party girl exterior fool you. She's a tough cookie and doesn't like people meddling too much in her personal life. Trust me, she'll tell you everything she wants you to know, but nothing more."

"God, that's a skill I would love to master."

"Wouldn't we all?"

Esme drives away from Reef Street along a beautiful coastal road towards another collection of villas, which I soon learn is the "standard" accommodation for most of the island's guests. There are around fifty villas, although because they are spaced out and hidden amongst foliage and palms, it's hard to believe there's more than five. Some over-look the gardens while others—the more expensive ones—overlook the clear blue Mexican Gulf.

"Hey, before I forget," Esme says, as she follows the winding road through the villa gardens. "There's a beach barbeque Friday night. It's the last Friday before the season starts. It's tradition and everyone goes. You can come with me and Shell, ok? We'll look after you, and you'll have an awesome time."

"Ok," I smile. That actually sounds like fun. After a turbulent couple of days and a first week in a new job and a new home, a beach barbeque could be just what I need.

Esme parks ups and we walk down to the main beach. We stand on the shore with our bare feet in the clear, shallow water and look out to sea.

"Those are our executive villas," Esme says, nodding towards a small pier half a mile west. It's the same one I saw when I was perched on the gate earlier today. I can now see it is lined with villas built on stilts, raising the structures out of the water.

"Next time I go to clean one you can come with me. They're so fucking serene, I'm telling you. Like nothing you've ever seen. They each have a tub that looks out over the water, and private infinity pools, and four poster beds. They're gorgeous."

"I would love to see them," I say, silently wondering if those were part of Connor's vision too.

"Over there is the marina," she points to a cluster of yachts moored a few miles further west. "Only four in slips at the moment. It'll be full next week, you'll see."

"Is that the Grand House?" I ask, pointing to a glistening white building that looks like it should live on the Atlantic Highlands.

"Yeah, that's where the Starlings live," she confirms.

"What are they like?" I ask, kicking my feet through the water and loving the way the wet sand feels between my toes.

"Eric and Maria... they're ok. He's a golf addict, always on the green. Never see him any place else. Maria? Now she's a firecracker. Always with some poor young man. She ain't never been faithful as long as I've been here, but I think Eric knows and I don't think he cares. It works for them."

I contemplate their situation for a moment. I try to be open-minded, but I don't get it. I could never be with someone I didn't love wholeheartedly, who I didn't want to be with above all else.

"Do they have kids?"

"Yeah, two girls. Blue—Bluebell—is seventeen. Violet is three years younger. They're both at school in England. Just left again, in fact. They'll be back for the holidays."

"Wow. It's another world," I sigh.

"That it is," Esme says. "Don't worry though, as soon as you get settled and you see all the crap that goes on behind the scenes, the shine will soon wear off."

"Great," I laugh, then she loops her arm through mine again and leads me back across the beach. It's getting late so she promises to take me around the west side of the island some other time. I don't mind at all. What I've seen so far is enough to excite me. I mean, I have an actual job now that requires talking to real people, new friends in the form of Hollywood icons and a beach barbeque to look forward to at the end of the week. And not only that, Esme got a text from Rhonda while we were out, informing me of my new digs. I am being moved out of 8A. Thank. God.

---

WE GET BACK to 8A and I shove my belongings back into my bag then follow Esme down the stairs and out of block eight. I am not sorry to say goodbye to that building. She leads me back towards the gate to block two and we make our way up to the second floor. Just as I push the key into the lock, the door to the next room opens. I don't need to look up to know

who is standing there, watching as I let myself into my new
room; Esme's professional but slightly awkward smile says
it all.

"So you're my new neighbor."

His tone is even and I can't read it. I look up finally, and
despite my determination to not be attracted to this man who
hates me, every hair on my body stands on end. He is leaning
up against the wall, his expression half pissed, half amused,
with a pair of grey sweatpants hanging low on his hips and
nothing—I repeat, nothing—on top.

"Yes, Mr. Johnson," I say, forcing myself to focus on his
face and not every single pack on his abs, "I am."

# CHAPTER EIGHT

RELIEVED DOES NOT EVEN CUT it. When Friday comes around,
I am ecstatic. I can finally say goodbye to my first week on
the island. That said, it's been a week of two halves. The first
couple of days I would be happy to erase from my memory
altogether. The last few have been better. I've settled into my
job with Carter's help, I've hung out with Esme a couple of
nights and I've enjoyed my much bigger, actually quite lovely
new dorm—for which I have Rhonda to thank. And Connor
has kept well away. I haven't even heard him come and go
from the dorm next door.

I put on the one outfit I have that looks marginally party-
like—a little emerald green skater dress that hugs my ribcage
and flips out around my thighs. It was cheap, but it's cute.
Then I make my way back to block eight, to Esme's dorm.

The door opens a crack and a tall glass snakes around it
filled with something fizzy and packed with limes and leaves.

"You can't enter until you've drunk half," comes a voice.

I chuckle and take the glass.

"It looks like a garden," I say.

"It's mint. Drink it," Esme orders.

I bring the glass to my lips and inhale the citrusy, peppermint aroma. The bubbles pop, misting my lips, and I take a sip. Suddenly, my mouth is flooded with saliva; it tastes amazing, whatever it is. I down half a glass, no problem.

"Done!"

"That's my girl. You may enter."

The door opens and Esme and Shell are grinning at me. I hardly recognize them without their housekeeping clothes on. Esme has the gorgeous Ghanaian figure of curves on top of curves, on top of curves, which she has wrapped up like a gift in an African print figure-hugging dress. Shell is wearing a long flowing maxi dress which, coupled with her dyed blonde buzz cut hair, makes her look even longer and taller, like the Statue of Liberty.

"Damn, honey!" Esme squeals. "I love your dress."

I spin around for her, buoyed by the alcohol now swirling in my bloodstream.

"We just need to doll up those doe eyes of yours, then we can hit the beach."

"Ah, I don't have any makeup."

"But I do," Shell replies, dangling a sizable bag between her fingers.

"Wow, you're not kidding." I settle down on Esme's bed while Shell gets to work with dark shadow and kohl pencils in various shades of grey, black and brown.

"What is this?" I say, taking another sip of the drink.

"A mojito," Esme replies, applying a layer of glossy red lipstick. "Ché gave me his recipe a while back. It's mainly tons of rum, tons of lime, tons of mint, a chunk of ginger and a dash of club soda."

"It's pretty lethal," I say, feeling the telltale warm fuzziness settling in my belly.

"Oh yeah, you won't need many more of those this evening," Shell adds. "But it's your first beach barbeque; we figured the Dutch courage might help."

"Well, if it doesn't, at least I'll be too far gone to remember anything."

Shell laughs. "So, what brings you here, Tawny?"

"Oh, nothing much. Just needed a change of scenery, that's all."

"I don't believe that for a second," she says, wagging a long finger. "Everyone who comes to Starling Key has a story."

"Like who?" I ask, intrigued.

"Hmm, let me see. Well, there's Maggie of course. Everyone knows about Maggie."

"Maggie from the hole?" I ask, doubtful of whether that's her correct title.

Shell nods. "Her name isn't really Maggie, but it's what we've come to know her as."

"Yeah, Maggie the Magpie," Esme adds. "From her penchant for shiny, glittery things like Rolex watches and diamond earrings."

"I don't get it."

"Used to be a petty thief. Got herself a record a couple years ago. Nothing too serious—she just really likes sparkly, pretty things."

"So, why put her in charge of the keys to everyone's room?" I ask, questioning the wisdom of whoever had made that decision. Probably Connor—he seems to have his hands all over everything here.

"Yeah, I can see why you'd ask that, but nobody here has much of any value and Maggie likes real glitz—none of this cubic zirconia stuff for her. Cartier, Chanel, Bulgari... they're more her kinda thing."

"But this is a luxury resort—those kinds of jewels and accessories must be everywhere."

"And that's why she works in the hole and not in house-keeping," Esme winks.

"Officially," Shell continues, tipping my chin so she can apply something black to my bottom lashes, "she's paid for her crimes—community service and such—but she and Connor know she has an appetite. He offered her this job to help her stay on the straight and narrow."

There it is again. Connor the saint who hates me.

"What about you guys? What are your stories?"

"I'm busy. You go first," Shell says to Esme.

"Ok," Esme starts. "Well, I came here to get away from an abusive ex."

I'm about to gasp in horror when Shell says, "keep your lips still", and applies something to them.

"He was this big guy in our neighborhood—everyone knew him, everyone was scared of him. He could have had his pick of any of the local girls within a five mile radius and he picked me. My mom thought it was an honor, so even when he started beating me, she wouldn't listen. Kept telling me how lucky I was, and not to fuck it all up. My dad left us when I was little and Mom struggled a lot, so the thought of her eldest daughter being taken care of by the most respected... well, feared... man in the town, was appealing to say the least."

"God, Esme," I say, as Shell finished my lips. "I can't even..."

"Hey," she shakes her head. "It was another life. I'm a

different person now. I wasn't when I left him; I was a shadow of myself. No one in the town wanted to hear about the way he was treating me behind closed doors. My only choice was to leave, but even that, to him was not an option —it would have been too embarrassing. He kept a close eye on me for a couple weeks but when he got complacent I made a run for it. It was the middle of the night. I stole a bunch of cash from his office, packed one bag, booked one bus ticket. Didn't tell a soul. Came down here. Begged for a job and haven't looked back."

"You came straight here?"

"No, I tried a few other spots first—some bars on Key Largo, a couple stores on Islamorada, then I came here. Connor was the first guy I saw and he gave me a job on the spot. It's as though he can see when someone really fucking needs the help and will work like a dog to repay him."

"And you do work like a dog, doll. I've never seen anyone work as hard as you," Shell says, zipping up her bag of tricks.

"I'm so sorry to hear all that," I say, staring at Esme. She looks so happy and content and at ease, it's hard to believe any of it really happened.

"Thanks Tawny, but it all worked out for the best. I'm happier here and I can live my life exactly how I want to."

"What about you, Shell?"

"I would love to tell you, honey, but my story is a little longer and we have a date with a beach."

"And you need to tell us about you," Esme adds.

"Seriously, there's nothing to tell," I assure them. "My mom died six weeks ago. She had Alzheimer's and didn't know who I was for the last four years. I was her sole caregiver. There was no one else to stick around for. That's it."

"I'm sorry to hear about your mom," Esme says.

"Yeah, that sucks," Shell says. "I'm sorry too."

"Thanks," I sigh, picking at my fingernails.. It was the first time since leaving New Jersey that I'd said the words out loud. *My mom died.* I still couldn't believe it, or quite a lot else, for that matter.

"So, any sightings of your neighbor?" Esme asks, changing the subject.

"Nope, none."

"Do you mean Connor?" Shell asks. "I saw him down by the marina earlier today with some of the guys."

"What were you doing down at the marina? Were you spying on Eddie?" Esme narrows her eyes at Shell who is now looking decidedly guilty.

"No. Yes. Maybe."

I can't help but laugh. "Who's Eddie?"

"He's one of the lifeguards. Tends to hang out at the marina end of the beach, which would explain why Shell here is familiar with the goings on down there." Esme winks.

"Anyway," Shells says, straightening up to full height and metaphorically brushing off Esme's teasing, "that's where I saw Connor. He's alive and well."

"Will he be at the beach tonight?" I ask, trying not to betray my obvious hope that he will be. Not for any other reason than he's pretty to look at, if you ignore his hawk-like stare.

"Yeah, he never misses the beach barbeques," Esme replies.

"Well, he can't can he?" Shell adds. "He's like the guest of honor. Everyone wants a piece of Connor."

"I still don't understand why," I say.

"Oh, Connor is amazing," Shell says. "And he makes sure we're all looked after, you know? He got us all proper contracts, he helps out with medical bills, and he's been known to support members of our families if they hit hard times. He's actually a good guy. I couldn't believe it when Esme here told me about the way he's treating you. He's never been mean to anyone as far as I've seen. Only you."

"I guess I am the only one who drove their car into the wall on the way in," I shrug.

"Right?" Shell laughs. "If you can do that sober, what are you gonna be like with a few mojitos inside you? I need to get me some popcorn."

Shell puts a mirror in front of my face and I have to look twice. I don't recognize myself. My green irises are framed with an expertly applied liner that makes my eyes look twice the size and three times as piercing.

"How the…?"

"Shell was a celebrity makeup artist in a former life," Esme explains.

I look up at Shell questioningly.

"A story for another time," she says, pulling me to my feet. "Come on. That beach is calling our names girls, and I'm famished."

I follow them both out the door, sneaking one last look at my reflection in the mirror. My eyes are dramatic and incredible, but my hair is still trussed up in a punishing bun. I pull the band out and let my curls fall down my back for the first time since I arrived at the Key. What had been a bag of nerves at the thought of earning more hateful glances from my next door neighbor has become something else.

A challenge.

I dare Connor Johnson to look at me and not like what he sees.

# CHAPTER NINE

 onnor

"HEY MAN," Carter says, poking his head around the door to my office. "It's late and people are asking after you."

"Just finishing up," I reply, making sure all the files are closed securely before I lock my computer in the safe under my desk.

"Here. I saved you a hotdog," Carter holds out a paper plate which I grab, devouring the food in a few mouthfuls. "And here's a beer. A proper one. You've earned it."

I smile. I generally limit myself to a couple of these things maybe three times a season. But after the week I've had, I think I deserve a proper beer. I take the bottle and follow Carter into the reception area. I glance, needlessly, at Tawny's desk. I've been pretty successful at avoiding her the last few days, and it's helped. I've been able to get on with everything I needed to, without worrying about how my body's going to react if I see those legs again.

"How's it going on the beach?" I ask, taking a few gulps of beer.

"Great. It feels like it's been a long time coming. Everyone's been so busy getting stuff ready for the start of the season. They know it's going to be a busy one. Don't be surprised if you see a few comatose bodies sprawled out on the sand..."

"Already? It's not even ten thirty."

"They've been drinking since four."

"Jeez." I take another long swig and reach the end of the beer. My empty bottle is swiftly replaced by a brand new one. "Where are you stashing these? Do not say your boxers."

Carter laughs. "Not tonight, bro'. I need to keep the General nice and warm."

"Who's the lucky lady?" I ask, shaking my head.

"Lucy from the spa," he grins.

"Lucy? Doesn't sound like your type."

"Short for Luciana. Martinez."

"Now, that does," I nod. Carter has one type and one type only: Latino girls. Has never wavered for as long as I've known him.

"Does she know her cards are marked?"

"Oh yeah," he grins again. "She's waiting by the kegs for me as we speak."

"Anything else going on I need to know about?" I ask. It's code for, what's Little Miss Ice Pack up to, but I don't expect Carter to decipher the message, not when his mind is clearly on Lucy from the spa.

"Nope. We just need to watch the volume as we're not too far from the retirement village. Saying that, most of 'em are deaf."

"Hey, watch it. They're paying guests." I shoot him a

warning glare. I don't like people talking shit about any of our guests, not even Carter, one of my oldest friends.

"Ok, man, sorry," Carter holds his hands up and a further two bottles clank. I down my second beer and throw the bottle in a trash can. Carter passes me a third.

We reach the northeast wall and walk around it's perimeter to the beach which lies to the east of the dorms. It boasts the same white sands as the rest of the Key but with fewer well-placed palms, and no decorative hammocks or luxury recliners. Instead, over the years, various members of staff have brought along garden chairs and benches rescued from dumpsters on the mainland and given a fresh lick of paint. Blankets cover a lot of the ground and old beer kegs have become makeshift tables. The beach is generally reserved as a place for employees to come and chill out after a long shift, or for some of our couples to make out and watch the sunset in peace. Those who want to socialize and down a few beers after work head to the northeast bar instead, in the courtyard right in the middle of the blocks, except on nights like this at the start, middle and end of the season. On nights like this, we all hit the beach.

The beach is jam-packed with people and my eyes scan the crowd as we get closer. I know who I'm looking for and I wish I wasn't. Luckily, Luca sees me first.

"Hey, Connor, how you doing?"

"I'm good, my friend. How was the cove today?" The cove is over the west side of the island, off the beaten track. Guests rarely go there but we still keep an eye out along its sands for anyone who might want to visit Starling Key uninvited.

"Non-eventful," he shrugs. "How about you? Everything ok with the shipments next week?"

"Yeah, all good," I reply, slapping his back. "Let's not

worry about that now; it's your night off. Enjoy it before the season really kicks in."

My eyes continue to scour the bodies sprawled across beach blankets, huddled around tables and splashing about in the water. I can't see her. Instead, I look for Esme, her new BFF apparently. It takes a while because the beach is so crammed full. Most of the people I recognize—permanent, year-round staff—but some are seasonal and not as familiar. Then I spot Esme and kick myself. I can't miss that bright African print dress amidst a sea of denim shorts and bikini tops. She's twerking to the music with Shell, another of the housekeeping team. My eyes grow ravenous. *Where is she?* Then I feel the wind knocked out of me.

That.

Is not.

Her.

I narrow my eyes and tune out the sound of Luca's voice. I'll blame my lack of hearing on the music. A third girl is shaking her hips, dropping into a squat then sliding her ass back up with a seductive smile and a flick of long red hair. She's spinning in the sand, her hands running through her curls seductively, her obscenely short dress flying up around her hips, showing off a thin black thong and perfect peachy ass cheeks. I know those ass cheeks. I watched them stomp away in a huff after I'd caught them falling off the security gate.

My eyes instantly flick to the people around her and my chest constricts. Every single guy in the vicinity is watching her, and probably drooling. I hate it, and there's absolutely jack shit I can do. I walk closer, my teeth gritted, ready to pounce on anyone who tries to make a move on her. She's lip-syncing to the song with her eyes closed. She looks happy and free, and... drunk.

She misses her footing and flops down onto the sand. Esme and Shell laugh and hoist her back to her feet. A hand leans in and holds out a joint. She takes it, her eyes already glazed, her smile wobbly but still sexy as fuck. The boy in question—a seasonal worker I assume, as I haven't seen him before—takes her gratitude as a green light to muscle forward and wrap an arm around her waist. Surprise flashes across her face and something inside me ignites. I stride forward, gently but firmly pushing bodies aside as I go. I can hear Luca behind me but his words don't register. Before I know it, the kid has landed on his ass in the sand and I've grabbed Little Miss Ice Pack by the wrist and I'm pulling her away from the crowd toward the shore. I feel over a hundred pairs of eyes on me but I can only see red.

"What are you doing?" She shrieks as I continue to pull her towards the sea, away from prying eyes and ears. "Let go of me, Connor!"

I stop and grab her other hand. Something tells me if I let her go she really is stupid enough to head back to the drug dispenser and her equally drunk mates, and given her track record, will probably wind up dead on the shores of Key West.

"Listen to me," I say, battling to keep my voice and my temper under control. When I finally feel as though I've got her attention, I loosen my grip slightly. "You need to sober up a little bit, ok? I don't need you being out of your mind on drugs and alcohol, or totally hanging the following day when our guests might see you."

She anchors her feet in the sand and looks me straight in the eye.

"Why are they going to see me? I'm all the way back here, behind the *northeast wall*," she spits out the last two words like they're an insult. "And I'm off work, might I add?

I thought I was entitled to enjoy myself. What's it to you if I have a few beers and a drag on a joint?"

"You need to not be hungover tomorrow. I might need you."

"For what?" she spits. "Rhonda told me I have this weekend off."

"There's no such thing as time 'off' when you live on the island, unless you want to stay in your dorm twenty-four-seven until your next shift. There's always a possibility you can bump into a guest, and they need to see you looking professional."

"I'm no more drunk than Esme is."

"Yes you are."

"Besides..." she says, ignoring me. "Why aren't you saying this to her? Why only me? I mean, look around, Connor. *Everyone*'s drunk."

"Because you are the face of our events team now. It's a position that we need to ensure our guests can respect. I need you to *not* be an idiot."

"There it is." She smiles like she just won the lottery. "You're still mad at me for driving into the wall and you're even madder that Rhonda took pity on me and moved me into the room next to yours. Right, Connor?"

I let go of her wrists and she folds her arms, defiantly. It's then I notice the snugness of the little green dress she's wearing. Her breasts are pushed upwards with the force of her arms. I swallow.

"You know, I'm really not that bad of a person," she says, firmly. "I'm not as stupid as you think I am."

There's a glint in her eyes I don't like. Actually I do like. I mean, her eyes... what the hell happened to them? I can't tear mine away. It's that which I don't like.

"Just, take it easy will you?" I say, struggling to truly justify why I've dragged her away like a criminal. "I don't know you, I don't trust you, and you haven't given me much reason to believe you're not going to fuck something else up, okay?"

She frowns slightly, her eyes dropping to my clenched jaw. She seems to realize who I am—her boss, for all intents and purposes—and her shoulders relax.

"Fine," she sighs. "I guess I have to prove I'm trust-worthy and capable of getting through a day without messing something up."

She kicks at the sand and I feel suddenly guilty. Again.

"Right," I grunt. "Go enjoy yourself but don't be fucking stupid."

Her eyes flick back to mine, holding them as she turns away, then I'm left feeling the water lap at my ankles as the skirt of her dress flips up and over her ass cheeks, taunting me as if on purpose.

"What was that?" Luca says as I reach him.

"A loose cannon," I reply, shaking my head at the offer of a fourth beer. I don't even know what happened to my third. It was still in my hand when I first saw Tawny but it clearly wasn't when I grabbed her wrists. I'm acting weird and even my boys can see it. I need to stay off the alcohol.

Luca raises his eyebrows.

"I'm just a little on edge this week," I try to explain. "We're getting closer to the casino opening, I've got Bianchi's shipments coming in next week, and I need to be completely focused on it, that's all."

"I know. But we got it. Everything's cool," Luca says.

"Where's Carter?"

"He left almost as soon as you guys arrived. With a lady friend."

"Fast mover."

"Nah, he's been working on her for a while. I think she just surrendered in the end."

I spot some empty chairs and jerk my head towards them. Luca follows and so does Isaac. We sit and I prop my feet up on a crate, the anger at seeing Tawny behaving like a stripper having left me feeling almost light-headed.

"So, to what do we owe this pleasure, Luca?" I tease. "Normally you're off with one of the seasonal lifeguards by now. What happened?"

"He's only interested in one girl," Isaac says, taking a swig of his beer.

"No, I'm not. I just haven't seen anyone I like yet."

"Who's the girl?" I say to Isaac.

"Autumn Lockhart. Dive team. She joined a few months back…"

"I know her. Great girl. Has a solid head on her shoulders."

"Exactly. That's why Luca here hasn't scored with her yet."

"Will you stop, Isaac? I'm not interested in her. She's a friend, that's all."

"A hot friend," Isaac laughs.

"It is possible to be just friends with a hot girl," Luca frowns.

"Well, you're not going to be short of options this season," I say to him. "I've spotted at least four pairs of eyes checking you out since we sat down."

And that doesn't surprise me. Luca is like a surf model. He's tan, with shoulder-length dirty-blonde hair and baby blue eyes. He's also the youngest of us all at a mere twenty-five. The rest of us are approaching, or have toppled over, the age of thirty.

"Yeah, well, we'll see. How about you Isaac?" Luca asks, changing the subject. "Seen any MILFs or cougars yet?"

Isaac isn't offended. He's the first to admit he's not the slightest bit interested in women his own age or younger. But give him a woman over the age of forty and he's horny as fuck. If they're married to a rich guy for whom a hole in one means only one thing, even better; those apparently tend to be dirtier because they've been deprived for so long.

"Well, none of the staff of course—way too young for me. But wait 'til the season gets going. I'm sure I'll have my pick then." He winks, knowingly. "What about you, Connor?"

Like the beach barbeques themselves, this is tradition: the pre-season sexpectations chat. Usually, all six of us participate, but no doubt there'll be a round two as the season takes hold. I give them the same answer I give every year.

"C'mon guys, you know it wouldn't be fair to you if I threw my hat in the ring. I'd clean up. None of you would stand a chance. Think yourselves lucky I have too much to do to be worrying about which women I'm going to be wining and dining over the next few weeks."

Fortunately, most of them are too guy-like to question a comment like that. We don't tend to go deep in our group. Sure, they probably think it's weird, the fact I rarely get involved with anyone on the Key anymore. I did in the beginning—a few one night stands here and there, but things always got complicated when they wanted more and I had to see them around the resort every day. Now, I make sure any sexual encounters I have happen off the Key. And I'm not off the Key very often, so... I may as well be celibate.

Carter, however, has known me since we both joined the Marines fifteen years ago. He knows exactly why I'm not the relationship type and he knows I won't ever budge.

It's getting late. The crowd doesn't seem to be thinning out and I need to get some sleep.

"Can one of you keep an eye on things here? I need to hit the sack; I've got to run through the shipment schedule with Mario first thing." Mario Bianchi is a mob man. Based in Miami, he and his underlings use various points along the Keys as gateways and ports for shipments of anything from drugs, to other illegal substances, to firearms. Over the years, we've become one of his most trusted partners, helping him get firearms onto the mainland. Highly illegal, highly unethical, highly lucrative. My conscience has got over the dirty nature of what we do, as long as the shipments don't become drugs, animals or humans.

"I got it," Isaac says, crossing an ankle over his knee and settling himself in for a long night. "I left the logbook in your safe for you to check over too."

"Thanks. I'll take a look. Night kids."

"Night, Connor."

I leave Isaac and Luca knocking back their beers and make my way across the sand towards the wall. Before I get halfway, someone grabs my arm from behind.

"Connor…" I turn to see Esme with a look on her face that is part apologetic, part panic-stricken. "It's Tawny."

I don't know why but my heartbeat speeds up a notch. "Where is she?"

"Over here," she says, gratefully, leading the way back down the beach to a circle of chairs and crates around a small fire. I'm filled with a mixture of anticipation and dread as we get nearer. Is she ok? What has she done now? How can she possibly fuck things up any further? I look beyond the people sitting around the circle, to a body passed out on the sand. Shell is stroking her hair and rubbing her back. My strides quicken and I'm standing over them in seconds.

"What's going on?"

"She's hammered," Shell says. "She's puked up, which is probably a good thing, but we can't get her to move, and she's too heavy for us to carry."

"She's conscious, right?" I bend down and put my hand to her throat. Her pulse throbs rhythmically against my fingers.

"Yeah, she keeps saying things but isn't making much sense. She's ok; I think we just need to get her to bed."

I straighten up and wipe the sweat from my brow. Seriously? This girl has made way too big an impact on my life since she arrived. I need to get some shut-eye but I've been roped into getting Little Miss Ice Pack into bed. I could ask Luca to do it, but for some reason I don't wish to interrogate, I don't want anyone else near her.

"Fine," I say. I bend down and loop my arms beneath her, lifting her up to my chest like a freaking baby.

"I'll check on her in the morning," Esme says and I nod.

"You better. Night ladies."

I feel Esme and Shell's eyes on me as I walk back up the beach carrying our newest arrival. Everyone else seems too drunk and preoccupied to notice. Instead of going back to the security gate, I take a shortcut to block two, around the top edge of the beach. It's quiet, apart from the sound of my boots hitting the wooden decking. Suddenly, I feel someone watching me. I look down and her eyes are open, studying my face, curiously.

"Wherewegoin?" She slurs.

"I'm taking you back to your dorm," I snap. I don't know why I can't be nicer to her. All she's done is pass out a little from alcohol.

"Canweshtopaminute?"

"What?"

"Ineedapee."

"I'm sorry?"

"I need to pee."

*Oh, you're kidding me.*

"Can't you wait two minutes?"

"Noimdeshperate."

Her eyes are actually pleading so I gently lower her feet to the ground, retaining a firm hold of her arms.

"Can you even walk?" I ask, doubtful.

"Igonnatry."

"Ok, well, go around that corner," I say, pointing to one of the storage bunks. "Hold onto the side of the building."

"Ok—hicc…"

*Oh Jesus.*

"If you fall asleep round there, I'm just going to leave you."

"Sushagenelman."

I instinctively turn away, even though she's disappeared round the corner and I can no longer see her. At least I don't need to carry her anymore; she can clearly walk just fine. I look out at the stretch of lights bobbing around from the boats at sea and inhale deeply. I need to get over this thing, whatever it is. I need to find a way to be around Tawny Graham without letting her bother me. I haven't got laid in a while, that's all it is. I've managed one week so far, but I've basically been a jerk to her, and people have noticed and are starting to question why. I have to manage it better and actually try to be nice. I make a decision here and now. I will be courteous to this girl. I won't avoid her. I have to push through it. I'm all mixed up because she's a novelty, that's all. I have to ignore the attraction.

Then a squeal almost pierces my eardrums.

# CHAPTER TEN

awny

*HOLY FUCKING MOLY, what's happening to my ass?*

"Connor!" I scream. "Help me!"

He's standing over me in a matter of seconds, pulling me up to my feet. He very gallantly ignores the fact my thong is around my ankles. Either that or he hasn't clocked it yet.

"Tawny, you ok?"

His voice is breathless and beautiful.

"No! I think I sat on a bunch of fire ants."

"Let me see," he whips out his cell and flicks on the torch, exposing my little puddle of pee and whatever had decided to attack me, as though the incidents of the past week haven't been mortifying enough.

"Did you sit on the cactus?" he sighs.

"Oh wow, is that what it was? What the fuck is a cactus doing back here?"

I am now, thankfully, S. O. B. E. R.

"It's a Key Cactus," he explains. "We built all this around it. Never had the heart to cut it down. It's one of the oldest things on the island."

"I don't care if it's older than Egypt," I say. "That thing is lethal and shouldn't be here."

"You're not supposed to sit on it," Connor says, failing to hide a smirk. I can't see it but I can hear it. I bend down to pull up my panties but stop as they hit my butt.

"Ow!"

"What?" He sighs, exasperated.

"I think I got spikes…"

"What?"

"The spikes," I say, cringing in combined pain and humiliation. "They're still in my butt."

That's it. Connor bursts out laughing and I'm just thankful he can't see me evolving into a human tomato.

"Asshole," I mutter, stepping out of the thong; there's no way I can wear it while these disgusting things are poking out of my skin. "I need to get back to my dorm."

I attempt to stomp past him but when I move, it's like I can feel a hundred daggers inching further into my ass. I stop and put my hands over my embarrassed face. It seems to remind Connor I'm a human being.

"Shit, I'm sorry," he splutters. "Can you walk?"

"No," I grumble.

"Shit, ok."

He seems to think for a second, then, before I have chance to consider my options, I'm flung over his shoulder, my bare ass on display to anyone who might walk towards us.

"Connor, no," I say, grabbing at his back. "I'm practically naked."

"Don't worry," he says and I detect a different tone in his

voice. He's no longer making fun of me. "We're taking a shortcut; no one comes this way."

He carries me along the decking, around the back of the northeast wall and through a gate I haven't seen before. Then we go through what appears to be a catering kitchen and storage area, before emerging right outside our block. Once inside the building, surrounded by electric lights flicking erratically, I feel his neck turn.

"Ouch," he whispers. He's looking at my ass and I'm nothing if not utterly mortified.

"Is it bad?"

"It ain't good," he says, striding up the stairs as though I'm light as a feather. "But don't worry, I got some lotion in my room."

He bypasses my dorm and I look longingly at the door as he fumbles in a pocket for his key. My head bobs up and down as carries me into his own dorm and lays me face down on a surprisingly soft, clean, white comforter.

"Don't move," he says, softly.

I'm painfully aware my dress is around my waist and my whole butt is on display and there's nothing I can do about it. Low point doesn't even begin to describe this moment in my life. I hear him turn on the light to his bathroom so I take the opportunity to look around his dorm. It is laid out exactly the same as mine, with whitewashed walls and a wooden floor. He has a queen sized bed, unlike my little single, and a couple more dressers, but otherwise, there's not much to differentiate the two rooms.

I turn my head as much as I can without embedding the spikes any further, and my eyes land on some photographs pinned to the wall. In the dim light I can just make out some of the guys from the security team—Carter, Isaac and maybe Hudson. In most of them, they're clasping beers with palm trees behind them, but a couple of them seem to show Connor and Carter dressed in army uniforms with nothing much in the background.

I hear footsteps coming out of the bathroom and I bury my face into the comforter.

"I can't believe this is happening," I mutter.

"For what it's worth," he replies, "neither can I."

I feel his weight sink into the bed and the warmth of his body against my thigh. I thank God I'm in near-shock, otherwise I don't know how my body would be reacting right now.

A couple of instruments land beside my head and I turn to see what they are. A pair of tweezers, some antiseptic wipes, lotion and a small empty pot.

"I need to get the spikes out first."

"Oh God," I groan and turn my face back into the comforter.

I feel his hand lightly press down on my left butt cheek, then a sharp tug, followed by pretty severe pain. I groan again.

"Man, you came down on that thing hard. These spikes are like an inch deep. Maybe we should take you to the hospital..."

"No..." I jerk my head up. A hospital is the last place I want to go, for a hundred and one reasons. "No, I hate hospitals. Hate them. Please can... can you try to do it? It'll be fine; I trust you."

I do not trust him. I really don't know if my ass is going to be fine after this. I mean, some cacti are venomous right? Where's Google when you need it?

"Please?" I beg.

He sighs, heavily.

"Ok," he says, finally. "But, look, um, this is awkward... I need better access. Most of the spikes are in the, um, crease…" I can almost hear the wince. "I need to raise you up."

"What do you mean?"

He speaks so quickly I almost don't hear what he says.

"DoyoumindifIputyouacrossmyknee?"

My eyes almost pop out of my head and I'm thankful only the comforter can see them.

"Oh, God," I groan. "If that's really the only way."

"Look," he says, quickly. "The other option is to go to hospital. It's your decision."

"Knee," I squeak.

"What?"

"Knee," I say again, more loudly.

"Right, ok." I'm grateful he sounds almost as uncomfortable about this as I do. He scoots down the bed and lifts my legs up. A small squeal escapes my lips as I feel the spikes again with the movement. As soon as my thighs are suspended above the bed, he slides beneath them and drops my knees, lowering my stomach to his jeans.

"There are about a hundred spikes here," he mutters, almost to himself.

"Guess I better make myself comfortable," I say, resting the side of my face on my hands so I can see him out of the corner of my eye.

"This is easier," he says, bending over me with tweezers poised. His eyes are narrowed in concentration and his jaw ticks occasionally as he surveys the damage. It definitely feels easier. I can still feel the sharp tug but the resulting pain isn't as severe and I find myself relaxing while he goes to work. Even the sound of each spike landing in the plastic pot is weirdly soothing. I try to make conversation but his one word replies tell me he needs to focus, so I let him. I close my eyes and the sensation of feeling unbearably embarrassed is replaced by something else, something like need. And something stiffening beneath my stomach.

I flick my eyes open to see if he's aware of his growing erection but his eyes are singularly concentrated on the task at hand. Occasionally, his fingers innocently rub over a spot where a spike has been, presumably to wipe away blood, but by the time he's finished pulling them all out, I'm a wet mess. He doesn't stop there. With the spikes all laid in the pot continuing to glare at me from their plastic prison, Connor takes an antiseptic wipe and gently applies it to each cheek. After a minute or so, he takes a tissue and pats the skin dry.

Only then does he take a deep, no doubt sobering breath and looks at me. There's something indecipherable in his eyes when they lock with mine.

"Just lotion now," he says, with a dry voice. I nod once, incapable of any other reply.

I watch him pick up the bottle, slowly, like he's prolonging the task, then squeeze out a small amount. He rubs his fingers together then brings them down to my bottom. I suppress a gasp.

I continue to watch him as his fingers glide across my skin in long sweeps and small circles. The lotion sinks in quickly and he goes to squeeze out more. I hold my breath against the unbearable exquisiteness of it all. What would he do if I turned over now and showed him what he's done to me? No, not in a million years. I couldn't do it. He thinks I'm pathetic, useless and a walking disaster zone and he does not hesitate to make me aware of that, at every opportunity. It would be just another embarrassing incident he would hold against me.

His fingers press against my skin again, this time moving out beyond the zone of injury. He's cupping the cheeks of my ass, does he know that? It feels like he's molding me into shape, and the longer he does it, the wetter I'm getting. I need to go.

"Connor," I whisper, because I no longer have a voice. His erection is like a steel rod beneath me.

He suddenly seems to snap out of a trance.

"All done," he says, lifting my thighs up and sliding out from beneath them to stand. I spin my head around and see him turn away, no doubt to conceal his giant hard on. He pushes a hand through his hair.

I gingerly pull my dress back down over my buttocks and get to my feet. I'm relieved I can stand without a million little sticks digging deeper into my flesh.

"Thanks," I say, quietly.

"I'll see you Monday," he says, not even looking at me.

"Ok. Sure." I shuffle towards the door. I am so wet and so turned on I can barely walk. I open the door and slide my feet through it, then as I turn to close it behind me, I catch his eyes. They are unusually dark, as though he's seen something deadly.

---

As soon as I get back to my room, I close the door and collapse back against it. My breathing is coming in short, fast bursts, as though I've been holding my breath under water. Without even kicking off my shoes, my fingers reach beneath the short skirt of my dress and find my clit. A low, unanchored moan leaves my throat and my head drops back against the wooden paneling. I can probably count on two hands the number of times I've masturbated in my life. This is the first time I've ever felt an urgent, unbridled need to. I don't think about what I'm doing; I just move my fingers blindly, stroking instinctively.

Within seconds I am biting down on my fist and sliding to the floor, the sound of an orgasm escaping through my knuckles as I imagine Connor's fingers in the place of my own. I pant hard as my orgasm subsides, then, just as I'm about to push myself back up to standing, there's a knock at my door.

I freeze, knowing that whoever is stood at the other side —unless they are deaf or completely stupid—knows exactly what they just overheard.

"You left your panties," Connor whispers, and my humiliation hits a new low.

I get up and open the door ajar, just enough to see his face and the black thong he's sneaking through the gap. The man looks half triumphant, half in hell.

"Thanks," I mutter, then close the door.

# CHAPTER ELEVEN

 onnor

I GET BACK to my room, close the door and put a palm up against it. With my other hand, I pull my aching cock out of my pants. I recall the sound of her panting and immediately see a liquid pearl appear on the head. I rest my forehead against the door and stroke the length of my cock, long and slow at first, imagining my hand is hers. My own breath comes in sharp beats and I quicken the pace. I recall the sound of her fingers sliding in and out of her wetness, only barely audible through the wooden door. Then the gasps as she brought herself close to the edge.

I grip myself harder and my elbow joins the palm of my hand on the door as I lean against it for stability. I can't have her but I can think about her. I can masturbate to the vision of her, to the sound of her own orgasm as she relieved herself of the same pent-up need that I'm feeling too. My forehead grinds into the door and I grit my teeth, straining to hold in a cry of release as I come. I can't make the same mistake she made. I can't let anyone hear. My hips spasm into my curled hand once, twice, and I'm empty.

I take some deep breaths, then step out of the pants I hadn't even stopped to remove when I returned to my room. I needed to come right there and then. Having her laid across me, butt-naked, had been hard enough, but then hearing her come only minutes after she walked out of my room, tipped me over the edge.

I clean up and take a shower. I feel slightly more sated for having taken care of myself but, unlike all the other times I take care of myself, I still feel need, and I don't know why. Actually, I do know why. I need the real thing. And that's a problem.

As I step out of the shower, I feel suddenly light-headed, as though the blood has drained from the top of my head to my toes. I grip the door frame for balance and wait for my vision to return to normal. As I wipe a newly formed light film of sweat from my brow, I remember the last time I felt this way and I'm filled with dread. I know what's coming. I know where it's coming from, and I know exactly where it's headed, and it's no place I'd send my worst enemy.

---

I PICK my way through the boxes of tools and machinery left out by the decorators. Only a few weeks until the casino will be ready to open to guests and visitors. I resist a smile. I won't celebrate until the first night is over, until the place has been christened and deemed a success. The casino is the latest of the projects I personally came up with and convinced Starling to do—a.k.a give me the money and green light to get on with. None of my projects have failed yet, and I don't expect this one will either. But no celebrating until the fat lady.

I walk around the outside of the main room giving it a quick once over. I know exactly where everything will go in the Pit—the Blackjack table, the Craps table, the Baccarat table, the slots. I know where the live poker will be situated—in a quieter corner at the opposite side of the room to the restaurant and bar. I know where the private poker room, Club Starling, will be positioned; I know where every single camera will be hung, inserted, hidden.

This casino is going to be a landmark development for the resort—for its reputation and for lining Starling's pockets. It will be good for SKS too. I'll need to hire more guys, promote the existing ones, give them greater responsibility, more money. I rub my palms together and allow myself a second to feel proud of what I've been able to do for these guys. Each and every one of them has a history they're running from and no other choice but to do this job, nothing to fall back on.

I push the door open and feel the tension roll off my shoulders. Sure, the job I created for myself is pretty stressful, and I only have myself to blame. But these guys make it all worthwhile. Isaac is at the far end of the poker table, shuffling the cards and stacking the chips, like the frustrated banker he is; Hudson is leaning back on his chair, his hulking frame bringing it perilously close to collapse; Jaxon is regaling Hud with some story that I'll no doubt hear in great, drunken detail later; Luca is stacking beer bottles and potato chips on a table in the corner with one hand while texting someone on his phone with the other. Carter hasn't arrived yet.

Hudson looks up first.

"Hey man, looking good out there."

"You mean the casino?"

"No, I mean you in speedos out on the boat this morning," he winks.

"Fucker." I was in no boat this morning; I was very much preoccupied with making sure a case of ammo got off the island without Starling seeing.

"Yeah the casino. We on track for the opening night?"

"Of course." Stupid question.

"Is 50 Cent still flying in?" Jaxon asks.

"Think so. Still waiting on Tobey Maguire. The PR guys seem pretty certain Matt Damon plans to show his face too."

"Did Diana Goldblum ever respond?" Luca asks, over his shoulder.

Isaac looks up. He's a fan of the fifty-something poker-playing actress.

"Not yet. The PRs are on it though. I'll chase them up."

"She'll get more than a poker game," Isaac mutters under his breath.

"Just 'cos she's a little older than you…" I start.

"A lot…" Hudson jumps in.

I ignore him. "…doesn't mean she's going to fall for your charms. She's a respectable lady."

"I only go for respectable ladies." Isaac looks genuinely hurt.

Jaxon fakes a cough.

Luca hands me a beer as I sit down and cross my feet on the edge of the table.

"Hey man," Isaac huffs, shooing my feet off the table. "This…" he strokes the smooth surface of the table. It isn't premium casino material but it's still Isaac's pride and joy, "…is where the magic happens. Show it some respect."

I hold up my hands and cross a foot over my knee instead.

"Where's Carter?"

"On his way," Luca replies, sitting down next to me.

"We need to talk about the marina," I say, shooting him a firm look. "The date's been confirmed, the boat is already on the water. We just need to do our part now—make space for the delivery and keep it quiet."

"For the load coming in from Mexico? It's all good," Luca nods. "We have one long-termer who is happy to move to Islamorada for a couple days, and two new yachts due in that I've diverted to Key West. As far as they're aware, we're doing repairs."

"And if Starling asks why the slips are empty?"

"Old Jaxon here is going down there with a sledge-hammer Sunday after dark. The Starlings will be in Miami that night, but we said we're doing repairs, so… we're going to do some repairs. No one's lying." He holds up his hands innocently.

I grin. "Good. This is the only delivery coming in by boat, but it's critical no one sees it. This is the only shipment by sea that doesn't have kosher goods on it. If we start getting questions, we'll be in deep shit."

"No one will see it, Connor," Hudson says, seriously. "We've all got our eyes on the prize and our necks on the line here."

"Ok, I appreciate it."

"And if we do get any passersby looking to dock for a night, I'll make sure Tawny knows we can't accommodate anyone."

"Shit. Tawny." My heart sinks and beats faster, all at the same time. "Does she know about this?"

"I don't think so, yet," Isaac replies. "But we'll have to tell her something soon. I can have a word with her…"

"No, I'll do it," I snap, earning surprised stares from all of them. "I mean, I have a few other things I need to discuss with her, and she's proven herself to be a bit of a liability up to now."

"She seems ok to me," Luca says, shoveling a handful of potato chips into his mouth. "And why would Rhonda put her on the desk if she didn't think the girl was up to the job?"

I keep my mouth shut and breathe angrily through my nostrils. "Well, we'll see."

"Maybe we don't have to tell her the whole tr…" Jaxon doesn't finish his sentence because the door opens and standing in the doorway is Carter. And Tawny. All five foot five, pale-skinned, redheaded curvaceousness of her.

My eyes are drawn to her immediately, as though they've been deprived of food and drink and she's an all-you-can-eat buffet. And all I can hear is the sound of her orgasm as she hit the floor of her dorm after I'd just massaged her butt with lotion and sent her packing. Remembering where and who I am, my eyes shoot to Carter and, without words, I demand to know what she's doing here.

"Hey guys," Carter says, cheerily. "Brought a guest!"

He avoids my glare and instead takes Tawny's hand and pulls her into the room. I can feel her green eyes on me the whole time and I dare not look back up.

"Hey," Hud leans across the table. "We haven't met. I'm Hudson. But you… you can call me Hud."

I can practically hear him wink. He's flirting, I realize with a surge of anger. And who wouldn't be tempted by him? Or by any of these guys for that matter. Those three hours we all spend in the gym every day pay off. Every single one of my guys is ripped, built like steel and has a face and person- ality for every possible female taste. Carter is the rocker with eyelashes that should be censored and muscles that look like they'd pop if someone stuck a pin in them. Isaac is the clean- cut, ex-CIA Italian charmer. Likes 'the thinking woman' and has an MBA in making cougars feel like teenagers. Luca is the baby-faced man-whore of the crew, well-known throughout the resort for being free and easy with his affections. Which many of our lady guests like. A lot.

Hud is the beefed-up, partially reformed bad boy. Ex-hitman, earned his stripes being a punching bag for his old man. The second he grew an inch taller, he hit back and didn't stop until his mom begged him to then shouted him down for hurting her husband. He walked out, took up beating crooks for a living and only looked back once, to make sure his little sister hadn't taken his place as the family punching bag. He and Jax go way back. But while Hud has no fond childhood memory, Jaxon is a family kid. Ex-stunt man. Was basically a wild child who liked adrenalin sports. His ma sent him to an outdoor pursuits camp to expend his greater-than-is-normal energy, and he never looked back. One near-fatal occupational accident later and he came to Starling Key to become one of my best men. Those women who like their men the flavor of quiet and darkly brooding, love Jaxon.

Carter pulls out a chair next to Isaac to let Tawny sit, then promptly takes the seat between me and her. Luca hands her a beer which she starts drinking immediately, as though she needs the Dutch courage. Damn right she's gonna need it. I'm fuming, because it's hard enough being around her during the day. I really don't need to have to focus on diverting my eyes, my thoughts and the blood that wants to rush to my groin, during my downtime too. She rewards him with a devastating smile. Fuck.

"Well, now that lover boy's arrived, I guess we can start," Isaac says, nodding at me for the final go-ahead. I raise one eyebrow in response. Luca sits to my right, with Hud and Jax between him and Isaac. I seem to be the only one who can sense the tension in the atmosphere so thick a knife could cut through it. Let the shitshow begin.

Isaac distributes the chips around the table. "Each one is fifty bucks."

Tawny sucks in a breath and I have to stop myself from hauling Carter out of the room and demanding to know why he brought her. The poor girl doesn't have any money; not only will she be embarrassed when she loses, she'll be even more broke than she is now.

"I'll spot you," Carter says to her. "It's cool. Put one in."

I feel my bones still as the blood pumps around them. *What is he playing at?*

She takes one of the chips between her fingers, studying it as though it's a precious gem. Then she pushes it towards the middle of the table, following Carter's nod. The rest of us push in two each, as usual.

Isaac shuffles the cards one last time then deals. Five cards each. I pick mine up last. I am seriously pissed. I've been looking forward to this evening, to relaxing and letting go, to just being a guy, with my guys. And now I have to be on guard. I have to watch what I say, watch where I look, be aware of how I breathe, be conscious of how my damn dick reacts. It hasn't been in the vicinity of Tawny Graham since she was laid across it, butt-naked. I silently reassure it that no amount of Tawny Graham is going to make it or me happy in the long run, but it isn't listening. I can feel it stirring in my boxers and I shift uncomfortably to conceal it.

I look at my cards. I tune out everything else and focus on them. When I do glance up, her eyes are deep beneath my skin.

"Now, you're new to this, right?" Carter asks her.

She slowly drags her eyes from me to him.

"Yeah," she says quietly. "I played a couple times at school but... I don't remember the rules or anything, really."

"Ok," Carter rubs his hands together. This is his dream date. Teaching a woman how to play poker. Then he flicks his eyes across to me and I can see the glint in them. I realize then, he's up to something. He's trying to piss me off. I have no idea why; Carter is my closest friend. He knows better than to make a play for her himself, so what's he up to?

"Can I see your cards?"

She holds them tightly and opens them out just enough for him to see. I know he won't take advantage of her; he's too nice a guy at heart, but it irks me that she's so trusting of him.

"Oof!" he says, glancing around the table. Ok, so she got good cards. Beginner's luck. Either that or Carter is bluffing, which he's shit at, so I believe him when he implies she got a good hand. I keep my eyes on my own; I refuse to be distracted.

"Are you kidding me?" Luca whines, winking at the girl my cock is relentlessly drawn to beneath the table. "This is your first time playing with us and you got a good hand already?"

"I..." Tawny looks back at him, confused, then her eyes flash to me and I feel rigid. "...have no idea."

"Yeah, bro'," Carter replies. "I think we're all screwed."

I look down at my own cards and feel quietly confident I don't fall into the category of 'all'.

"Let's start with Isaac then, and go clockwise," I say, moving on.

Isaac moves two chips to the center of the table and I take a swig of beer, my eyes zeroed in on my hand.

"I fold," Jax says, throwing his cards face down on the table and taking a giant swig of beer.

"Hud?" I say, turning to face him.

He says nothing but pushes two chips of his own into the pile.

"Luca?"

Luca clicks his tongue against the roof of his mouth while we wait on his decision.

"Call." He pushes two chips in. I'm next up.

"I call." I push two chips forward, then throw in a third. "And I raise you fifty." I turn to glare at Carter.

"Man, I fold," he grins, then turns to whisper something into Tawny's ear. I can feel the blood pumping through my temple.

Everyone looks at Tawny. We know she has no clue what she's doing, but Carter seems to have a lot of confidence in her hand. She looks up and slides her eyes across all of us. They're sparkling with challenge.

"I call one-fifty," she says, pushing three chips in. "And I raise you one hundred." She pushes in a further two chips and slowly withdraws her hand.

"I'm out." Isaac folds.

"And me." Hudson.

Back to me. I stare at my hand. Two pairs. I'm pretty confident it's the better hand out of mine and Tawny's; Carter has a useless poker face and he's hamming it up for the drama.

"Raise you another fifty," I say, pushing another chip forward. Confident, but cautious.

Carter leans into Tawny again and the back of my neck breaks into a sweat. She picks up a chip, then another. "I call and raise you fifty."

"So, we're at three-fifty," Isaac says. "Connor?"

He wants to know if I'm prepared to raise again but I'm done. I can't bear to watch my best friend sidle any closer to the girl sitting opposite me, taunting me with everything she's got, whether she knows it or not. I look her straight in the eye for the first time since she entered the room.

"Call you fifty," I say, pushing one more chip to the center. "Now, show your hand."

She slowly lowers her cards to the table. Four Queens and an Ace of Clubs stare up at me—four of a fucking kind.

"Congratulations." I force a smile, then lay down my two pairs.

Carter cracks up. "Ah man, I told you, didn't I?"

I ignore him and push all the chips towards Tawny. She looks up at me through thick red lashes, almost triumphant.

"Beginner's luck." Her smile is cocky but I catch her staring at the chips as though she can't believe she just won.

"Nice one," Luca says, pushing back his chair to grab more beer and potato chips.

"Isaac, man. Deal me a better hand this time, huh?" Jaxon looks across at our dealer with a feigned expression of utter boredom.

Isaac rolls his eyes, shuffles and cuts the deck. "It's not always about the hand, Jax, I keep telling you."

I want to leave, but I don't want to look like a petulant child, so I force myself to remain seated for a second game.

"Another beer?" Carter asks Tawny.

"I'd love one, thanks."

I bite my tongue. It's none of my business if she wants to drink or not, or even if she wants to get as blind drunk as she did on the beach. I can't help myself.

"Go easy. I don't want to have to carry you back to your dorm again."

Her eyes flick up at me and swarm with something—a recollection. Which was precisely my intention. Carter narrows his eyes; I neglected to update him on that little incident. She takes the bottle from Luca and tips it back, taking a long drink, her eyes glued to me.

Isaac deals again. I look at my hand. Aces and damn spaces. Hudson is as still as stone—his classic poker position. I notice Jax start an eye roll, then stop abruptly. Luca betrays nothing as he shovels more chips into his mouth. Isaac studies his hand intently, while Carter throws an arm around Tawny and whispers into her ear, making my knuckles curl.

Isaac pushes a chip forward. Jax does the same. We all look at Hudson.

"Fuck it. I ain't convincing anyone I got a good hand. And I need to pee." He throws his cards down and heads for the bathroom.

I push two chips in.

Carter lays his cards down. "I'm out," he says, then leans over again to Tawny.

"Call," she says, flashing her eyes at me, before pushing two chips in.

"Out," Isaac says, dropping his cards and leaning back with his beer.

"Raise you fifty," Jax says pushing another chip into the pile.

"I'm out," Luca huffs.

I'm pretty confident I have a good hand and I'm convinced Jax is bluffing, but my blood is boiling so hot I can barely concentrate.

"Out."

Carter raises his eyebrows, then pulls Tawny closer to him and whispers something else in her ear. She laughs and pushes a chip forward.

"Raise you fifty, Jax."

"Ah man, I don't trust you," he laughs back. "I reckon

you lied about not playing before. You're really a pro, aren't you?"

Tawny grins mischievously. "Yeah, maybe I was bluffing."

"Really?"

"No. I'm totally kidding. I have no idea, honestly."

"Ok, I raise you another fifty," Jax says, grinning.

Tawny looks up at Carter, then back at her cards. "I'm out."

"No way!" Jax laughs. "Let's see your hand."

She lays down the cards—a pair.

"Now let's see yours, Jax," she says, excitedly.

His face is the picture of smugness as he lays down his hand of *nothing*, then slaps his hands together.

"Ah, man?" Carter groans.

"I don't get it," Tawny says, frowning.

"He was bluffing," Carter explains, then turns to Jax. "You're usually shit at that. What happened?"

"I lost too much fucking money, that's what."

Luca piles more beers onto the table and Isaac shuffles again. I sit back and watch as the evening I'd been looking forward to unfolds into one long, uncomfortable nightmare. Carter is speaking to Tawny quietly and there it is again. An open-mouthed laugh, presenting perfect white teeth. She doesn't look at me, even though the tension in the entire upper half of my body must be traversing the table. Instead, she sinks backwards into Carter's chest and he plants a small kiss on the top of her head. *Fuck this.*

I stand up, shoving the chair backwards so hard it hits the wall. Everyone's eyes are on me now, for entirely the wrong reasons, and I don't even care. I slam my empty bottle on the table and walk to the back of the room and grab a fresh one.

Cocking it to Luca with my thanks, I walk straight past the table towards the door.

"You leavin', man?" Carter asks, his voice littered with cockiness.

"Yeah. Early start. It's been a pleasure."

I yank open the door and feel her eyes boring into my back. I resist the burning urge to look back and instead I walk through, letting the heavy door close behind me.

# CHAPTER TWELVE

awny

My eyes are glued to the door until my brain computes the simple fact he is not coming back. Carter's plan—which he updated me on as we made our way to the casino—to annoy Connor into submission is either working or has completely backfired. I feel Carter's hand on my thigh, giving it a small squeeze.

"Last game, guys, then I'm taking the lady home," he says.

"Does Lucy know about your... um... arrangement?" Hudson asks, frowning.

Carter squeezes my shoulder.

"There's no arrangement here," he grins at me. "We're just trying to get under Connor's skin is all."

"Why?" Luca is completely oblivious.

"Because he's been giving the poor girl a shit time since she arrived and she doesn't deserve it."

Jaxon nods.

"And she has to work with us now, right?" Carter looks at me and I raise my eyebrows in agreement. "He needs to get over himself, or all our lives are going to be miserable."

"Well, I just hope you know what you're doing," Hudson mumbles. "He looked ready to break someone's arm."

I don't say anything. Not because I don't dare and not because I'm embarrassed that the big boss guy apparently hates my guts. But because I'm confused. No, I'm utterly bewildered. Only days ago, Connor Johnson was gently extracting cactus thorns out of my butt and getting obviously turned on by it, yet it appears he can't bear to be in the same room as me.

---

AFTER THE NEXT GAME, Carter and I leave and head to the beach. I jam my third beer into the sand and watch the white grains stick to the condensation around the bottle. There's no breeze, but the night air is cool.

"Don't take it personally, T," Carter says as he sits heavily on the beach beside me.

I sigh and look out across the sea. It is black, like the night sky, and calm, reflecting the light of the stars and making the horizon twice as bright though indistinguishable.

"You keep saying that to me, Carter, but how can I not take it personally? He's nice to everyone except me."

He turns to face me. "Look, you know Connor doesn't trust you, right?"

"All I do is book excursions for guests and ask them about their dietary requirements. It's a beach resort. Very little can go wrong."

"Well, there's the rub," he says, taking a swig of beer then wiping his wrist across his mouth. "To us, it isn't just a beach resort."

"What do you mean?"

"Ok," Carter takes a deep breath. "You know how I was saying we do a lot more here than just security?"

I shrug. "Yes."

"We all have a past that means we can bring a certain something to the running of this place. We all have connections and ways and means of making things work. Take Connor, for example. He's the one with the brains and the ideas, but I'm his defense. If someone overcharges us, or tries to get away with sub-standard work, Connor sends me in. They don't fuck with me."

"Do they fuck with Connor?"

Carter laughs, loud. "Oh no, they don't fuck with him, but he doesn't have time to do the, um… shall we say, house-keeping. And I like it. I like scaring the living daylights out of people who don't always deserve daylight."

"What about the others? Isaac? Luca?"

"So, Isaac is ex-CIA and a mathematical genius. He sorts out all our finances. Those reports Connor gives to Starling every week? Isaac does those. Why do think he holds all the chips at our poker games? He's a frustrated investment banker; he loves that shit."

"And Luca?" I raise a skeptical eyebrow.

"Hey, don't be fooled by his beach bum aesthetic. Luca is a salesman through and through; he handles all our supplier negotiations. If we get big corporate parties on the island or we need to hire a company to build a new bar for example, he handles all the back and forth. He can barter like a fake handbag dealer on speed."

I can't help but laugh at that. I hadn't talked much to Luca but he didn't seem like the salesman type, just a sandy blonde surfer dude who happened to be built like a truck, just like the rest of them.

"What about the quiet one?"

"Oh, Jaxon? Jax, he's our tech whiz kid. He used to be a stuntman you know."

"Really? He seems way too shy for something like that."

"That's why he was so good at what he did. He didn't try to steal the limelight from the big actors—and he filled in for some serious names—he just got on with the job. He's always had a weird inclination to dice with death. No idea why, happy childhood and all that. He just loves living on the edge, throwing himself off cliffs and crashing insanely expensive cars, all to make some other guy look tough."

"So what made him stop?"

"Brain injury," Carter sighs. "He was doing a rooftop chase, missed the roof of a building, fell fourteen floors onto a roof below. Doctors said he should have been dead three times over. It was touch and go for a while, but he came round. But his brain had moved and now..." he tugs at the label around his beer bottle and doesn't meet my eyes. "He's kinda living life on a tightrope. Anything could happen. He has to stay indoors whenever there are fireworks; he can't fly on a plane; he can't even go on fairground rides in case something knocks his brain even a little. He could fit, it could cause serious damage and he might never recover."

"Is security really the best profession for him?" I ask.

He laughs, darkly. "Good point. But, you know, Connor listened to his story and still hired him even though he knew we could only use him to a quarter the extent we'd use anyone else. But Connor knows that Jaxon possesses a rare gift, a kind of ridiculous optimism about his own mortality.

He's fearless. The number of times we have to hold him back from jobs for his own safety… He would do anything for the team, and he reminds us every day of why we're lucky to do the jobs we do."

"And the other guy, Hudson?"

"Hud. Yeah, he and Jax go way back. Hudson is probably the softest, most dangerous guy you'll ever meet."

"I don't understand. He seems pretty cool."

"He is. That's what I mean by 'soft'. He could entice anyone into his orbit, but once he has you, he takes no prisoners. Connor and I fought alongside some hard guys in the Marines, but no one, and I mean no one, came anywhere close to Hudson."

"Is he a veteran too?"

Carter throws his head back and laughs hysterically.

"I'm glad I amuse you."

"No, it's not you, it's just the idea of him being in any of our armed forces. Holy hell, he would be one lethal weapon against the enemy, that's for sure."

"So, what was he?"

Carter finally stops laughing and eyes me cautiously. "He was a hitman."

"An assassin?"

"Not quite. He didn't kill anyone for religious or political reasons. In fact, considering the job he did, he very rarely killed anyone. He didn't need to. He did other things. Physical torture, mental torture, breaking bones, breaking minds."

"So, what's his role in the security team? Not breaking bones, I hope."

"No, he's our main muscle. No one messes with him. He mans the marina a lot of the time and manages most of the typical security stuff—the wider team, the CCTV set-up, protects the high value assets, that kind of thing."

"Ok," I nod. "So you all do a lot more than security, but you still haven't explained why this is more than a beach resort to you."

Carter pushes his thick fingers through sweat-damp hair.

"We have a few side hustles going on. We do a bit of private work—investigative stuff, bodyguard stuff. And we also, um, we have a kind of courier business on the side."

"A courier business?"

"Yeah. Um, we help clients move shit around. Sometimes it comes in by boat and we need to get it to the mainland. Sometimes it comes in from further down the Keys and it needs to change hands a few times before it reaches Miami."

"What kind of 'shit', Carter?" I have a feeling the 'shit' he's referring to is not legal, which makes my blood run cold.

"Um, ok…" he starts, then mutters under his breath, "no turning back now."

"Carter?"

"Firearms. Guns. Ammo."

"What?" My fear is confirmed. "How long have you been dabbling in this stuff? How often? Who with?"

"It started about three years ago and it's frequent enough now but small shipments only. We're not in too deep, T. We just do favors for a couple of groups up in Miami. It makes us a bit of pocket money and you never know when we might have to call one of those favors in. It buys us protection."

I make a conscious effort to steady my breathing. Connor is a crook. They're all criminals. Thoughts I'd managed to lock away for my own good begin to sneak into my consciousness. My old life isn't the only thing I've traveled to the Keys to get away from, but no one can know that. And it appears the very thing I'm running from is right here on my new doorstep.

"Who knows about it?"

"Most of the staff," he shrugs. "And they know why we do it. It's to help them, ultimately. You know, Connor did a great job getting everyone proper contracts and all, but the pay is still shit—you'll find out. And some of these guys are sending money home to their families. When it comes to serious medical bills, their moms needing a new refrigerator because hers broke and she's been storing milk in a bucket on the back porch for four months... that's the kind of thing we spend it on."

"So it's not to line your pockets?" I raise an eyebrow.

He shakes his head. "We don't line our pockets more than anyone else's. We earn more than most of the staff here but our wages are still pretty poor, compared to what we made in the Marines, anyway."

I try to wrap my head around everything he's telling me when he shifts to position himself between me and the sea I'm staring out at.

"Can we trust you, T? Please say we can trust you."

I watch his jaw tense and release, then nod.

"Of course, Carter. It's just... this is a whole new experience for me and I don't know what to think. I lived a... somewhat reclusive life before I came here."

Carter takes my hands in his and squeezes them.

"I guess Connor didn't want me to know all of this?"

Carter sighs. "No."

"I haven't put a foot wrong again since I started this job, Carter. How can he trust everyone else and not me?"

Carter hesitates, then rubs his eyes. "Ok. It's got nothing to do with how well you can do your job or how well you can keep a secret."

"Then, what is it?" I look back at Carter and his face has taken on a different expression. Gone is the cocky self-assuredness of twenty seconds ago. In its place is a solemn look.

"You remind him of someone."

"Who?"

"Someone who let him down a long time ago."

I repeat. "Who?"

"His fiancée."

The wind is sucked out of my lungs as my stomach plummets to the floor. Connor is engaged? That explains why he didn't make a move on me after he'd taken all the cactus spikes out of my ass.

"How did she let him down?"

"They were childhood sweethearts. Met when they were about twelve years old, something crazy. I think they started dating when they were like sixteen years old. He joined the Marines soon after—followed his dad's footsteps—and she was fine with it. Came from a military family herself so she knew the drill. They stayed together for almost ten years, then right before he came home from his final deployment to Iraq, she went off with his *supposed* best friend."

I listen without breathing. I don't know why this information is so important to me, but it's important enough for me to not want to pollute it with the sound of my own breath.

"That was five years ago. As soon as he came back and discovered she'd had an affair with his bestie, he packed up and moved here."

I finally release a breath. I'm aware I might be looking slightly like a crazy person for not breathing so I take a swig of beer and pretend to act normal while I prepare myself to ask the obvious question.

"What does that have to do with me?"

Carter's lip curls up, almost sadly, at one end.

"You're a dead ringer for Clarisse," he replied. "Could have been separated at birth."

I suddenly feel incredibly tired. Now I understand why Connor's been so weird towards me. Somewhere deep inside, I'd kind of hoped it was just a case of a boy teasing a girl in the proverbial schoolyard because he secretly likes her, but apparently that isn't the case at all. I remind him of someone else. I remind him of how it feels to have a broken heart.

"Right," I say. "Is he likely to ever get over it?"

Carter shifts back to sit next to me and we both look out at the darkened horizon.

"I don't know, T. We've had other girls on the island who also have red hair like you have, and freckles, similar height, similar figure, you name it. I don't remember him being quite so... I don't know... *bothered*. Maybe it's because it's been five years now. Maybe it's because you drove a Chevy into the wall. Who knows? All I really know is you shouldn't take it personally. He can't hold something against someone he really doesn't know, right?"

I feel hollow and heavy at the same time.

"I've got to go," I say, heaving myself up to standing. I look down at Carter. He looks apologetic. "Thanks for telling me, I appreciate it. And thanks for the beers and the game. I had fun."

"Until I dropped that bombshell," he said, obviously aware my mood had sunk, drastically.

"Nah, I'm tired, and it's Sunday. I need a decent night's sleep."

"Ok, well," he gets to his feet and pulls me into his predictably firm chest. I can feel his long hair brushing against my neck. "You sleep tight, T. I'll see you tomorrow."

I pull away and smile, despite everything I've just learned. I like Carter and finally feel as though I've made another friend. After Esme and Shell, I now have a whopping three. I mentally high five myself.

"Night, Carter."

I make my way back to my dorm with heavy feet, heavy arms, heavy everything. I was stupid and idealistic to ever imagine that Connor might be attracted to me in the way I wanted him to be. He is a Greek god for one thing. What I also now know is he's a fractured, bitter man who may or may not be hellbent on making my life here miserable, all because I look like someone who once hurt him.

I reach the top of the stairs to my floor and see light coming from under Connor's door. I fight the urge to knock on it, to take his face in my hands and assure him I'm nothing like her. But of course I don't. Because I don't have a freaking death wish. So I open the door to my apartment, strip out of my clothes and land heavily on my bed. The night is completely silent, which is why I hear it. The click of a switch as Connor shuts off his light.

***

"You have to come, darling." Barbie's tinkling voice lights up the phone, drawing a smile from my lips. "Fitz makes a marvelous picnic—he's quite the Gordon Ramsey, you know. We've found the perfect spot in the cove and we can travel there in style."

"In style?" I ask, mindful of the limited modes of transport available on the island.

"Golf buggy, of course," she giggles.

"Of course," I reply, reminded of the fact the Reef Street community don't get out an awful lot. I make a mental note to look into how I might change that. "Then I would love to.

Thursday, right? I take lunch at twelve-thirty. Maybe I could bring a buggy to you and pick you up?"

"That sounds perfect, darling. Can't wait."

She hangs up, leaving me—in the way only Barbie does—feeling much lighter for it, and filled with optimism.

I turn back to my 'research' into the vast array of excursions available around the Keys, and become so engrossed I don't realize someone is standing over my desk, until I hear a throat clear. My heart thuds inside my ribcage as my eyes scan slowly upwards from the crisp white shirt drawn taut across a hard chest to the open collar, light shadow of stubble, tensed jaw and piercing blue eyes of my boss.

"Can I help you?" I say, forcing some confidence into my tone. He attempts a small smile which doesn't quite carry up to his eyes. It doesn't surprise me. He hates what I represent; it all makes sense now.

"We're moving the boats out of the marina," he says, his voice completely emotionless. "I need you to keep the place clear for the next two days. Don't let anyone else dock."

"Ok," I nod. "Can I ask why?"

"Repairs," he says, simply.

I blink slowly. Fine. I can't make him share the kind of stuff Carter shared with me. He seems to sense my resignation because he adds: "We need to fix some of the boards before the season really kicks in. We need the marina to be clear so we can do a thorough job."

"Ok," I reply, knowing he's lying. "Noted."

He holds my gaze for a long, fairly excruciating moment, then taps his fingers on the desk before walking away. He gets about four paces then turns back around.

"Good game last night," he says. "Congratulations on your win."

I shrug. "I honestly have no idea how to play. That was

beginner's luck at its best. So, you'll be pleased to know I won't be participating again; I will almost definitely lose every cent I made."

"That's a shame," he says, to my surprise. And even more to my surprise, he sounds as though he actually means it. But he doesn't elaborate. He turns and walks straight out the double doors.

# CHAPTER THIRTEEN

onnor

"Is that your cell again?" Hudson asks, as we drive back
through the main gates. It's been one drainer of a day driving
to Miami and back, but with the casino build almost
complete, we've had to meet with various contractors and it's
easier to get deals done in person. I pull my phone out of my
pocket and check the screen. *Jeez.* I cut off the call for the
tenth time that hour.

"Who is it?"

"Don't recognize the number."

Hudson winds down the truck window and shouts his
thanks through the intercom to whoever let us through. He
turns back to face me.

"What's the plan now?"

"Can you go check the marina is empty and the Starlings
have left? It's past eight so they should have. Then I guess we
can give the boat the all-clear for tomorrow."

"Sure."

I spin the truck into a space outside the main building and step out.

"Where will you be?"

"I'm going to take a quick shower before I head over. Call me?"

"Will do." Hudson taps his cap and breaks into a run towards the marina.

I notice Tawny's light is on as I pass her room and resist the urge to knock and see how she's doing. My feelings towards her are all over the place. One minute I'm infuriated that she's had the audacity to show up to one of our poker games, the next I'm fantasizing about her mouth wrapped around my cock when I see her sitting outside my office. Even the simple act of telling her not to book any boats into the marina almost stretched me to my limits. Rhonda has got her in the Starling Key uniform now but I think that's made things even harder. It might not be the short skirts making my mouth water anymore, but knowing she's got the standard issue stockings on beneath her bottle green skirt suit and spiked heels is an equally pervasive type of torture. And her looks have changed somehow over the course of the last couple of weeks. She's a natural beauty already, but she's been styling her long auburn hair and wearing a little makeup. Black kohl makes her eyes pop out of the pale, creamy skin, and her lips shine with an allure that makes me want to nibble them. But it's her attitude that gets me off the most. She felt my hard on and that's put me in a compromised position. She must know that every time I chastise her, it's because she's got under my skin. What she doesn't know is I need her out from under my skin, before a moment of weakness claims me and I do things to her I know I'll regret.

I peel the clothes off my sweat-ridden skin and throw

them into a laundry basket. Tidiness is one of many strengths
I took away from my time in the Marines. I step into the
shower and turn my back to the steaming hot water. Fixing
everyone's shower was one of the first things I did as soon as
Starling handed over the keys to the cash. There's nothing
worse after a long day in the sweltering Florida heat than a
limp and lifeless shower. I let the water pummel my back for
a few minutes, and allow my eyes to roam the tiny bathroom.
They land on the bottle of lotion that I rubbed onto Tawny's
ass and the image takes me right back to when I was sitting
on my bed with her strewn half-naked across my lap.

The thought makes my dick twitch. Without thinking, I
reach down and wrap my hand around it. I try to imagine
Tawny's slim, delicate fingers are curled there instead of my
own rough ones. My cock thickens and lengthens in my grip.
With my other hand I take the soap and squeeze some along
my length, then I massage it in, watching, imagining it's
Tawny's hands doing the work. I stroke along the length and
massage my balls then return to my cock, massaging the
head. I imagine it sliding into Tawny's mouth. I place my free
hand against the glass and close my eyes.

Tawny's lips pull gently at the delicate skin around the
head, making sucking noises as she pulls away. I stand there
gagging, desperate for her to take me deeply, pull me down
her throat. My hand works the full length of my cock and
Tawny sucks forcefully, her cheeks hollowed, her eyes
closed. I place my hand behind her head and carefully
encourage her to take more. She opens up and pulls me down
until my head touches the fragile skin at the back of her
throat. Her finger nails dig into my ass, holding me in place. I
gently pump my hips driving myself into her then drawing
out again; I'm making love to her mouth and she's repaying
me with sweet moans as I thrust into her, and little gasps as I

pull out. Fuck. I tighten my grip around my cock and some-thing happens. I'm there. Faster than I've ever been there before in my life; not even when I lost my virginity. Tawny's eyes open and fix on mine, her moans grow louder, her nails dig deeper. Her throat opens and she rams me down it, pushing me and pulling me, as I've lost all sense of rhythm. I explode and empty myself down her throat while she moans in satisfaction and swallows it all.

I stand there, leaning up against the glass with hot water beating against my back, and I'm shaking. Everything has gone white—blinding white—and the sound of gunshots penetrates my brain. They pepper the air around me, getting closer and closer. It doesn't matter how fast I run, how loudly I yell to the others—the pat-pat sound continues to claw at me, until a terrifyingly loud explosion sounds right next to my ear. I'm thrown several yards sideways and I black out.

I'm sitting on the floor of the shower with hot water raining down on my head and I know what just happened. I had a flashback, and it wasn't my first. I reach out to turn the shower handle and climb slowly to my feet. Color begins to come back into the room, calming my heart rate, but I know not all the moisture on my skin is from the shower; it's sweat. I climb out of the cubicle and take deep breaths while I dry off. I thought I'd got past the flashbacks; I haven't had one in four years. I hope, with every beat of my heart, this one was a one-off.

I throw on a pair of suit pants and a clean shirt, leaving it unbuttoned until I'm completely dry, then my cell phone rings.

"Hudson. We good?"

"No, Connor. There's a boat docked. No idea who it is; they're not booked in."

Panic pierces my skin and every hair stands on end. The

boat from Mexico docks in less than twenty-four hours and I can't afford for anyone to see it. Of all the dodgy deals we've done, this one takes the title. The boat is *full*. With nothing but guns and ammo.

"Are you fucking kidding me? Does anyone know about this?"

"I don't know," Hudson replies. "You're the first person I've called."

I think quickly. "Ok, go down to the boat, pretend you've just come on shift, didn't know a boat was docking, find out who they are. I'll call the guys, see if they know."

"On it." Hudson hangs up and I dial Carter. He answers on the first ring.

"Sup?"

"Did you know there's a boat in the marina?" No time for pleasantries.

"What? You sure?"

"Hudson's down there now. Who the fuck signed it in?"

"I've been with the guys all evening. No one knows about this."

We both think of the same person at the same time.

*"Tawny."*

"Fuck," I growl, and hang up.

Seconds later, I'm banging her door down.

She flings it open and I'm momentarily stunned. She's wearing a Yankees shirt about three sizes too big for her and her long hair is all about her shoulders in one unruly, delicious mess.

"To what do I owe this displeasure?" She snaps. My face must say it all.

"Do you know anything about a boat in the marina?" I ask through gritted teeth.

"Yes, I do," she says, planting her hands on her hips,

oblivious to the fact I now want to smack something over her pretty little head. "And if you answered your damn phone, you would know too."

"What?"

"I've been calling you for the last six hours!"

"That was you?"

"I'm so pleased you have my number programmed into your phone." She makes a pretend pout and, absurdly, it makes me want to laugh.

"Why didn't you try Carter?"

"I did. He's a ghoster too, it seems."

"A what?"

"Doesn't matter."

"So who is it? Who owns the boat?"

"Some friends of Mr. Starling."

I sink my face into my hands. "Tawny, did you not hear anything I said to you this morning?"

"What? About the fact you wanted the marina free and clear of boats so you could do repairs? About the fact I was not to book anyone in?"

I look up, the exasperation abundantly clear on my face. "Yes," I sigh, dramatically.

"Ok, so what happens when Mr. Starling comes up to you and goes, 'so, hey, my buddy wants to park his boat here overnight' and you go 'oh, sir, no, we're doing repairs tonight', and he goes, 'what repairs?' and you go, 'repairing some damage to the decking', and he goes, 'but I was just there—there's no damage'. Do you go 'no sir, you are blind, stupid and sorely mistaken. There is damage, you just can't see it. Because it *isn't... actually... there?*'"

She says the whole spiel as though she's two different people—physical actions and everything. One second she's hopping over to the left, pretending to be me (or her—I'm a bit lost), the next she's hopping to the right, pretending to be Starling talking to some imaginary person. I can't do anything other than stare at her in disbelief.

"C'mon Connor, am I gonna lie to Mr. Starling? You know the only thing I could do was let the guy dock in then call you guys and tell you, so you can, y'know, fix it."

"Shit." I thump the doorframe. I know she's right, but that doesn't make the situation any less hugely inconvenient. "How long are they staying for?"

"Couple of nights, Mr. Starling said."

"The shipment is happening tomorrow."

"What shipment?"

I size her up, trying to figure out what she knows. I have a sneaking suspicion Carter has talked to her, but exactly how much she knows, I've no idea.

"I know about the side hustle," she says, answering my thoughts. "Carter explained everything. Is that what this is about? There's a bunch of stuff coming in by boat?"

"Yes," I sigh. There's no point in lying about it now.

"Look… why don't we set up a dinner or something for Starling's friends. Maybe Arnaud wants to try out a new taster menu or something. We could invite them, get them away from the boat somehow, and bring the 'shipment' in while they're away."

I pinch the bridge of my nose and consider her idea for a second. My eyes drop to her milky legs tapering down to her ankles, one of which is decorated with a small silver chain and… a toe ring? Even that, I find insanely hot.

"That might actually work," I say. "Arnaud's team can create something quickly, I'm sure. We just need to find a couple of people to wait the tables—all the guys we have are working tomorrow night."

"I can do it," she says, eagerly. "And I'm sure Esme and Shell will help if you toss a few bills their way."

I think it through. I still don't trust Tawny not to drop an entire tray of hors d'oeuvres onto the diners; such is her track record.

"Ok. Can you ask Esme and Shell? Rhonda will have spare waiter uniforms. Have them talk to Claudette—she runs the waitstaff here, she can give them a few pointers."

"What about me?" She asks, a look of disappointment on her face.

"I want you to keep watch over the west villas—they're closest to the marina and we don't want anyone wandering over that way and seeing something they shouldn't. If anyone looks as though they might attempt to do that, you call me and Carter straight away."

She goes to speak but I stop her.

"And don't worry; we'll both have your number plugged into our phones."

She seems content with my reply and I stand there trying to think of something else to say, just so I can prolong this moment. I just want a few more minutes so I can imprint this picture on my mind—Tawny Graham standing before me looking like she just got out of bed, probably naked under that top.

I want to be that top. I want to be the fabric hanging loose around her, skimming her breasts and the curve of her bottom. I realize I'm staring and she's looking back at me with a mixture of curiosity and something else I can't put my finger on.

I clear my voice as something tells me it's probably croaky after that analysis of her figure. "Let me know when you've spoken to Esme," I say, stepping back.

"I will do," she says.

I continue backwards until I hit the wall, then I return to my room, shut the door and lean back against it. I take out my cell and pull up my missed call log. Selecting the most recent number, I add it to my contacts list. I type the name Tawny and allow myself to feel a small rush of excitement as I enter her name into my cell. I normally add a family name, even with employees, but I don't want to. I want to leave it like this—casual, close, familiar. I mean, I pulled ninety-eight thorns out of her ass the other night—you can't get much more familiar than that.

I let my eyes linger on her name for a few more seconds, then I pull up Carter and press call.

# CHAPTER FOURTEEN

Tawny

I LEAN BACK on my hands and let the sand warm my feet as Barbie paddles in the sea, her turquoise kaftan blowing in the soft breeze.

"This is her happy place," Fitz smiles beside me. I turn to see his eyes filled with the kind of love that should never be unrequited—pure, unconditional, unwavering. "I thought she was in her element in the Hills, hanging around the studio crowd, being pals with the greats… But she puts on a good show. The most convincing non-actress I ever met. Deserves an Oscar several times over."

"You don't think she was happy there?"

"She was happy enough at one time, but she was living someone else's dream. I knew Ralph, her husband. He was a charismatic guy—too charismatic for his own good. Had an affair with a small time actress—Polly Brennan her name was. I remember her well. Party girl. She'd been in more laps than a napkin. It broke Barbie's heart when she found out."

"How awful…"

"But she stayed with Ralph 'til the end. He hated himself for hurting her. I think he did truly love Barbie, but it wasn't long after that he had a heart attack. He died where I'm sure he always wanted to. Right there on the studio floor, surrounded by some of the most famous faces in showbiz. Even Hitchcock was there that day."

"Poor Barbie," I say, my sentiment sounding mismatched against the sight of her dancing, carefree, amongst the foam.

"She moved south after that, went back home for a while, came to Florida a few years later. That's when I caught up with her. Figured she'd had enough time to grieve." He leans into me a little and nudges my elbow. "Didn't want to muscle in before I was welcome, y'know?"

I grin down at him.

"When we heard about Starling Key and the Reef Street development, Barbie pretty much packed her bags there and then. She'd fallen in love with the Sunshine State and wanted to settle somewhere. This place is perfect. It has everything— sun, sand, sea… Not much of the other S but, you know, I'm no spring chicken…"

"By 'S' I take it you mean 'sparkling wine'," I say, arching an eyebrow.

He laughs heartily and Barbie glances over at us, wondering what's so funny.

"This place is home. Probably the last one we'll ever have." He looks on at Barbie and the skyline, wistfully.

"I doubt that," I say. "But if it is, it isn't half-bad."

"And the people…" he continues. "Everyone who works here is an absolute gem, including you. How are you settling in? Esme is wonderful. Have you made many other friends yet?"

I sigh without thinking.

"Oh dear. That doesn't sound good."

"Oh, it's not anything bad. It's just... I think I've actually made an enemy and that kind of overshadows any friendships I've made."

"An enemy? In who?"

"Connor Johnson."

I feel Fitz's face pan around towards me. "An enemy? I didn't think that man could make any enemies."

I shrug.

"I mean, he's always so kind and helpful. Not always the most personable, but I never heard him say a bad word about anyone. Not that he would in front of me anyway, but... he doesn't seem like he would."

"Well, I somehow managed to crash my car into the wall when I arrived..."

"That was you?" Fitz cackles, prompting Barbie to tiptoe out of the water towards us.

"Then I tried to climb over the gate to the northeast wall and set off a load of sirens..."

Barbie flops down beside us.

"Sirens?"

"Sirens, alarms, whatever. Then I sat on a cactus and got a load of spikes in my butt..."

"Wh—what?" Fitz cackles again.

"It's a long story. I won't get into it. And then I allowed a boat to dock in the marina when I shouldn't have..." I sigh, heavily. "I've messed up a lot."

"That's not messing up," Fitz says. "I mean the crash was an accident, right? I heard you saved a raccoon from certain death?"

"Yeah, I guess."

"I don't know why you would want to climb the northeast gate or sit on a cactus, but… I doubt that's a reason why Connor would dislike you. The marina booking? Shit happens. So you made a mistake. Sounds like that's all you did."

"Yeah, well, Connor doesn't see it like that."

Fitz glances at Barbie who hasn't said anything yet; she's clearly mulling something over.

"This cactus," she says, finally. "Why on earth did you sit on it?"

"I fell. I was trying to pee. I'd had a few drinks, Connor was trying to get me back to my dorm…"

"And, um, how did you get these spikes out of your butt?"

"I didn't." I feel a crimson blush creeping up my cheeks. "Connor did."

Barbie claps her hands together and Fitz collapses back on the blanket with a triumphant groan.

"Connor doesn't hate you, Tawny," he says. "He likes you. He got too close for comfort is all."

"He was just being a gentleman. He couldn't just leave me there covered in cactus spikes."

"He also didn't need to do that himself," Fitz says, arching an eyebrow. "He could have got Esme or Shell, or one of the first aiders to do it."

"He didn't want me to feel any more embarrassed," I say, waving away any suggestion that Connor might have actually *wanted* to help that night. "And that's not all. If my sheer clumsiness hasn't been enough, apparently I remind him of his ex."

"Ah, right," Fitz says, glancing up at Barbie.

Barbie takes my hand and rather than squeezing it like I

expect, slides a glass of gin and tonic into it instead. "Then there's nothing you can do except wait."

"Wait for what?" I say, smiling gratefully and taking a sip.

"For him to get over it and realize what a good thing he could have with you."

I almost spit out the drink. "Oh, that's not what I want. I mean, he's my boss. I just want him to not hate me."

Barbie and Fitz stare at me as though they're not buying a single word.

"So, you're not attracted to him?" Fitz asks, surprised.

"Well, um, no. Um…" I mumble.

"Of course you are," Barbie cuts in. "You're a red-blooded woman. Of course you're attracted to him. That man has been crafted out a block of perfection. Everyone on this island is attracted to Connor Johnson, even Fitz."

I'm about to howl laughing but Fitz nods. "Oh yes. If I played for the other team…"

I clap my hands over my ears.

Barbie pries them away and brings her face up close to mine.

"But I think you're the one he's interested in. So what if you look like his ex? You're his type, clearly. It won't take long for him to realize you are not her. You just need to enjoy the chase my dear. You know what they say: a hard man is good to find."

Fitz covers his face and groans.

"Please don't tell anyone about this," I say to Barbie.

"About what?"

"Ha ha," I laugh, sarcastically.

"No, I'm serious. I'm one of the best at keeping secrets, honey, because I can't remember a damn thing."

LUNCH WITH BARBIE and Fitz was the perfect distraction, taking my mind off the task ahead this evening. But now it's here, I'm almost light-headed with nerves. Esme and Shell are dressed in the signature Starling Bay waitstaff uniforms, eagerly awaiting their special guests in the private dining room in the main building. Connor is stalking around the office on his phone making sure everything's working to schedule, while Carter and Hudson are invisibly manning the marina. Jaxon is on camera watch and Isaac is at the front gate, while Luca is preparing to chaperone Starling's friends to the main building for their hastily prepared special evening.

And me? I'm crouching in the damn mangroves looking out for any guests who might wander a little too far west of their villa. I'm praying the battery on my phone doesn't die out because the little built-in torch is the only thing saving my ass from freak cactus attacks and anything else my bad luck would have me run into.

I can see movement by the marina so I check my watch. It's seven forty-five, only fifteen minutes to go before dinner is served. I recognize Luca's silhouette as he moves around the front of the yacht. It's followed by four figures who I assume to be Starling's friend, his wife and two kids. Although judging by their height, I wouldn't call these kids 'kids'—more like adults, maybe even people my own age. They walk along the pathway to the waiting caddy and climb in. Seconds later, I hear the engine start up and the small vehicle makes its way up towards me. I'm far enough away from the road that I know they won't see me, but that doesn't stop my nerves from rattling around in my chest. I crouch deeper into the foliage as they pass and breathe a sigh of relief once they're away and heading towards the main building. Then I turn my attention back to the marina.

Seeing nothing of note, I settle down on a patch of grass, with my elbow on my knee and my chin on my palm. The island is quiet; most of the guests have retired to their villas or are dining in the restaurant in the main building, which thankfully looks out west, not directly south to the marina.

Just as I start to feel my eyelids getting heavy, a small light in the distance grabs my attention. I look out to sea and watch as the light comes nearer. Then a figure to my right comes into view. Connor. My heart thumps loudly as I watch him approach the marina. Like magnets, the light closes in on the edge of the docks and Connor's feet hit the decking which had been duly smashed and repaired by Jax in an attempt to provide cover for what's happening right now. A boat— bigger than I'd first expected given the size of the dot as it approached—glides into one of the slips and Connor secures it to the dock. Then a couple of guys get out of the boat carrying large bags. More bags appear to be handed out and placed on the decking. My eyes search for Connor who's suddenly disappeared, but land on him again quickly. He's pulling what looks like a trailer along the decking. The three of them load the bags into the trailer and pull it along the decking to the edge, where they secure it to the back of an SKS truck.

I look around, thankful to see no movement anywhere except at the marina. I still want Connor to hurry. I don't know what kind of danger he could be in if he got caught but the thought of anything happening to him makes me feel strangely sick. Connor seems to exchange a few words with one of the men, something changes hands, and then he walks back to the truck. He fastens a sheet over the top of the trailer and seems to double check the connection between the trailer and the truck. I silently implore him to hurry.

Finally, he gets into the truck and starts to pull away, just as my phone buzzes silently in my hand.

I look at the ID and answer immediately.

"Hey Esme, how's it going?" I whisper.

She doesn't answer my question. "Tawny, the son is heading your way. I can't get hold of any of the guys. You have to distract him."

"He's on foot?"

"Yeah. I reckon he'll be passing the west villas in a couple of minutes. Can you text Connor?"

"I can but he's in the truck; he won't see it. What do you mean by distracting him? How the hell do I do that?"

"Do anything you can, Tawny. Just keep him away from the marina until the boat's gone."

The line clicks and I stare at the phone. I look up towards the main building and, sure enough, I can see a figure walking around it along the footpath that will eventually lead back to his father's yacht. I pull out my cell and thank God I still have ten percent battery left. I punch out a message to Connor quickly and hit send, then I crawl along the edge of the mangroves towards the beach line. It will look less suspicious if I appear to be heading back from the beach than if I'd been cowering in the mangroves.

I roll my denim shorts up until my butt cheeks are confidently poking out beneath, then tug my shirt sleeves over my shoulders revealing the thin red strap of my bikini top, then I saunter towards the main building, aiming for the son.

As I approach, I give him the widest, flirtiest smile I can summon. It feels unfeasibly fake, but he slows when he sees me.

"Hi," I say, tucking my hair behind one ear. "What are you doing walking around these parts at this time of night?"

He stops about three feet in front of me and I get a close

look at his face. He's good-looking—tall, blonde, pale-skinned—and well-dressed in a polo shirt, stone-colored shorts and leather sandals.

"Maybe I was looking for you," he deadpans. My chest tightens and I'm lost for words. "I'm kidding," he laughs. He holds out his hand and I recognize the accent as British—public school British. I reach out and let him shake mine.

"I'm heading back to the boat," he says.

"Oh, that's your boat in the marina?"

"Yes, well, my family's."

"Of course. She's beautiful," I say. It isn't a lie; I salivated over Lady Denver from the safety of the events desk this morning.

"She is indeed." He looks over my shoulder at the target of his affection with a slightly weary look in his eye. "But she needs a rest. We've been traveling for three months."

"Three months, really? Where have you been?"

"The south Americas, mainly."

"That sounds incredible."

"Have you ever traveled?"

I resist the urge to smirk. Only if you count a road trip from Monmouth County to Starling Key.

"No, not yet. But I'd love to one day."

"What's your name?" He asks me, suddenly.

I hesitate, wondering if should give a different name, but I don't have time to think one up. "Tawny."

"Tawny. I'm Franklin. Frank for short."

"Frank," I say, nodding my approval. "I like it."

"So, Tawny, what are *you* doing wandering around these parts on your own?"

I smile. Touché. "I work here."

"Really? That's cool. What do you do?"

"I'm still quite new. I just started looking after events,

although 'events' is quite strong a word. I mainly book excursions for guests, but I think there's a lot more we can do. There are so many options around here and with an aging community on the island, we could definitely provide more tailored trips and experiences."

"Sounds like you're ambitious."

"I don't know about that. I've just had a few ideas, that's all."

He cocks his head slightly and looks at me. He really is a good-looking guy.

"What?" I ask.

"I'm just thinking how lucky you are to live on this resort. It's paradise here."

I can't help it. I beam from ear to ear, because it's true, it is paradise here and as much as I begrudged coming here in the beginning, I am starting to appreciate it. I love the sun, the sea air, the tropical feel, the fact it's so far from anywhere.

"Where do you live?" I ask. "When you're not sailing around the high seas, that is."

"London mostly," he says, kicking the sand beneath his foot. "And the Arab Emirates."

"That sounds exotic."

"Dubai, maybe. London, not so much."

"Well, exotic or not, I'd love to go to London."

I look out at the black night, wistfully. I've always dreamed about traveling, but with looking after Mom, and not having a lot of money, I never expected I would. Living on Starling Key may be as close to traveling as I get.

"If you can get past the shitty weather, you might like it," he laughs.

"Can you tell me about it?"

"Now?" He asks, failing to stop a grin spreading across his face. I realize I do want him to tell me about it now. I nod and sit down on a grassy sandbank alongside the footpath. He shakes his head and sits beside me.

"Ok, sure. Wow, where do I begin?"

He turns to face me and pulls one knee up to the bank giving me the full benefit of his handsome face, then he proceeds to tell me about London—not the touristy bits that I expected, like Buckingham Palace, Downing Street, the Houses of Parliament—but the life of a local. He tells me about the small boroughs that make up the city, the differences between north and south London, the little quirky events that happen every year like summer street parties, and festivals in the Royal Parks.

I'm so enraptured by his stories and the completely unexpected picture he's painting of a city I thought I knew because I've watched every episode of Ted Lasso, that I don't realize someone is standing behind us, staring me down.

A cough makes me jump and I look up to see deep blue eyes penetrating my skin.

"Connor! Hi! Um, Connor this is Frank, Frank this is Connor, my, um, boss."

"Good evening," Frank says, jumping to his feet to shake Connor's hand.

It's awkward. Oh God, it's awkward. Connor looks like a wild animal. Something must have gone wrong with the shipment. I glance over my shoulder and see the boat gone, only a small light in the distance, heading away.

"Evening, sir," Connor says, adopting his guest-friendly face. "How is your stay so far?"

"It's fantastic," Frank says. "We couldn't have docked in a better place for a few days. The dinner was delicious—your chef is very talented. And Tawny here has been a delight to chat with."

I can't look at Connor. There's something about his

demeanor that half-frightens me. He is rigid as a rock and I can almost feel anger rolling off him in waves. Thankfully, Frank doesn't seem to notice.

"She's been indulging me, asking about life in London. I'm sure she's not half as interested as she lets on."

I flick my eyes up to him and then kick myself knowing it probably looks as though I'm batting my eyelashes.

"No, I am. It's a hundred percent genuine," I say.

"Well, Tawny has an early start in the morning and we don't want to keep you," Connor says, his words short and clipped. "I'll walk you back Tawny," he adds, pulling my arm until I'm standing awkwardly between the two of them.

"It's been really nice to meet you Frank," I say, hoping my face adequately conveys how disappointed I am at our conversation being cut short.

"I'm here for a couple more days, Tawny," Frank says. "Maybe I'll see you around."

"Tawny has a few errands to run in Miami," Connor says and I hear the snap in his tone. I spin around to face him.

"I do?"

"Yes," he replies, still looking at Franklin.

"Ah," Franklin nods, his eyes slightly narrowed. It's as though the two men have come to an understanding about me. That I am off limits.

"In that case," Franklin drops his eyes to me and leans towards me. "It's been a delight speaking to you. Thanks for brightening my evening." He kisses me on the cheek and his perfectly shaven skin lingers slightly against mine, as though to taunt Connor. "And good luck!" He says brightly before shooting Connor a bemused look and spinning on his heel, the gravel crushing beneath his leather sandal.

I spin around again and face Connor square. He looks like he's about to kill someone, but right now I don't care. I want to know why the hell I'm suddenly going to be running errands off the Keys.

"Miami?"

His jaw ticks and he turns to head back to the northeast wall. I stomp after him, almost running to keep up with his giant strides.

"No one's mentioned anything about going to Miami. What do I need to go there for?"

He doesn't slow down, seemingly content with the pattering of my sneakers on the gravel behind him.

"Am I going alone?" He still says nothing and it's infuriating. I reach out and grab his arm.

"Connor!" I hiss.

He turns to face me and I stop immediately, shocked at the expression on his face.

"What?" He steps forward bringing his face about an inch from mine and growls at me through gritted teeth.

I want to step backwards because he's intimidating me, but I also want to lean forward, just a little, because this is probably the closest I will ever get to his lips.

"Why am I going to Miami?" My words come out in a whisper and I can feel his hard breath against my face. Our eyes are locked in some sort of weird battle of wills. Then his eyes drop to my lips and he wets his own. I'm aware my entire body has heated up by at least two degrees.

After several seconds he pulls back, letting a pocket of cool air flood the space between us.

"I'll tell you tomorrow. Meet me at the entrance to the northeast wall at seven."

He starts walking again.

"What about the events desk?"

"Carter is going to keep an eye on it."

He keeps walking while I stand, watching him go.

"Did everything go ok tonight?" I ask after him.

When he stops again he doesn't look back, but his voice is different.

"Yeah. It did. Thanks…"

He dips his head slightly to one side as though he's talking to the floor just behind his feet. "…Tawny."

He hovers for a moment, then walks away. Beneath the thin cotton of his shirt I can see the bird, it's wings moving in harmony with each stride. If I squint my eyes and focus on its feathers, I could swear it is flying away.

# CHAPTER FIFTEEN

onnor

I CAN'T UN-SEE THAT. I can't rewind the clock and erase my head of the vision of Tawny Graham flirting with that stuck-up limey. She is either an incredibly good actor or there was genuine attraction there. And I didn't like it. Not one little bit. And Miami, what the fuck? I have to go there myself to run some highly confidential errands, but I usually take one of the guys with me, not Calamity Jane.

*Shit.*

I know I'm an asshole leaving her standing there, but I'm burning up and can't let her see any more of my anger; it's obvious enough I'm pissed, I don't need to labor the point.

And now I'm going to have to spend the day with her tomorrow, feeling her proximity in the passenger seat like a thorn in my side. God, I could marvel at the way I cut my nose off to spite my face.

I bypass the shower and head straight for bed, burying my face in the pillow before I get a chance to imagine hers.

---

SHE'S WAITING outside the gate as I approach, with a resigned look on her face. Guess she's been looking forward to this as much as I have. We walk to the parking lot in silence while I scroll mindlessly through emails that I've already read. It would be awkward if we weren't both seething so much.

She heads towards one of the SKS trucks and I swallow a smirk as I take a turn towards my Corvette—my pride and joy. When she sees I'm not following, and her gaze moves between me and my car, I get an eye roll.

"Get in," I say, as I sink into the driver's seat.

"This is such an asshole's car," she mutters, having apparently forgotten I'm her boss.

"Watch your mouth."

She sits down in the unexpectedly low seat with a thud and her dress rises up her thighs.

"Sorry, *sir*."

I turn on the engine and allow the roar of it to drown out some of her attitude before spinning the car out of its spot onto the main drive. She's doing her best to appear completely unaffected. I drive up onto the highway and we spend the next hour in silence—Tawny probably taking in the sea view, me mulling over in my head how to get through the next eight hours without fantasizing about throwing her over the bridge.

She speaks first.

"So, what is it you've roped me into today?"

"Just some drop-offs and pick-ups."

"Of what? Drugs?"

"Of course not drugs. Money."

"Whose money?"

"Associates."

"What kind of associates?" I can hear the despair in her voice, no doubt at the lack of detail I'm giving her.

"They're just people I do business with. Connections."

"That sounds cryptic."

"It's meant to."

She's silent for a minute, then she faces me again.

"Weren't you in the Navy or something?" *Is she kidding me?*

"The Marines."

"Is that the badass version?"

"Depends who you ask."

She shakes her head. "Haven't you had the good of our country drilled into you? Like, this isn't exactly model citizen stuff we're doing today, right?"

"Yes."

"Yes to which question?"

I hold back a smile. I'm enjoying infuriating her. "To both."

"God," she huffs and turns to face out the window. I'm momentarily relieved because the intensity of her eyes on me is making me feel uncomfortable.

"Yes, I have had our good old American values drilled into me, and yes, you are right. This isn't model citizen stuff, but it's the American Dream, isn't it? Equal opportunity, allowing the highest aspirations and goals to be achieved? I don't recall there being any mention of legal parameters in the definition."

She falls quiet and her face is turned so I can't see her expression. After a few minutes and a heavy sigh, she turns to look ahead.

"Can I tell you a secret?" She says.

"Sure. You know pretty much all of ours."

"This is a bit weird for me." She seems to be choosing her words carefully. "I've never been one to get involved with anything like this."

"Like what?"

"Anything that's, well, naughty."

"I find that hard to believe. What kid doesn't get up to mischief at some point?"

"No, I'm being serious. I've always been a total goodie two-shoes, a teacher's pet. Never stepped a foot out of line."

I can't help but laugh. "Seriously? You're like the biggest liability I've ever met. I would have thought you'd be on every possible detention register."

"Hey!" She playfully smacks my knee then withdraws her hand very quickly. "You have seen me at my absolute worst. I have never had so many unfortunate things happen to me in such a short space of time as I have since I got here."

"So you don't usually crash cars, fall off security gates, get hammered and sit on a cactus, or stand so close to someone you get a nosebleed if they move?"

It's her turn to laugh now.

"Wow, when you put it like that, I do sound like a liability."

"Thank you," I grin.

We reach the mainland and I continue along the highway.

"No, really. I was a straight A student before I left school, never bunked off, I never picked up guys, never forgot anyone's birthday. I did everything that was expected of me. I never rebelled. This is all kind of new to me."

I'm not sure which part of the sentence to respond to. I know I should probably start with the straight A part but my thoughts are still stuck on 'never picked up guys'. I don't know why but my chest feels suddenly warm.

"You know, you don't have to be a part of this," I say, instead. Something about her demeanor makes me think she's wary of what we're doing. "After we get back, we can always move you so you don't see what's going on so closely. If, you know, it makes you feel uncomfortable."

She takes a long pause before speaking again. "It's ok," she says quietly. "I know everyone's kind of in on it. And I like it at Starling Key. I like the people, I like what we all do, I like that it's sort of a family. I want to be a part of it. I feel like, if I pretend I don't know what's going on, I'm doing it a disservice, or I'm judging it in a way. I don't see anyone breaking bones or killing anyone; I don't see any real harm being done."

"What about the Starlings? Don't you think we're screwing them?"

"Maybe," she shrugs. "But it's not like they don't have enough money themselves. And a lot of what they make is because of... well, you apparently. And I like that you've done good by everyone, you know, with their contracts and insurance and all. You're like a regular Robin Hood."

"What?" I shake my head to rid it of the misconception she just gave me a compliment. But I can't wipe the smile off my face; it's been a long time since I've really enjoyed someone recognizing me for what I do, let alone someone who happens to be obscenely attractive, even if the way she looks is a little too close for comfort.

"Anyway, I like being a part of it is all."

She turns away again and I find myself craving her gaze. This is going to be one hell of a difficult road trip, and not for the reasons I'd braced myself for. We drive the remaining distance to Miami in relative silence, only breaking to comment on the traffic, the weather and the views. It's a lot more easy and more comfortable than I'd expected, and I like having her next to me, just like I like having her name in my phone.

"What's the first stop?" She asks, as we make our way through the suburbs.

"84 Manaqua Drive."

"Ok," she checks the navigation. "Just a few roads over. Do you want me to go in, or you?"

"Me," I reply, a little too sharply. "You need to stay in the car at all times."

She does a double take and I can tell she's not used to being ordered around, but likewise, she gets that it's not puppy handlers we're dealing with here.

"And lock the doors as soon as I'm out."

She nods. "Left here, then two blocks on the right."

"Thanks." I turn the corner and drive the car slowly along the road until number 84 comes into view. It's a typical nondescript house with a bare front yard and driveway, curtains drawn, very little in the way of life. There's a truck on the drive but other than that, there's nothing to suggest it's even occupied. Knowing Bianchi's mob as I do, it's likely some sort of safe house, used for tactical purposes as opposed to being someone's actual home. I pull up to the sidewalk and reach into the bag Isaac gave me. There's a small pile of envelopes bound with an elastic band. I take the top one and turn to Tawny.

"Lock the doors, ok?"

I climb out of the car and walk up to the front door. I ring once and knock twice, as usual, then I wait. After a few seconds, the door opens and a man appears. He doesn't look like one of the Bianchi's, although he must be connected to them somehow—they wouldn't put just anyone on the receiving end of this package. He nods then looks past me to the car. Instinctively, I step sideways to block his view, but not before I see a look flash across his face. A look I can't pinpoint. It could be recognition, or simply appreciation. I brought along a stunning girl, what else should I expect? He takes the envelope and eyes me curiously before closing the door. I head back to the car and wait for Tawny to unlock the doors. It dawns on me she could have left me here in the street if she'd wanted to—I'd probably deserve it—but she wouldn't. She's a good person, and that's why keeping my distance is so damn hard.

"Where to next?" She asks as I start up the engine. I sense the curtain twitching as we pull away and make a mental note to bring a nondescript truck next time; the engine on the Corvette is possibly a little too conspicuous. I don't why I brought it today. Actually, I do know. It was to impress Tawny Graham. *Fuck.* My conscious mind and my subconscious mind are completely at odds and making my head fucking spin.

"Wynwood. Then up to Little Haiti."

"Ok, take a right turn at the end of this block."

———

WE FIND ALL the houses no problem and I have to conclude that Tawny is a way better navigator than any of my guys; they're all too busy staring out the window at city girls and talking shit about whatever game was on the night before.

"We're all done," I say, getting back into the car after the last drop.

"Well, that was easy enough. And you're getting free money out of this? Man, they neglected to mention *this* profession at my school career talks."

"There's more to it than dropping off envelopes, T," I say, then I freeze. I actually freeze, halfway through pulling out onto the road. A car speeds past and honks its horn at us.

"Like what?" She asks, smoothly. She knows exactly why I stopped. I called her 'T', the cute name Carter has adopted for her. It feels too friendly, too much like I'm past whatever problem it is that I have with her.

It feels wrong.

And it feels so fucking right I want to punch myself in the face.

I pull out properly and put my foot down, as though driving fast is going to propel me away from the situation.

"These aren't just your average run of the mill criminals; they're pretty hardcore. A lot of them deal in much graver commodities than the kind of shit we're shifting for them. I'll move firearms, but no drugs, no animals and no people."

"These guys smuggle animals?"

"I don't know for certain if these guys do. I don't particularly want to know. But it happens. A lot. Just not via Starling Key."

"Don't you ever worry the authorities will find out?"

"No, I don't."

"How can you be so sure?"

"We do a lot of important people a lot of favors. And we call them in from time-to-time. It's called networking."

She laughs, filling the car with a sound so beautiful I almost forget where I am.

"Not where I'm from."

Her stomach rumbles and I realize we've been driving all day without stopping for food. "How about we get something to eat? There's a great place in North Key Largo."

"That would be amazing. I'm actually starving come to

think of it. Maybe I've been having too much fun with you to notice," she teases. "Imagine that."

I laugh but there's a part of me that agrees with her. I'm enjoying this day a little too much.

We pull into the parking lot and she follows me into the café. It's actually more of a diner than a café but I've been coming here for the last five years and it was definitely a café when I first arrived. The food is so good, Angie and Trey have expanded it over the years.

"Connor Johnson!" I hear Angie's voice before we've even stepped foot inside.

"Hey Ange, how are you doing?"

"I'm great. Haven't seen you in a while. What brings you up here?"

She reaches us and throws her arms around my neck, before spotting Tawny hovering awkwardly behind me.

"Oh, I'm sorry, I'm Angie. Welcome to Trey's Café."

Tawny beams at her. "Thanks, I'm Tawny. It smells so good here."

"Well, let your mouth water all you want, honey, it's on the house. Come, sit." She leads us to a table overlooking the water. "So, Connor, how's life on Starling?"

"Oh the usual," I say, sitting down. "Nothing much to report."

"I hear the casino's almost ready?"

"Yeah it is. Are you going to come down for the opening?"

"I'll try, honey, but you know how it is. Getting pretty busy here again."

"I can see," I look around. The place is packed. "I'm surprised you even had a table."

"I always keep one spare for VIPs."

I arch an eyebrow. "VIPs?"

"Of course. You kept me afloat in 2017."

I laugh at that. "Well, in that case…"

"Two beers?"

"Sure. Thanks Ange."

She walks away, threading herself through the packed diner to the bar, leans over the counter and pulls out two ice cold beers, then she winds her way back and places them, dripping with melted ice, on the table.

"Do you want to see the menu or shall I surprise you?" She grins and I know what that means. Trey got a new recipe he wants to try out.

"Surprise me." I look at Tawny, whose face is lit up, her eyes dancing as she takes in the vibrant scene. "T?"

Part of me is really fighting calling her that, but it feels so insanely right, I can't help it.

"Um, yeah, I'll have whatever Connor's having."

Angie shoots me a knowing smile and walks away.

"You know, they serve deep-fried Key Cactus here," I say.

"Are you kidding?" Her mouth contorts into a grimace and I can't contain an evil laugh.

"Yeah, I'm kidding. Whatever she brings out, I guarantee you'll love it."

"I have no doubt about that. This place is full—there are people lining up outside now."

"Doesn't surprise me." I take a swig of beer.

"So, you're a regular?"

"Used to be. I used to come here all the time when there was a lot of building work on the island and very little in the way of decent food. No need to now though since we have Arnaud. I eat pretty well these days."

She grins. She knows how lucky we are to have Arnaud, a Michelin starred French chef, right on site.

"Were you the one who found Arnaud?"

"Actually," I say, picking at the label on the bottle. "He found us. He heard about the renovations and the developments, and he approached Starling. He's a golf nut. Wanted to live in the Keys. It worked out well for all of us."

She's quiet for a few minutes and I pretend to stare out the window when actually I'm watching her out of the corner of my eye. She's picking at her own bottle, nervously.

"Why do you do this, Connor?" she says. "Did you always want to run a resort?"

"Well, officially, I don't run it."

"Yeah, but, you do. And everyone knows it. Apart from Starling."

I allow myself to feel a little smug.

"Anyway, don't avoid the question."

"Ok," I smile. "I never imagined running a resort to be honest. I only ever wanted to be in the Marines."

"So, what changed?"

I feel cold suddenly. I don't want to taint the surprisingly nice day I'm having with the truth about why I'm here. I take a sobering breath. I'll give her the edited version.

"I was deployed to a new base in 2016 out in Iraq. It was brand new. We didn't think anyone knew it was there, but we were wrong. It was hit after just a few weeks. I lost all but three of my men."

She watches me carefully, as though she's processing every single word.

"How old were you?"

"Twenty-six."

"Weren't you a little young to command a base?"

"I wasn't officially the Commander. I was a Major. But my two superiors were killed about four hours prior—a drone attack. That's when we knew the base had been spotted. It was my job to protect everyone from that point on and I didn't."

"Surely, if they'd already found you, there was nothing you could do?"

"I could've got them out of there." Even as I say the words, I know it isn't true, and I've been through enough debriefs to know that moving an entire base with all its equipment and vehicles in the timeframe given was not only against orders, it was also impossible. I know deep down I'm not to blame for what happened. But that doesn't quell the guilt or the shame. It doesn't erase the despair and the loss etched across the faces of all the men's relatives at each funeral I attended. And it doesn't prevent the blinding flashbacks I've started having again.

"It wasn't your fault," she says, her hands reaching across the table. My fingers are still picking at the bottle even though the label has already come off without me realizing it. They stop when her hands cover mine. For a brief moment, I allow myself to feel the warmth of her touch. I look down at her palms cupped over my knuckles and time seems to slow down. I can't look up; I don't want to break the spell. I lift a thumb to gently stroke the soft skin of her finger, and watch goosebumps appear on her arms.

"What about you?" I say, quietly. "Why did you come to Starling Key?"

She pauses and I can hear her breathe.

"I have no one to stay in Monmouth County for. My dad died of a heart attack eight years ago when I was fourteen. My mom died ten weeks ago."

I don't move. "Jesus. I'm sorry, T."

"It's fine. She had Alzheimer's so it happened slowly. I quit school at sixteen to become her caregiver. When she died, I had to sell the house to pay off Dad's debts. I didn't have anywhere else to go and Aunt Millie wouldn't have wanted a twenty-two-year-old girl cramping her style. She was the one who helped find me this job. That's why I'm here."

"You don't have any other family?"

She shakes her head. "My grandpas died before I was born and my grandmas went soon after; I don't really remember them. Dad had a brother but he also died young and had no family of his own. So, yeah, it's just me and Aunt Millie, who thought it best to ship me three states south to start a new life."

"That's really shit, T. I can't imagine losing both my parents at your age."

"It could have been worse," I say. "And I don't need pity; I'm doing fine."

I am no longer sitting in a diner opposite a girl I've been trying to avoid like the plague until today. I am in a bubble of shared emotion. There is no need for words. Despite the fact she's just told me the same story I know she's told everyone else, I have a feeling there's more to why she's here. And in these few seconds I know she's hurting; I can feel it in my fingers as she presses down gently. We are both hurting; we are both keeping dark truths locked up inside, and in this moment I feel closer to Tawny Graham than I've felt with anyone in a very long time.

# CHAPTER SIXTEEN

 awny

I DARE NOT BREATHE. It was only meant to be a simple gesture of comfort as he relentlessly picked at the label on his bottle. But now we're both staring at our fingers which are slowly threading through each other, exploring tentatively. I want to look up, to see if his eyes will tell me what he's think-ing, but I don't want to break the spell. But then, it doesn't matter, the food arrives and we pull our hands back as though we've been electrocuted.

Connor takes a deep breath in and out and looks up at Ange. "What do we have here?"

"This, honey, is Trey's latest Special: Cuban-spiced Red Grouper Tacos."

She puts two plates down and my eyes almost pop out. "These are not tacos; these are works of art."

Ange laughs. "Well, Trey does pride himself on the presentation."

She points out the different elements of the dish. "So, this is the tortilla, obviously. This is the spiced grouper. Here's a lime and ginger salsa—Trey's own recipe. Rice and beans. Radish salad, and cilantro. Enjoy!"

"Oh my," I say, still unable to take my eyes off the plate. "I will."

"Thanks Ange, it looks amazing."

"You're welcome. I'll send Trey out to say hi in a while." She turns to walk away then stops and turns back. "Oh, and you're just in time for the open mic starting."

"You do open mic nights now?" Connor gives her a look that suggests he's not a fan.

"Every Thursday. It's actually pretty popular. The locals love it. And it's still early, so it'll be pretty tame, don't you worry."

"Bring it on," Connor smiles, unconvincingly.

"This is incredible," I say, chewing on a bite as Ange leaves us alone. "I don't think I want to eat anything else ever again. Just Cuban-spiced Red Grouper Tacos."

Connor takes a bit of his own and groans. "God, I miss this place," he mutters.

I want to know more about Connor's past and the Marines, so I try to get things back on a more positive note.

"So, what did you learn in the Marines that made you who you are today?"

"Wow, that's a good question." He finishes his first taco and wipes his mouth with a napkin. "Well, first off, discipline. The ability to focus, and control. We were trained to be in full control of everything we say, do, and feel, at all times. It was so we could act and behave a certain way under pressure, but it's helped me a lot in my civilian life too, as you've probably guessed."

I smile and nod in agreement.

"There were a lot of times where we had to operate on hardly any sleep. I mean, we were completely exhausted, from traveling, from simply learning and being aware of new surroundings, acclimating to hot weather, especially with heavy clothing and artillery on our backs. Stress and exhaustion can play havoc with the mind, so that's where it begins. Control your mind, control your ability to survive."

"I have so much respect for anyone who fights for our country. It sounds like an ordeal."

"It wasn't all bad. There are things I really miss about it."

"Like what?"

"Like the brotherhood, the camaraderie. I miss the friendships I made. When you're forced to live in close proximity with a bunch of strangers it's amazing how quickly you can break down barriers and form tight bonds. It doesn't take long before you would throw yourself under a bus for one of them. It was like having a brand new family, you know? I guess that's what I like so much about Starling Key. Most people live on the island and have been there a few seasons. We've become like a family, I guess."

"It certainly feels like that," I reply. "It's nice. As a new person, that supportive feeling makes it easier to settle in—for the most part."

"I guess that isn't helped when the head of security decides to stick you in the smallest, stinkiest dorm on the island."

"Well, no. That didn't help."

Connor wipes his hands and reaches across the table to take mine again. "I'm sorry I did that, T." His eyes are full of apology. I shake my head.

"I know. I'm sorry I drove into your wall."

"I'm sorry I made you stand and watch while I fixed it."

"I'm sorry I stood so close you accidentally gave me a nosebleed."

"I'm sorry I didn't give you the code to the gate."

"I'm sorry I tried to climb over it."

"I'm sorry I didn't tell you your butt was on display when you stomped off."

Blood floods my cheeks and I laugh. I try to pull my hands away but he holds them fast. His smile falls and he looks at me seriously.

"I'm sorry I've been an asshole to you. You didn't deserve any of it."

I nod, timidly. The atmosphere around us has shifted and I suddenly feel out of my depth. I flick my eyes up towards the bar and see Ange standing at the other side watching us with a fond smile.

"I deserved some of it," I say quietly.

"No, you didn't. I'm going to be on my best behavior from now on, ok?"

I want to ask him why he's been an asshole to me—have him tell me himself, in his own words—but the moment has passed. He's picked up his last taco and is grinning as he bites into it. The new silence is broken almost immediately by the squeal of a microphone. Connor rolls his eyes.

"Ladies and gentleman." One of the waiters is up on stage leaning into the mic. "Let me introduce the first act of the afternoon: Keeley Summers."

There are a few claps and some shuffling on stage while a young brunette perches on a tall stool and rests an acoustic guitar on her thighs. It seems the entire diner is holding its breath, waiting to see if the next ten or fifteen minutes are going to be cringey or bearable. She gently strums the guitar and sings a soft first line and the room sighs with relief.

"See?" I turn back to Connor. "It's not so bad. She actually sounds really good."

"Hmm," he replies, chewing his last mouthful.

"I remember once being at an open mic night, before Mom got really dependent. This guy read the most beautiful poem by F Scott Fitzgerald, something about starting over. I hadn't really heard of Fitzgerald at that point but it prompted me to read the Great Gatsby, then Tender is the Night, and then pretty much everything else he's written…"

"Woman after my own heart," Connor says, raising his eyebrows.

"You like F Scott Fitzgerald?"

"Sure I do."

I swallow back my surprise. "Well, anyway, I don't know how people do it. I could never put myself on stage like that in front of everyone."

"Yeah," Connor pushes his empty plate to one side. "You wouldn't catch me dead up there."

"No? Not even karaoke?"

"Least of all karaoke. No, I have a weird fear of stages."

"Are you kidding me?" I'm genuinely shocked. "You're practically on a stage every day at the resort—people look up to you, they follow your lead, they look to you for all the decisions. That's kind of like being on a stage."

"It really isn't. I'm not standing up in front of a crowd, holding court and feeling everyone staring at me. That is not me at all."

"So you wouldn't make a thank you speech or something to all the teams at the resort, for example?"

"That's different—that's about them. This…" he gestures towards the stage, "is about the person standing up there. They're inviting scrutiny. I would never in a million years want to bring that upon myself."

"Connor Johnson," I say, smiling at each new snippet of information he gives me, "you are endlessly surprising."

He smiles back, his beautiful blue eyes glittering. "I aim to please."

———

AFTER WE'VE SAT through a second perfectly lovely open mic performance and thanked Trey and Ange profusely for the delicious dinner, we climb into the car and head back to Starling Key. We sit in comfortable silence while a million thoughts fly around my head. I think back to when I first sat in Connor's car that morning, fuming because I knew being forced on this trip was supposedly punishment, for what, I've no idea. But as the day progressed, I feel like I got to know him a lot more. I like him, and I have a pretty strong feeling he might like me. Connor shuts off the engine and I climb out, almost regretfully.

"Where are you going?" he asks as I take off in the opposite direction to the northeast wall.

"I'm going to go and sit on the beach for a little while," I say. I need to get some air, to blow away some of the pent-up need that has been bubbling beneath my skin ever since our fingers entwined across the table.

"Mind if I join you?"

*Ok, so that plan backfired.*

"Sure," I shrug.

"Hold up a sec," he says and pops the trunk of his car. He pulls out a bottle of white rum.

"Let's go one better than the beach," he says. "Ever been inside the executive villas?"

"No. Esme was going to show me but hasn't been able to yet."

"Well, the Hemingway has just been vacated, the villa furthest south. I'll show you."

He catches up with me and we walk down to the pier. The sun is about to disappear below the horizon and the sky is an awe-inspiring kaleidoscope of pinks and oranges. We reach a small gate at the end of the pier. Connor unlocks it and lets me walk through onto the decking. We leave the shore behind and make our way along the wooden pathway between the pristine white villas.

There are four on each side, the ones to our left overlooking the Mexican Gulf, the four to our right overlooking Starling Key and beyond it towards the mainland. We catch glimpses of people moving about inside the villas, voices chattering, bodies splashing in the private pools and the clear blue sea. Then we reach the very end villa.

Connor unlocks a wooden door and holds it open for me. Unfortunately, I can't move because my jaw is on the floor. I've never seen luxury like it. I vaguely notice a slick, minimalistic kitchen equipped with small, discreet, top of the range gadgets, and a serene white seating area lined with tropical plants, original artwork and sculptures. But what stuns me the most is the opposite wall of the villa. It just isn't there. All I can see is expansive blue ocean, extending for miles and miles. The peaks of the waves are pink reflecting the setting sun.

"It's ok, go in," Connor says, smiling.

I step inside and slip off my sandals. The temperature is perfect, the space tranquil and calming. I turn to my left and see the most stunning bed I've ever seen. It is dark mahogany, Indonesian style, with decadent mosquito drapes cascading down each side. To my right is a sunken bath overlooking the edge of the villa and the sea beneath, and beyond that is a shower. The cubicle hangs over the water with clear panels all the way round. I walk towards the opposite wall which I now realize is made of glass, and bring my face as close to it as possible without touching the polished surface. There's an infinity pool below and a small concealed seating area.

"Come on, let's sit out there," Connor says. He presses a button and the glass slides to the right revealing some steps down to the seating area.

He watches me sit down on one of the rattan chairs with a bemused look on his face.

"What's so funny?" I ask.

"You look like you've just sat down in a hot seat. You're not going to get electrocuted if you touch anything you know."

I relax a little. He unscrews the top of the rum bottle and hands it to me. I take a few mouthfuls, gratefully, then hand the bottle back. He stares at the rim for a few seconds then puts it to his mouth.

"So, you designed this place?"

"Sort of. I had ideas but an architect really brought it to life. The brief was simple really, create a villa that makes you feel as though you're living in the sea."

"I think it's achieved that," I say. "It's breathtaking."

He smiles to himself, as though my compliment really does mean something to him. He passes back the bottle and I drink down some more.

"How much does it cost to stay here for a week?"

"Depends on the time of year but if you were to come now, during peak season, between forty and forty-five thousand dollars."

I hand him back the bottle before I have a chance to choke on the rum.

"Who has that kind of money?" I mutter.

"Oh you'd be surprised," he says, staring out at the sea.

"There are a lot of people out there prepared to pay an arm and a leg for a week in paradise."

"When are the next guests due?"

"Day after tomorrow."

"Have you ever stayed in one of the villas?"

"Nope. Never really wanted to. Don't think it would be too much fun on my own."

He takes a swig of the rum while I get to my feet and walk to the edge of the decking. There's a discreet silver ladder leading down into the clear water, and I'm suddenly overwhelmed by an urge to jump into it. Instead, I look out across the expanse, my eyes becoming accustomed to a darker sky now that the sun has disappeared.

"Cuba is just a few hundred miles that way," a voice almost whispers in my ear and I jump. He's standing right behind me, wedging me between his body and the sea. He dangles the bottle over my shoulder.

"Are you trying to get me drunk?" I take it from him and swig a little more rum. We've devoured almost half the bottle already.

"No. I've seen what you're like when you're hammered and I have a duty to protect all the cacti on the island."

I elbow him gently in the ribs and feel his hands on my shoulders.

"Thanks for bringing me here, it's beautiful," I say quietly. Then I can't help it; I blurt out what I really want to do.

"Can I go in the water?"

He steps backwards. "Right now?"

"Yeah. Right now. It's gorgeous here."

"You don't have your bathing suit…" He almost chokes on the last word.

"I'm wearing underwear though," I smile. "Would you mind? I know I probably shouldn't, but…"

"No, it's fine," he rushes out. I take a closer look and his cheeks are an adorable shade of pink. "I'll just get you a towel."

He disappears back inside the villa and I decide to spare him any further blushes by stripping out of my dress quickly and sliding into the beautifully crisp water. It's deep here but I can see the sea bed clearly, despite the quickening darkness. I push myself away from the edge and duck beneath the surface, kicking my legs behind me. When I emerge and push my soaked hair back off my face and open my eyes, Connor is standing at the edge of the decking with a strange look on his face.

"Are you gonna come in?"

He shakes his head and tightens his lips. "I'm good."

"The water is still warm," I say, before ducking under again and swimming further out. When I pop up again, he looks almost panic-stricken.

"Will you stay a bit closer to the deck?" He asks. "You've had quite a bit of rum, and it's getting dark, T."

"Are you worried about me, Connor?" I tease. "Less than twenty-four hours ago you couldn't have cared less what happened to me. In fact, you'd probably have pushed me right in."

"That's not true," he snaps, and my smile falls. I've hit a nerve.

"So, why did you make me go to Miami with you?"

He doesn't reply, he just grinds his jaw and there it is, the look I'm most familiar with. Connor is exasperated with me.

"Come on, you didn't need me there."

"Yes, I did," he says in a low voice. "I never do those trips alone."

"So, why didn't you take Carter?"

"He was busy."

I shoot him a sideways glance as I twist and turn in the water. "I don't believe that." I know exactly why he made me go. "Admit it, Connor, you were pissed that I did such a good job distracting Franklin, you wanted to knock me down a little. Going to Miami was the first thing that came into your head."

His breath is tight as he hovers by the steps. "T, come a little closer, please."

"Admit it, and I'll come closer."

"I'm not admitting that, because it isn't true."

"So, tell me the truth." I've pushed Connor into a corner —one he is clearly not used to being pushed into—and I'm thoroughly enjoying myself.

He takes another tight breath in. "Yes, you did a good job distracting the guy. Too good. You were gloating and it pissed me off."

"I was not gloating…"

"Please T, will you come out now?"

"Only if you agree that I was not gloating."

"Ok, fine. You were not gloating. Now, will you get the fuck out of the sea?"

I don't reply. I swim up to the steps and climb out, slowly, to infuriate him. I reach the top and allow him to wrap a towel around my shoulders. His eyes beat down on me, his face inches from mine, with an emotion I cannot decipher; he looks almost scared. Have I just scared him by being in the water after sunset?

"So, why did you make me go?" I whisper. "How could I have been 'too good' when all I did was talk to the guy?"

His eyes roam my face and my legs feel as though they're turning to jelly. After the day we've spent together and the things he shared with me, I thought I felt closer to Connor. But right now, in this moment, with his eyes staring me down and his words absent, I feel more distant from him than ever.

"You seemed to be enjoying it," he replies. "And I didn't like it."

"Why?" I press.

He says nothing so I lean in, bringing my lips up to his ear. "The part I enjoyed the most was when you showed up. That was my favorite part."

I settle back down on my heels and search for his reaction.

"Tawny." My name comes out of his mouth with a rush of air, as though it's been sitting on his tongue, trapped, waiting. It emboldens me.

"I know you want this," I say, watching his lips go dry. He wants to lick them but he's stopping himself. "I felt you when you were removing the cactus spikes."

He starts to shake his head.

"That was real," I say, my voice firmer now. "I did not imagine that."

His head continues to move from side-to-side, his eyes still anchored on mine.

"It doesn't matter," he says, finally.

"Why doesn't it?" I can feel the moment slipping away. I have to keep a hold of it. "Carter told me about your fiancée."

His head stops moving and his eyes narrow.

"That we look alike," I continue, quickly. "I'm not her, Connor."

In a beat, he turns and takes two long strides to the door of the villa. Then he twists back around and drops a key onto a rattan chair.

"Lock up on your way out," he says. Then he's gone.

# CHAPTER SEVENTEEN

onnor

THE DESPAIR that fills me hits the ground with each pounding stride as I walk away from the villa, leaving Tawny Graham dripping sea water onto the deck. I can't believe Carter told her about Clarisse. That's really pushing it. I expected him to tell her about other stuff—work stuff—but not my damn personal life. I whip out my cell and dial his number.

"Hey man, what's up?"

"Why the fuck did you tell Tawny about Clarisse?"

"Ah, ok, that. Listen, she's convinced you hate her, ok? She can see the way you behave with other people and how you treat her so differently. The fact she's a clumsy nut isn't going to cut it forever, and she can see right through it. I couldn't lie to her."

"You had no business saying anything."

"Well, I'm sorry Connor, I am. But you would have done the same thing if you'd been in my shoes. Besides, it's true isn't it? Tawny reminds you of Clarisse. That's why you're giving her such a hard time."

"Carter…" I warn.

"Look man, I know it's hard to admit, but I know you Connor. I'm saying this as your best friend; you need to get over it because it isn't right treating her this way. It's unethical for a start, but it's also… it's pretty nasty, and it kind of undermines your authority."

"What do you mean?"

"Well, it's affecting how you make decisions. I mean, who went with you to Miami today? Were you gonna tell one of us? It's our gig too. You're getting lost up in your head over this girl because, what? She brings back difficult memories? Or is there another reason?"

"No," I snap.

"Then why did you take her to Miami? I saw you heading down to check how she was doing with the yacht guy last night. What happened?"

"Nothing. Nothing happened. I wanted to keep a close eye on her, that's all."

"Why, Connor?" He's pushing me. "Why do you want to keep a close eye on her?"

I reach the main building and see Carter walking towards me. I hang up. He strides up to me and stops. He can see right through me and I know there's no point in lying anymore—to him or to myself.

"I like her," I say to his face.

He beams. He positively beams, and I could jab one in his jaw.

"He confesses," he smirks.

"Fuck off, Carter. It doesn't mean I'm going to do anything about it." I go to walk past him but he sticks a heavy black boot in front of me.

"Why?" He puts a hand on my shoulder but I refuse to look at him.

"You know why."

"And you know Tawny isn't Clarisse. She's nothing like Clarisse. Ok, so she looks similar but... Man, you know I never really liked Clarisse. There was a reason for that. She always seemed to be looking over your shoulder for someone better to come along. Stupid bitch didn't realize she would never find anyone better than you. But when you came back from Iraq and she'd gone? I wasn't surprised. Tawny is nothing like that, Connor. She really fucking wants you, you know. I can tell. Anyone with two eyes can tell. She isn't looking over your shoulder for someone else; she's looking right at you."

"She deserves better," I say, quietly.

"What makes you say that?" Carter drops his hand and squares himself in front of me. He's losing his patience.

"I'm carrying a sack-load of baggage and you know it."

"What bag..." Then he gets it. "Connor, are you ok?"

I pause and take a deep breath. "The flashbacks have started up again." Finally, I look at him and see the fear in his eyes.

"Shit, man, you need to take some time off. We don't need a repeat of what happened last time."

I shake my head. "It's only one time so far."

"It was only one time last time, until it wasn't. What's triggered it?"

"I have no idea." I can't tell him the flashback immediately followed the most intense orgasm I think I've ever had, while I fist-fucked to thoughts of Tawny Graham. It was accompanied by an overwhelming sense of resignation—that what I'd fantasized about could only ever be just that: a fantasy. "All I know is my brain is too volatile, too precarious. The only way I can keep the flashbacks at bay is if I know exactly what's happening and when. I'm no control freak, Carter; I need everything to work perfectly, because if it doesn't, I fucking fall apart. That's why nothing will ever happen with Tawny; I won't be able to control the way I feel."

I stare at him, willing him to see I'm telling the truth. It takes a lot to admit what I just have, and I would only admit it to Carter. He takes a deep breath and shakes his head.

"I just want you to be happy," he says, with a sigh. "I miss the old Connor. The one who used to get a kick out of sleeping in, pulling pranks, flirting with girls. I know you went through hell and back in Iraq, but seriously, you became a different person after that, and I want my old friend back—the one who wanted to be happy."

I force myself to stare through the memory of who I used to be, unaffected. "I am happy, Carter. I don't need a woman to be happy."

He holds his hands up in surrender. "Alright, man. I'll back off on the Tawny thing. I won't tell her anything else."

"Thank you. Now, are you going to move so I can go to bed?"

He grins and steps to one side, slapping me on the back. "Night Connor. Go get your beauty sleep. Not that you need it," he sniggers. He calls after me as I walk away. "Such a waste, man. You're so hot and you're just gonna let these poor women salivate over you from a distance? It's a travesty!"

I ignore him. "Night Carter," I say, as I make the walk back to the northeast wall.

THE FOLLOWING day I walk into the reception and see Tawny's desk empty. Despite the way things went down last night, my stomach still clenches at her absence. As hard as it is seeing those big eyes and gorgeous legs every day, I find myself craving it the second I wake up.

I move through to the meeting rooms and hear voices coming from the first one I reach. There's no sign on the door to say it's been booked out so I knock briefly and open it.

Four guests from the retirement village look up from whatever it is they're studying on the desk and consider me warily, as though I'm intruding on my own offices.

"Morning everyone. How are you doing?"

"Oh, Connor," Barbie says. "We're planning a week-long itinerary of excursions. My birthday's coming up you know. The big seventy-five!" She claps her hands together, glee-fully. "You know, my darling, you'd make the perfect birthday present. I've always wanted a boy toy."

"You're such a flirt, Barbara," I say, grinning at one of my favorite ever guests.

"Only with a lucky few," she winks.

"Do you have everything you need?"

"Oh yes," she nods, enthusiastically. "We're in excellent hands. We are not worried about having things arranged; all we are worried about is how we manage to do all the amazing things your wonderful events manager has suggested..."

"What amazing...?"

At that exact moment, I hear her Jersey twang.

"Sorry about that wait, everybody. The coffee machine gave up the ghost; I snuck into Connor's office and borrowed his..."

At that moment, Tawny appears carrying a tray laden with cups of coffee, water and snacks. She sees me and her cheeks color instantly.

"Hey Connor! I just borrowed your coffee machine… but I guess you already knew that." She shoots a devastating smile at me then offloads the drinks and sits down, resuming her discussion with the retirees as though I'm not even there.

"Tawny?"

"Yes, Connor?"

"Come see me when you're done."

"Of course, boss," she smiles.

I close the door and already I can't wait to get her in my office.

---

A HALF HOUR LATER, Tawny knocks on my door.

"Come in."

She's confident yet sort of humble as she walks into the room and waits for me to signal she can take a seat.

"Is everything ok?"

"What are you doing with our highest-paying guests?"

She takes a deep breath and splays her fingers across my desk as if she's gripping onto some form of courage.

"Connor, you have to get past this idea that I'm somehow incapable of doing anything right. You have to give me a chance." Finally, she looks up and suddenly it's me who wants to look away.

"I want to make it up to you. I shouldn't have said what I did; it's none of my business and it was inappropriate of me. I want to help, I found a gap in our offering, and I've been getting to know these guys. I can enhance what we offer—the boat trips, the outings to other Keys, different experiences. We can give them more of what they like."

"How do you know what's even available for them?"

"What do you think I've been doing every day while I sit

at that desk with nothing to do? I've been researching. Well, daydreaming mainly, of all the things I would love to do if I had the chance. I already had a list of things that looked like fun."

I sigh and look back at her. Her big green eyes are wide and pleading, her pink lips pulled into a concentrated pout, willing me to give her that chance. My eyes linger on them a little too long.

"Fine." I sit back in my chair and watch the relief roll across her face. "I will need to sign off the final itinerary."

"Of course." Her face has lit up and it's because of me. I just gave her my approval; my forgiveness for her pushing me too far.

I follow her out of my office and see the retirees standing in the foyer. They look up as Tawny approaches and smile excitedly.

"We love these ideas," says Fitz. "We just need to make sure all the timings work, you know, with our meds…"

"And naps," Barbie adds.

"Absolutely," Tawny smiles back. "I'll just need to run the final choices past my boss." She turns and shoots me a wink as I walk out of the foyer. I can't help it; I feel as though my insides have turned liquid and I want to hold on to the feeling with both hands.

# CHAPTER EIGHTEEN

*Tawny*

"I HEAR Barbie's birthday celebration got off to a great start today?" Esme says as we hover next to Che's bar. "She was squealing as a bunch of them went flying past me on a buggy this afternoon. Where did you send them?"

"Boat trip round the smaller Keys with a BBQ thrown in —and probably gin."

"Ah, that explains the squealing." She waves at a group of her housekeeping colleagues as they thread their way past. The bar is packed tonight with everyone wanting to blow off steam after a few weeks of the season being in full swing. "What else have you got lined up for them?"

"Mangrove kayaking, dolphin spotting, live music mini cruise…"

"All sounds very decadent."

"…and then a Ghosts and Gravestones Trolley Tour."

Her jaw drops. "Until that. Seriously? Do I have to say it?"

"Say what?" I ask, innocently.

Esme leans in so no one else can hear—not that anyone would, Camiro's Latino beats are pumping around us pretty loud.

"They're kinda heading that way themselves, you know? To gravestones?"

"I think that's why they chose to do it. A sneak preview. I showed them all the options—that's what they chose."

"Here you go, ladies." We turn back to the makeshift bar to see Ché holding out two of his famous mojitos. Esme takes a long sip from a straw.

"Ah, I needed this. Thanks Ché!"

"Tough week?" I ask her.

"A little. That aging rock star we had here until a couple days ago left the room in a terrible state. Took Shell and I a whole day just to deep clean the bedroom."

"That's grim."

"How about you? How was Miami?"

"It was actually ok," I say, squinting as the sour notes of the lime touch my taste buds. "A whole day with Connor and he didn't kill me."

"That's progress, right there. And everything went ok with the shipment?"

"As far as I know."

"I heard you did a great job distracting the son." She shoots me a cheeky look.

"From who?"

"The guys. Carter maybe. I forget." Esme grins, then reaches out to tap someone's shoulder. When the person turns around I recognize her—she's the girl I saw doing shots and holding her own amidst guys twice her size when I watched out the window of 8A.

"Hey, Autumn. Have you met Tawny yet?"

A tan, heart-shaped face looks across at me, with large brown eyes and beach-tousled long blonde hair. She's incredibly pretty. I would be intimidated if she wasn't smiling so kindly. "Hey, Tawny. You're new here?"

"Reasonably. Six weeks."

"I'm surprised I haven't met you already. Welcome to the Keys."

"Autumn's one of our Dive Masters," Esme explains. "World record holder too, aren't you? The best of the best."

"Once upon a time," Autumn smiles. "I'm probably a little rusty now. Don't get to do the deep dives so much anymore. Need to keep things nice and simple for the guests," she explains. "Do you dive?"

I shake my head. "No, but I'd love to try one day."

"Well, just let me know. I love taking newbies out for their first dives. But I'll warn you, it's addictive. Especially around here with the amazing coral reef."

"I'll keep that in mind," I say, but my eyes have drifted. They've landed on Connor and are watching him as he makes his way, slowly, through the packed yard towards us. I'm glad I apologized about what I said in the villa but I know I touched a nerve. When I climbed out of the sea and he pulled me towards him in a towel, he looked as though he wanted to devour me right there. His eyes agreed with everything I said even though his shaking head said 'no'. I have no idea where I stand with him, especially when his lips say one thing but his eyes—and his cock—say another. All I know is I live for every morning, knowing I'm going to see him emerge from his office at some point and look me up and down like I'm his next meal. Those mornings, and the memory of our day in Miami, where I felt like I might be getting to know the real Connor. The Connor I saw before he spectacularly shut me down and left me in a puddle on the deck.

"Oh, hey Connor," Esme shouts.

"Hey," he says, coming to stand with us. He looks tired, but as handsome as ever.

"Tawny was telling me about the amazing trips the retirees are taking this week. I saw them earlier—they were having a ball."

"Yeah, I saw them too," he replies, then looks at me properly for the first time. My nerve endings tingle as I feel his gaze on my skin. "In fact, I need to talk to you about that. Do you have a minute?"

I feel Esme nudge me gently with her elbow, as though the butterflies now coursing through my belly haven't put me on edge enough.

"Sure. Here?"

"No. I can hardly hear myself think." He jerks his head towards the alleyway behind the bar so I follow him across to it, then around the wall and out onto the staff beach. The peace and quiet of the sand and the ocean is almost deafening as we emerge into its embrace.

Connor leads me down the beach and sits beneath one of the palms where I join him. "Is everything ok?"

He sighs and looks at the beer in his hand. I realize Esme must have taken my mojito as I followed Connor out of the yard in a daze.

"I owe you yet another apology," he sighs.

"No you don't." I'm genuinely confused.

"Yeah, I do. For storming off and leaving you in the villa. I shouldn't have done that."

"I shouldn't have said what I did. It was none of my business."

"I don't blame you for saying something. And what you've been doing with the excursions and the trips for Barbie and her friends... I want you to know I really appreciate it. They seem to be having the time of their lives, and that's down to you."

"It's easy to please happy people," I smile.

"Well, anyway. I'm sorry."

"You need to stop apologizing Connor. I just hope we can get back to the way things were when we left Key Largo. I don't think I'm wrong in saying you were enjoying my company, and I was enjoying yours... I just want to be friends."

He looks up sharply.

"Just friends?"

I can't breathe. His eyes are piercing me, asking me to bear my soul, right now. I stare at him, open-mouthed, because I don't know what to say.

He drives the bottle into the sand and puts an arm around me, bringing me close to his chest. I would be confused if my blood wasn't pumping loudly through my ears, the sensation of being held by Connor Johnson overwhelming every cell in my body. He's stroking my hair and I don't want him to stop. But more than that, I want to know what's going on, why his actions are betraying his words, why he can't be clear with me about what he wants. I gently push him away; I need answers.

"Connor, listen to me. This isn't fair what you're doing."

"What do you mean?"

"One minute you're walking away or turning away from me, the next you're demanding I go with you to Miami.

You're obviously turned on when you're getting damn cactus spikes out of my butt…" I hesitate at that last point, and Connor breaks a small smile. He's adorable when he smiles. The blue of his eyes shines and the small wrinkles at the side of them deepen. He looks older than his age but it suits him.

"I'm going to lay my cards on the table." I take a deep breath. "I like you Connor. I really like you. I don't know why—you've treated me like shit for the most part, but I know you have a heart of gold. And every time you come after me, or you touch me accidentally-on-purpose, or you seek me out like you have done tonight, it gives me hope. Then you go and shut down somehow by snapping at me, or storming out of a villa. Then my heart breaks a little and I'm back where I started. It's like having whiplash."

He looks down at the sand between us.

"I'm just a Jersey girl, Connor. I don't have the experience you have. All I want is a normal life—a job, friends, maybe a boyfriend someday, then, I don't know, a home, a dog. I don't want the world. I don't want the bad boy either. I'm not that girl."

He looks up at me through those stupidly thick lashes of his and my heart cries a little. It already knows the response it's going to get. It's going to start building a little wall around itself right now, then when I'm alone, in the quiet of my dorm, it will weep. I can already feel it breaking. It's broken before, when I lost my dad, and then my mom, and then my home, but it's never broken before because of a boy —or man, in Connor's case—and I can already tell it's an entirely different kind of pain.

"Fuck," he sinks his head into his hands.

That's really all the answer I need, but I still want to hear the explanation.

"You're right, and I'm sorry."

He sighs, as though he's been hoping this conversation would never happen, as though he could just carry on seeking comfort in me when he wants it, and rejecting me when he doesn't.

"I like you too Tawny, I do." He lifts his chin bringing his eyes level with mine. "But nothing can come of it. Nothing good anyway."

"What do you mean?"

"It isn't just about Clarisse," he says, turning his head and looking out to the sea. "I have baggage I'm not ready to unpack, let alone allow anyone else to see."

"What kind of baggage?"

He sighs with a heaviness that sinks into the sand around him. "It started in Iraq. After my base was hit, me and the other guys who survived had to prepare the bodies to be flown home. We had no idea if we'd be hit again, our eardrums had taken a massive beating—all any of us could hear was a ringing sound. We didn't know if it was temporary or if we were deaf for good. Every time I closed my eyes, all I could see was white—that's what the explosion looked like to me—and debris curling up into the sky. It took three days for rescue teams to arrive and collect us all. I had bone fractures and muscle tears in my right arm and leg—the doctors were amazed I'd managed to haul the bodies of twenty-seven dead soldiers to a site where they could be collected. They were amazed I could walk, or even function.

I was taken to a hospital where I was surrounded by other veterans, many who were injured far worse than I was, and I had the constant thought that despite everything I'd been through, everything I'd seen—the needless death and destruction—I was fucking lucky."

He shakes his head bitterly.

"I checked out as soon as I was given the all-clear. I was

offered therapy but I declined it, thinking that after seeing the men and women in the hospital with hardly any limbs at all, half their skulls whipped away, blind, you name it, I couldn't indulge myself with *therapy*."

He practically spits out the word.

"I thought I'd be fine if I went home, let Clarisse look after me for a few weeks, then sort myself out with some civilian job, but... settling back into civilian life is difficult enough, let alone coming home to discover your fiancée had been sleeping with someone else the entire time and doesn't want you back."

He claws his fingers through his hair.

"So I left. I came straight here. A buddy told me Starling was hiring and wanted some serious muscle. I applied, came down here to interview. The minute I saw the Key—and it was nothing compared to what it is now—I fell in love. I gave that interview everything I had. Luckily, Starling gave me a break. I don't know what I'd have done if he hadn't."

"But you're still carrying the baggage," I say.

"Yeah. it doesn't go away; it just gets heavier. For the first two years I had pretty bad nightmares and panic attacks. At first I hid it from the guys, because, you know, this is not the job to do if you suffer from anxiety."

His laugh is bitter.

"But Carter saw right through me. He wasn't on the base that blew up but we'd served together in the years before. He knew me better than anyone. He made me go to therapy. So I tried it once. Fucking hated it. He still goes on at me about going for more, but... it's not me, Tawny. It's not how I deal with stuff."

"So you deal with stuff like you have obsessive compulsive disorder instead?" I ask. "Everything has to be exactly right, exactly in line with the plan, not a hair out of place, otherwise it triggers some sort of reaction in you?"

"Yeah, I suppose."

"It's not healthy, Connor."

"But it's made Starling Key what it is," he says, firmly. When he turns back to face me, there's a different look in his eyes. A look that says I'm not going to win this fight.

"If I wasn't the way I am, we probably wouldn't have the sea villas, the spa, the diving center. We wouldn't be raking in thirty mil every year. We have all this because I don't tolerate anything less than the fucking best."

"Because you're afraid that anything less than the best will trigger an attack?"

"Something like that."

"Do you realize how absurd that sounds?"

"I don't care, Tawny. Do I question you about how you got here?"

Now it's my turn to stare at the sand.

"I know there are things you aren't telling me. But I don't need to know. I take you exactly as you are, past or no past, it's none of my business."

My cheeks are flushed and I can't look at him.

"I'm sorry to say that to you. You're the sweetest, kindest, most infuriating woman I know. I need to keep my life simple, and that means not getting into relationships with anyone other than my teams. But it kills me that I can't give you what you need."

I look up to see him rubbing his eyes.

"But you want to?" I ask. I can more easily live with him not acting on his desires if I know for sure he has them in the first place.

He stares at me, his eyes roaming my face, from my hairline, around my cheeks, along my jaw, across to my eyes, to my nose and to my lips, and there his eyes linger.

"You've got no fucking idea, T."

I can't help it. I launch myself at him, kissing him full on, on the mouth. He sucks in a gasp and doesn't move at first, but then I feel his large hands at the sides of my face. He pulls away to position his mouth on mine exactly the way he wants it—everything has to be done Connor's way—then he kisses me, as though I'm oxygen and he needs me in order to breathe.

His mouth moves against mine, gently sucking in my lips, dragging his teeth along the soft skin. I can almost hear the hiss of chemistry as it floods my system, and a deep moan from the foot of his lungs followed by an involuntary pause tells me Connor feels it too. He pulls me close and I sink deeper into his body. His tongue nudges softly at my lips, tentatively asking for more. I moan, open-mouthed, letting him slide in, then his tongue chases mine, hungrily. I clutch at his back, needing more, so much more. His hands clasp my hips, pulling me up to straddle him. As I sit back down over his thighs I can feel him. There's no denying he's as turned on as I am.

His hands are in my hair, tugging at the band holding it in place, so I reach up and loosen it, letting my hair fall over our faces. He pulls back and I see his eyes are completely glazed.

"Fuck, T," he breathes, then his mouth is back on mine.

I'm burning all over. I've never felt anything like it. I've lost my virginity but my sexual encounters with boys have been nothing to write home about but this... *this*... is insane. It's just a kiss but it's the most sensual, mind-blowing kiss I've ever had in my life.

Instinctively and without thinking, my hips start to rock. It elicits an untethered groan from Connor's throat which I'm instantly addicted to. I rock again, just so I can hear it. I'm rewarded. Not only with another groan but a rock from him. His hands are on my ass and we begin to move together, in rhythm. His hair is tufted between my fingers and my tongue is roaming his mouth while he stokes the fire between my thighs with his growing erection.

"Oh God, Connor," I say, my voice alien. I can feel something stirring in my groin and I try to rock against him harder but his hands stop me. Gradually, he slows the rocking until we've stopped. If we weren't still kissing, I'd be panting from frustration. Instead, he continues to fuck my mouth with his tongue, exquisitely. If my mouth could orgasm, it would have had multiple by now. I can feel his fingers push through my hair and I have the distinct feeling this is close to being over and I want to cry. How can anything that feels so good and so perfect be wrong? Surely, what's happening now is enough to convince Connor it's right.

His fingers stay entwined in my hair as he pulls back. My lips suddenly ache. He places a small kiss on my lips. And another. And another. And between each one, he says my name.

Finally he stops and looks me in the eyes.

"Do you want this?" I ask again.

"How could I not want it?" He says, his voice thick with emotion—so much emotion he looks as though he's in pain. "If I didn't care about you, I wouldn't have stopped myself."

"Then don't care about me," I say in a gasp.

His lips curl into a bittersweet smile.

"It doesn't work like that. I care about you too much and I can't guarantee I won't hurt you. I'm fucked up, T. I have to live a certain way or I can't function. It's selfish but it's necessary. You asked me to trust you, and I did. Now I'm asking you to trust me. Trust me when I say if we were together I'd be your worst nightmare."

I can't argue with him but I can't argue with the way I feel either. Before the kiss I could just about cope, but now… Knowing we share such sexual chemistry, that a kiss could feel so good, that two bodies could align in such perfect rhythm so effortlessly, I'm not sure I can carry on in the same way anymore.

"Then I can't do this, Connor," I say, and I can feel the tears welling up. "I can't stay on this island, seeing you every day, being around you, watching you at a distance, never being able to touch you. I should leave."

His eyes suddenly fill with panic.

"Not yet." He holds my hands as if that might stop me going. "Please just stay until the end of the season. If you feel the same way come April, I won't stand in your way, but please… you've become such an important member of the team and everyone loves you. If you leave now, I'll never forgive myself."

"That's all well and good for you but what about me? What about my feelings? My sanity?"

"I'll give you a different job, somewhere we won't come into contact a lot, ok? I'll respect that. It'll be fucking hard not seeing you, but if it's the only way you'll stay…"

The sexual chemistry raging in my veins is now replaced by anger.

"And what if I fall for someone else on the island?" I say, testing him.

His eyes turn a different hue and despite the darkness, I can see the muscles clench in his jaw.

"I won't stand in your way."

My shoulders collapse and I sink my face into my hands. I know in this moment he isn't going to budge. No amount of sexual attraction is going to make him change his mind, and I'm not a total imbecile; I know when begging is not only futile but foolish.

When I get to my feet, he starts to apologize but I hold up a hand. There's nothing more to say. I shake my head, sadly, then I make my way back up the beach feeling his eyes watching me go.

# CHAPTER NINETEEN

 onnor

I FEEL EMPTY. My heart, if I still have one, has gone with her. My dick is still straining against my jeans; it hasn't got the memo. I have to wait for it to process the message nothing is going to happen before I can even think about getting up.

I turn and look out to sea. I've had this conversation once before but it wasn't with someone I couldn't stop thinking about or preceded by a kiss that sent fucking dynamite through my bones making me question everything. I have no idea how I was able to put a stop to it. I can only imagine it was my military training kicking in, recognizing my brain and body had checked out so my subconscious needed to step in and take over.

I also didn't care this much the time before. If I remember correctly, I just carried on as though nothing had happened. The girl was assigned another job, she eventually left and I honestly can't say I noticed when she'd gone. But, fuck… the thought of Tawny leaving the island makes me feel sick. The thought of Tawny falling for another guy makes me feel like breaking someone's bones.

Moving her is the right thing to do. I can't do my job if she's around, knowing what she tastes like, knowing how she feels rolling back and forth over my jeans-clad cock, knowing how she sounds when she's close to the edge—those small, uncontrollable gasps each time I rocked into her. Jesus, this is not helping my hard on.

I think about the casino, the opening night plans, the guest list, the catering, anything. After a few minutes, it's safe for me to move, so I push up to my feet and follow the path Tawny trod, even though she's long gone, in every way.

---

THE NEXT DAY, I'm walking back from the Grand House after my weekly meeting with Starling, when Carter calls.

"Hey, man. Haven't seen you all d…"

"Connor, I'm at the hospital."

"What? Is everything ok?"

"It's not me, it's Lucy."

"Shit. Is she ok? What's happened, Carter?"

He's silent.

"Carter, is she ok?" I say again, more firmly this time.

"Yeah, she's ok, but…"

"But, what?"

He's silent again. When he finally speaks, almost a minute later, he says the last thing I ever expected to hear.

"She's lost the baby."

THE WHEELS of the truck screech as I pull into the parking lot. I slam the door shut and run towards the main entrance. I burst through the doors and almost knock over an elderly couple on their way out.

"Hey, mister!"

"I'm sorry," I shout, jogging up to the front desk.

"Maternity ward," I pant. "Where do I go?"

The lady grins at me and it takes me a couple of seconds to realize she probably thinks I'm about to become a dad myself. I don't even contemplate it. Never have done. I can't have a kid; I couldn't do that to anyone.

"Straight down the hall, through the double doors, turn left, take the elevator up to the third floor. You'll see signs."

"Thanks." I run off down the corridor, hearing her shouting for me to walk, but I don't. This is Carter we're talking about, my best friend. And he's broken. He won't ever say that, but I've never heard him sound so desperate and so worried. Then there's Lucy. I can't even imagine what she must be going through right now. I had no idea they were pregnant; nobody did. Carter didn't go into detail over the phone but it sounded serious. She's on the maternity ward now but she was admitted straight to ER with some sort of life-threatening complication. I will the elevator to go faster than it's leisurely, rickety pace. As soon as the doors open, I rush into the main corridor and follow signs to the maternity ward.

I see Carter pacing and I jog up to him. When he looks up, he's as pale as a sheet.

"How is she?"

Carter's eyes are distant, as though he's living someone else's life.

"She's not good Connor, but at least she's alive."

"What the fuck happened?"

He sighs, heavily, then nods to a row of seats. We sit down and I look at the ground, waiting. I don't want to rush him.

"It was ectopic."

I don't even pretend to know what that means, so I wait for him to explain.

"She was pregnant but the egg didn't embed itself in her womb like it should have. It embedded itself in one of her fallopian tubes. We had no idea. Apparently no one does, not until the egg starts to grow."

I turn my head to look at him. He's staring at the wall opposite, saying the words as though he's trying to remember everything the doctors have told him.

"It grew. She started getting these pains and we googled it, and apparently stomach pains in early pregnancy are common, so we didn't think any more about it. But this morning, she was in the middle of a treatment and she collapsed. Pearl called me and we got her to hospital. She was delirious by the time we got here. I thought…"

He stops talking and holds a hand over his mouth as though he can't bring himself to say the words. I put an arm round his shoulders.

"It's ok, man."

He takes a couple of deep breaths, then continues.

"We nearly lost her, Connor."

I shake my head. "What happened?"

"The tube had burst. She had massive internal bleeding. The doctors told us if we hadn't gotten her here when we did —and I mean, I hauled ass down the highway—we could have lost her. She was that close."

I keep my arm across Connor's shoulders while I try to process everything he's just said.

"How long have you known she was pregnant?"

"Three weeks. She was nine weeks along…"

I rub my face with my free hand. I don't believe it. Carter was going to be a dad. I didn't even know he'd been seeing Lucy all that time.

"They've stopped the bleeding, right?"

He rests his elbows on his knees and wrings his hands.

"Yeah, but they have to keep her in a few nights for observation."

"Ok," I nod. "Is Pearl still here?"

"No, she took a cab back about twenty minutes ago. She needed to get back to running the spa. You just missed her."

"Is she ok? It must have been a shock for her too."

"Yeah, she's fine. She was great actually. I was fucking helpless, I didn't have a clue what to do. Pearl was the one who made sure we got Lucy into the truck and here on time. She was the one who told me to put my foot down. She spoke to the doctors. I had no fucking idea what was going on."

He sinks his head into his hands. I've never seen Carter like this before. He looks completely lost.

"How are you doing?" I say, bringing my arm down and nudging him with my elbow.

"I'm doing shit, Connor," he says, without looking up. "But seriously, I have no right to even complain. Lucy nearly died."

"But she didn't. And you've both been through something horrible. It's ok to feel shit about it."

He sighs heavily and looks up, perching his chin on clasped hands.

"I'd just got my head around the idea of being a dad. I mean, it still seems surreal that that could've happened. When I first found out I was petrified. I couldn't see how we could make it work, you know? We both live on the island, in dorms for God's sake, and neither of us are making much money. I didn't know how we were going to do it. Lucy was worried too. Then after a couple days, I found myself getting excited. Was it gonna be a little girl? A little girl I could protect and nurture? Or a little boy I could go watch play sports? I felt optimistic. I promised Lucy we'd manage, we'd find a way."

"And you would have, Carter. I could have talked to Starling about a different kind of accommodation, or we could have come up with some other arrangement."

His shoulders collapse. "It doesn't matter now."

"Hey," I say, trying to make the best of an awful situation. "Not this time, but if you guys get pregnant again, we'd sort it, is all I'm saying."

He shakes his head. "I don't know, man. I don't know if that'll happen."

"What makes you say that?"

He pauses and stares at his tattooed fingers.

"Just… a feeling I have."

I don't press him.

"Have you seen her since she came out of surgery?"

"Only briefly. The doctors are still in with her."

"Ok, well, I'm going to go grab a coffee. I'll bring one back for you."

"You don't need to stay, man. I'll be fine."

"Carter." I spin round and fix him with a determined stare. "I'm not going anywhere. You're practically family, brother. I'm staying here with you."

He watches me steadily, then gives me a weak smile. Then I turn and head down the corridor in search of caffeine.

# CHAPTER TWENTY

awny

I BURST through the doors to the emergency room waiting area with Esme hot on my heels. Both of us abandoned our work the second we got the call and I drove along the highway in my newly repaired truck like a bat out of hell. The waiting area is full and our eyes scan it madly for a sign of Barbie.

"Where is she? I can't see her." Esme says, panting.

"Me neither. How come it's so busy?"

"God knows."

We weave our way through dozens of people, then I see her. A pop of pink hair in a sea of blonde and brown, draped in a turquoise kaftan—her uniform of choice—clutching a cell phone and a patent pink purse, as opposed to her usual gin and cigarette.

"Over there!" I point to the far corner where Barbie is talking to a nurse.

We push our way through the crowded room to reach her, and the relief on her face at seeing us is palpable. Instead of saying anything, she bursts into tears and collapses to the floor. The nurse and me and Esme all reach out to catch her and spectacularly miss, so she ends up in a crumpled pile on the hospital floor. The three of us hoist her up and set her down on a seat which has been hastily vacated by a nearby visitor.

"Barbie, you ok?" Esme asks, both of us crouching down to face her.

She looks from me to Esme and back to me, her eyes streaming with tears, and nods.

"And Fitz?" I ask. "Is he ok?"

"He's doing much better," says the nurse behind me. "He's had some painkillers and we're setting the break in his leg. He won't be mobile for a while, but he's doing well."

"Oh, thank goodness," I gasp, pressing my hand against my chest. My heart is beating so fast I fear it might pop out at any second.

"What happened?" I look up at the nurse.

"They were on a boat…"

I nod. "The live music cruise."

"He fell and landed awkwardly on his right leg. It's broken in two places and he may need to have a hip replaced when his leg has healed."

"Oh my Lord," Esme says.

I sink my head into my hands. "This is my fault. I was the one who suggested the cruise."

"It was an accident," Esme says, rubbing my back as I crouch beside her. We both look up to face Barbie.

"Was anyone else hurt, Barbie?"

She shakes her head through the tears and strokes a hand down my cheek. "Everyone else is fine. It wasn't your fault. I just…" she hiccups, "I just… I thought we might have lost him."

Esme clasps Barbie's knee. "He isn't going anywhere, Barbs. It was just a break. You heard the nurse. He just landed awkwardly. Old Fitz Bellamy has got a long life ahead of him yet."

Barbie sniffs and nods, childlike. "I was so scared," she says, her unusually small voice trembling.

"It's ok, Barbie," Esme says. "Everything's going to be ok. And we're here. We'll stay with you."

"That's right," I echo. "I'll go grab us some drinks while we wait. I don't think it will be long before we can go see him."

"The machine's broken in here," the nurse chips in. "You'll have to go next door."

"Ok," I say, then turning to Esme, whose hands are now cradling Barbie's. "I'll be right back."

---

THERE's a line for the coffee machine when I finally find it, so I stand dutifully at the end of the line and wait. As much as I try to fight it, I can't help but look around at the signs and posters promising swift, efficient medical treatment for a variety of illnesses and conditions. I hate it. It reminds me of all the times I went with Mom to the hospital, and how each time we went, the doctors would tell me her condition had worsened. It was like running a marathon backwards. There were milestones in the progression of the condition but each one, once achieved, signaled something worse than the last. It wasn't like Mom got halfway along and she was a little bit closer to a coveted finish line, on her way to gain a grand prize, she was on her way to total senility. I dreaded each milestone. The closer Mom came to making the next one, the further away from me she drifted.

I am lost in my thoughts when a hand touches my shoulder. I jump, assuming I'm holding up the queue. But when I look up and see Connor, my heart does a little dance. My head knows nothing will ever happen with him; my heart is taking a little while to catch up.

"Hey," he says, softly. "Did you just get here?"

"No, I've been here the last half hour. I haven't seen him yet, but the nurses say he's doing great. Barbie's the one I'm most worried about."

He looks at me like I've grown two heads.

"Who are you talking about?"

"Fitz. He had a fall. Isn't that why you're here?"

"Fitz Bellamy? He's had a fall? Is he ok?"

"Did you not hear what I just said?"

"I thought you were here for someone else. So he's ok?"

"Yeah, he's doing really well according to the nurses, but Barbie, I'm not so sure."

The person in front of me takes their coffee and I'm standing facing the machine. I press the buttons for two coffees and turn to face Connor again. My heart jumps up into my throat and I suddenly know for certain I can't let him move me to another part of the resort. It's agony being this close to him and not being able to touch him, but the thought of hardly seeing him at all is far, far worse.

"What do you mean? Did Barbie have a fall too?"

"No, but she's not coping very well with this happening to Fitz. She's a wreck actually. I know she's a drama queen and she probably just faked a faint when we arrived, but she can't stop crying. It's like she can't function without Fitz."

"Why are you shaking your head?" Connor asks as I take

the coffees and he steers me back out to another waiting area, where we sit.

"They're meant to be together, Barbie and Fitz, and he's besotted with her, but she's too proud to let him in. I don't know if it's because she feels it wouldn't be respectful to Ralph—her husband—or she's afraid of getting hurt again if anything else happens to Fitz. I just don't know. But…" I'm almost afraid to say anything because, in a way, Barbie and Fitz's situation mirrors my own. One of them is prepared to give themselves wholeheartedly, the other is holding back. "It's better to spend a few years together with someone you love and be hurt when they die, than to spend no time together in that way at all. They'll still be hurt when something happens, but they'll have had no years of that love to treasure forever."

I feel an arm around my shoulder and I can't help it, I snuggle into his warmth. I only hope he can't feel my racing pulse through my skin.

"They really mean a lot to you, don't they?"

I sigh. "They've become like family to me. And that's what frightens me."

"What do you mean?"

I take a deep breath and look up into his eyes. They seem lighter and warmer and entirely focused on me.

"Well, since I haven't had much success in holding onto family and friends in the past, I worry that if I get much closer to Barbie and Fitz, and something happens to them, which it inevitably will one day, I'll be broken all over again. I love them both, but I'm petrified that inviting them into my life like this is going to be the end of theirs."

"Tawny, it's not like you're cursed or anything. Of course nothing will happen to them, and even if it did, it wouldn't be your fault. You can't let something like a fall frighten you away from being close to these guys. If you enjoy their company and they enjoy yours, you shouldn't let fear stop you."

I suddenly feel angry with him. Here he is telling me I shouldn't let my past affect how I live my life now, when he's doing exactly the same thing.

"Connor, do you realize how hypocritical you sound?"

He sits up straight and glares at me.

"You're telling me not to let fear stop me from being close to people, but isn't that exactly what you're doing?"

He continues to stare at me with laser like eyes and I can see his chest moving up and down with effort.

"It's not the same," he says, quietly.

"It's fear, right?" I press. "Fear of losing control?"

"It's more than that."

"Then what? What is it Connor? You want me." I say, taking care to keep my voice down. "You said it yourself. And it seems you can't stay away from me—you didn't have to sit and talk to me right now, especially after you said it would be best if I moved to a different part of the resort. You're making it difficult for me to get by without thinking about you every minute of every day. It's not fair. If you really can't stay away, I deserve to know why you won't let it happen. It isn't just that you might lose focus. I deserve to know exactly what I'm up against."

He throws himself forward onto his knees and shoves his fingers into his hair, pulling at it as though the pain will ease everything else around him—including the conversation he clearly doesn't want to have.

Finally, he lifts his head and looks straight ahead at the opposite wall.

"I have PTSD."

I suck back a breath. I know PTSD. When I took Mom to

respite residential, there would always be someone there suffering from severe post-traumatic stress disorder. More often than not, they were veterans. Like Connor. I should have guessed. He's been through so much, and he's had nightmares in the past. I should have expected there to be more to it, and there is.

"How bad is it?"

"In the last few years I've been able to manage it, but… it's gotten worse again in the last few weeks."

"In what way? What happens to you?" I feel as though I'm prying, but he's doing what I asked. He's telling me what I'm up against.

"I'm getting flashbacks again. Detailed, dynamic, incredibly real visions, as though I'm back there when the explosion happened. They affect me physically. I come around and I'm often shaking, sweating, confused and completely overcome by guilt."

"Because you couldn't save everyone?"

"Yes. Because I survived and they didn't."

He breathes out, heavily.

"Some of them had families, sons and daughters waiting for them to come home. I didn't even have the fucking fiancée I thought I had waiting for me to come home." Bitterness drips from his tongue as he speaks.

"Why have they gotten worse recently? Has something happened to trigger it?"

A small smile curls the corner of his lip.

"Well, this is the irony. They started happening again after you got here."

I feel the need to grip the seat because the room is slowly spinning. Instead I just grip the coffee cups even tighter.

"You're a distraction," he continues. "I worry that I can't do my job the way I need to do it when you're around. My focus is off. You might think it's easy for me to turn this away, what you and I have, but it's really fucking hard because I can't stop thinking about you."

He rubs his face while I try to compose something resembling a sentence.

"I think…" he squeezes his eyes shut, "… my attraction to you is threatening the structure I've created that keeps me afloat."

"Structure?"

"I need to have things done a certain way; I need to feel as though I'm in complete control of everything. I know it isn't normal, but it's how I operate, and it works. It's got Starling Key to where it is now. And it's the only way I know how to cope."

"You know it's not a normal or sustainable way to live, don't you? You can't go on like this. You've simply created another condition… obsessive compulsive disorder."

He sighs again and I almost think I've gone too far when he replies.

"You're right, but I'd rather contend with that than deal with the flashbacks."

"But that doesn't make any sense. You have OCD yet you're still getting the flashbacks."

He turns again to look at me. This time his eyes are laden with sadness. "Because of you. You're creating a compulsion within me that I can't control."

My heart is hammering against my chest. I can't believe what I'm hearing. I can't believe what Connor is admitting to. I stir something inside of him that he can't resist. I want to crash through it and make him surrender, but I also want to stay the hell away, for his sake. I have no idea what to say. Should I apologize? I mean, I've done nothing wrong. Instead, what comes out of my mouth surprises even me.

"You can move me to wherever you need to. I don't want to be the reason you suffer. I want your flashbacks to end and if that will only happen if I'm out of sight, then do it. I won't hold it against you."

He covers his face with his hands and groans in a low voice that I don't recognize as Connor's. Then I remember why I'm here and notice the two cups of coffee—now cold—in my hands.

"If you didn't know about Fitz's fall, why are you here?" I ask.

Connor's head snaps up.

"Shit. Carter."

"Carter?"

"Well, not him exactly. He's ok."

"Then who's not ok?"

He turns his entire body to face me. "It's Lucy, Carter's girlfriend."

"Lucy Milano, the spa therapist? I didn't realize they were dating. I mean, I know he had a thing for her, but…"

"Well, whether they were serious or not, they were expecting a baby."

"What?" I whisper, clamping a hand over my mouth because, as soon as Connor said it, I realized he was using past tense. They *were* expecting a baby, not they *are*. "What happened?"

"The egg attached inside one of her fallopian tubes instead of her womb. It grew and the tube burst. She almost died."

I close my eyes. I don't know Lucy all that well. Carter introduced me when I first started at the resort, and we've exchanged a few words since, but we aren't close. Still, I feel her pain almost physically. My mom always used to say I feel too much for my own good, and she was right. Sometimes, other peoples' pain cripples me. Which is why I want Connor to move me out of sight; I can't continue to cause him pain.

"That's awful," I whisper. Then I open my eyes. "How is she? And how is Carter?"

"She's out of surgery now but she's being closely watched by the doctors. The condition she had was life-threatening and there was a lot of internal bleeding. The doctors need to keep her in for a few days to monitor her."

"Of course. That's understandable. And Carter?"

I look up at Connor hopefully. I really like Carter and, despite his tough, tattooed exterior, I know he's a huge softie at heart. He must be in pieces.

"He's in shock," Connor replies. "I don't know. He's disappointed. He was looking forward to being a dad." Connor shakes his head, smiling. "I'm just as shocked as he apparently was when he first found out. I didn't think that was what he wanted but I guess we never truly know what we want until its staring us in the face."

The words hang in the air until I can't take the close proximity anymore. I stand up slowly.

"I'm so sorry to hear all this. Will you give them both my love?"

Connor nods. "You leaving?"

I walk to the trash can and throw both cups of coffee into it. Esme won't appreciate cold coffee, especially as I've left her with a particularly volatile Barbie for the last half hour.

"I should go and see Fitz," I say, standing over Connor one last time. Connor nods but doesn't say anything. "I'll check in with Rhonda first thing tomorrow and find out where my new role is. I'll ask for a different dorm too. A different block…"

"No," Connor says, standing up to face me. "You shouldn't have to move room again. I'll move into the main building temporarily. I'll figure something else out from there."

I might be compassionate and empathic, but in that moment I feel so angry with Connor that he would rather succumb to his destructive mental illness than do something about it and give himself a shot at happiness. I can't look him in the eye until he places two fingers beneath my chin and pulls it upwards so I can't avoid it. For a few seconds we drink each other in and it's agony. This man is everything I want, and I can't have him. A small sigh leaves my lips without me realizing and it seems to knock Connor out of a trance. He leans forward and presses his lips to mine. A spark of electricity rackets through my body, gluing us together. He reaches a hand round the back of my head and pulls me into him, kissing me deep and slow, his movements full of unspoken words.

His hand remains at the back of my head when he pulls away momentarily, and the words, 'stop me' tumble from his mouth. I let his tongue glide against my own one last time, then I do as he asks. I place my hands against his hard chest and push him backwards.

"Stop," I say, feeling the ache of withdrawal pummel my lips. I watch his eyes fall, sadly, then I turn and walk away.

# CHAPTER TWENTY-ONE

onnor

I FEEL, again, as though my heart is walking away from me, dragging a whole bunch of arteries along with it, because something is causing me pain and it's more than just an aching heart. I know what she's thinking. Why don't I just do something about it, get help, fix the PTSD. But it isn't that simple, and if she'd asked me, I would have explained that to her as best I could. I tried therapy once before at Carter's insistence. The boys had had enough of me flaking out of jobs, becoming unreliable, hiding away sometimes for days on end. They needed a boss, someone to guide them, someone to deal with the unreasonably dramatic whims of Eric Starling. And I wasn't there.

I eventually relented and went to see a civilian therapist, someone who tried to get me to talk about my parents, my upbringing, all things I figured were irrelevant to the real reason I was having flashbacks—the incident in Iraq that lost me twenty-seven men and any sense of deserving happiness. When I explained that my dad was also a Marine who died during deployment to Afghanistan, that my mum subsequently turned to alcohol and is still today in and out of rehab, and that I was raised from age twelve by my grandparents, I swear the therapist thought she'd struck gold. Actual dollar signs appeared in her eyes. I politely sat out the session, then I thanked her and left, resolving never to return. Instead, I self-medicated mainly with alcohol, before devising a way of life that ensured I was able to suppress my memories to the point I could function.

The truth is, I can't go through therapy. I just can't. Because I know it isn't just the incident in Iraq I'm going to have to deal with, it will be the pressure placed on me from as far back as I can remember, to follow in my father's footsteps. I never had a passion for the armed forces, as much as I respected them, but I never thought I had another option. I resent that. I resent not being allowed to think about what I really wanted to do with my life. My dad was strict. Everything he learned as a Marine himself, he brought home. I knew how to be a good soldier from the age of six. My mom worshipped him, and so everything he thought was right for me, she went along with. And he was just too big to fight against. That's one of the reasons I work out as much as I do. I need to feel big, bigger than my father who, even though he's now passed, he still exerts a larger-than-life influence over me. Becoming physically bigger makes me feel as though I'm the one in charge.

I'm thirty-two years old and my life is already mapped out within the parameters afforded me by the regime that keeps me sane. I know it's fucked up, but I don't know any other way.

I want Tawny Graham more than I've ever wanted

anybody. The torture of not being able to act on my desire causes me physical pain. I don't want to move her, but I can't think of another solution. I hate myself for messing her around and I hate myself for not being able to make things right. I hate myself right now, pure and simple.

I stand and throw the cold coffees in the trash, and turn my thoughts back to Carter.

# CHAPTER TWENTY-TWO

awny

I'M surprised when Connor pulls his truck into the parking space beside me, I didn't think he was driving so close behind. He gets out and helps me and Esme load Barbie into a golf buggy. I try not to pay too much attention to the way his biceps round out beneath his shirt as he lifts her, and the way his back flexes, his muscles dancing, when he places her gently in the seat. I'm constantly floored by how perfect his body is—his broad shoulders and back tapering to a solid waist and tight ass beneath his dark jeans. It makes my heart ache to know that his body is a front, that he is anything but perfect. I love and hate his imperfections in equal measure. I love that they make him who he is. I hate that they stand between us.

"Are you sure you're going to be ok?" I ask Esme.

"I'll be fine. You just get some rest. You're on shift tomorrow; I have the day off, and it's late."

"I'll come by straight after work, Barb," I call to the woman in the front seat who now looks shockingly frail—an absolute shadow of her former self. She nods and dabs at her eye with a beautiful silk handkerchief. It never fails to surprise me just how decadent and old-Hollywood she and Fitz are, and not for the first time that evening, I thank God I've met them, and beg God to leave them with me for just a little while longer.

"Is Carter staying at the hospital?" I ask Connor, as Esme manages to spin the wheels of a freaking golf buggy and chugs off down the road towards the retirement village.

"Yeah. I left him curled up on a chair next to Lucy's bed."

I run my hands down my neck and attempt to squeeze some tension out of my shoulders. I can't take on anyone else's pain tonight. I walk towards the northeast wall and Connor follows. We reach the gate and Connor unlocks it silently, letting me through. I hate that we move together as though we're two halves of the same coin. I hate that I know how his lips feel on mine. I hate that I know he wants me but he won't let it happen. I hate that I have to survive around this, continue with this job, this life, knowing I live so close to something I want but that I can never touch. I hate it all. And yet, I love it all too.

I can't bear the thought of not seeing him every day. I can't bear the thought of moving jobs so we don't see each other every morning and afternoon. But I can't bear the thought of him suffering because of me, more.

We reach the entrance to Block 2 and Connor holds the door open for me, probably for the last time. Our eyes meet as I pass and for a breath we stare at each other. I want so much in this moment to hold him tightly. I know we need each other. I also know that need won't get any closer than the other side of a bedroom wall. But if that's the closest I can get, if only for tonight, that's what I'll take.

I move past him and walk up the stairs slowly, prolonging the inevitable. I reach the top and take out my key. As I put it into the lock, I feel his hand rest on top of mine. I can feel his breath in my ear, the warmth of his chest against my back. I dare not look up. Then I feel his other hand slide around my waist, pulling me back towards him. My back and hips fit perfectly into his torso, as though we were designed for each other. He pulls the hand holding the key back out of the lock and wraps it around my front so that he's hugging me from behind, and he nestles his face into my shoulder.

"I can't fight it anymore," he breathes into my neck. My eyes flutter closed and I nod, my cheek brushing against his nose. He unwraps his arms and keeps hold of one hand, then he leads me into his room and closes the door.

We're hardly inside the room and my pulse is thundering in my ears. I watch him walk to the window and close the curtains. Part of me can't believe what's happening. I dare not move in case I'm misjudging the whole situation. But as he walks towards me, his eyes darker than I've ever seen them, his jaw clenched and his chest rigid, I know he definitely wants this, and I shake with nerves.

Despite looking as though he wants to eat me alive, his touch is alarmingly gentle. So gentle I start to question if it's real. His hand reaches up and cups my chin, pulling my mouth towards his. He moves his lips so slowly I'm scared he'll stop, so I inch my tongue forward. The need for more of him is excruciating. A hand reaches around the back of my head, tugs out the band holding my hair up in a reckless bun and fists it, holding me in place. I can feel the rest of my hair fall like a blanket down my back.

He pulls back until I withdraw my tongue, then he presses

his mouth against mine once more, taking it agonizingly slowly. I almost sigh with relief when I finally feel the tip of his tongue against mine, tasting me delicately, exploring me as though he has all the time in the world. Meanwhile, I'm acutely aware we're still standing at the door and my legs are getting weaker by the minute. I clamp my hands to his waist and grip his t-shirt. His tongue probes deeper, muffling the small quiet moans that keep escaping my throat. I pull him towards me for more stability and feel him hard between us. His fist tightens in my hair and he continues the relentless exploration of my mouth until I can barely take any more. I pull back reluctantly and look into his eyes.

"Connor… I can barely stand."

The expression on his face immediately changes, from one of complete absorption to one of guilt. His hand leaves my hair and I'm lifted suddenly. My legs instinctively wrap around his waist, and he carries me to his bed, then sets me down gently, as though I might break into a million pieces. He crawls up over me but doesn't lower his body, only his face, and his lips find mine again.

After an eternity, he reaches a hand down to part my legs then he sets his knees between them and sits back on his heels. I look up at him and almost cry at how stunning he is. His hair flops over his eyes as he looks down at me—at my collarbone, my chest, my stomach, my thighs—and his jaw clenches as he wets his lips.

"What do you want, Connor?" I whisper.

His eyes travel back to mine and they seem even darker than they were before we kissed. He doesn't answer. Instead, he begins to unbutton my dress. He starts at the top button and works his way slowly down, past my breasts and my stomach, hardly touching me, and with a focus that is completely unwavering. My dress falls aside with each button unleashed, putting my pink lace bra on full display, then I watch his Adam's apple move as he reaches the buttons below my waist. I'm so turned on I just want him to rip the damn thing off but he seems set on prolonging this as much as he can. His Adam's apple moves again and the last button pops open, revealing distinctly *un*matching blue satin panties. My breath is starting to come out in small pants and I'm painfully aware it is bordering on hyperventilation.

His eyes flick up to mine with a desperate look in them. He crosses his arms, grips the bottom of his shirt and pulls it over his head, then drops it to the floor. Now it's my turn to stare with unwavering focus. His body is perfection—of course it is; anything Connor puts his hand to has to be perfect, even himself. I marvel at the indentations defining his abs, and the way I can see the synchronicity of each muscle and the way they connect with each other as he moves.

I'm mesmerized until I feel his fingers hook over my panties. My eyes shoot back up to his and he's watching me, as though asking for permission. I have no idea how to respond. I don't even really know what he's asking, but I nod anyway. Something tells me that whatever Connor does to me tonight, it is going to feel amazing, and perfect. His eyes don't let go of mine as he gently pulls the satin down over my stomach. I push my hips up to let the fabric pass over my bottom. Then Connor lifts my thighs up in front of him so he can slide the panties all the way down my legs and over my toes. I'm usually a little ticklish but each inch of skin touched feels as though its burning. Then, he rests my ankles on his shoulders. I feel exposed and vulnerable but, in a weird way, completely safe. As he bends forward, my calves slide down his back until my knees are hooked around his neck. His eyes drop to my center and I hold my breath. I've read about this in books but it has never happened to me. Nothing like this has ever happened to me. Losing my virginity was a goal. And one which I achieved with minimal fuss. There was certainly no pleasure involved, just 'get in, get out'.

I feel his breath first and it makes me jump, but his hands come down firm onto my hips, pressing me down, holding me in place. I realize he hasn't answered my question—what is it he wants? Is his answer… *this*? I can't imagine going down on a woman is a pleasant experience for a man, just as I don't expect sucking a man's cock to be a pleasant experience for a woman. But it doesn't take long before I am seriously questioning my theory. Connor kisses me between the legs, and I have to force myself to relax. Then I feel his tongue. It is scorching hot against my folds. He licks me, applying pressure as he drags the length of his tongue across my clit. My back arches and a untethered cry comes from deep inside my chest. Until that point, I didn't know what to do with my hands but now they act of their own free will, pushing my fingers through his hair and gripping it for all they're worth. I don't know what that was, but I need more of it. Now.

He does it again, longer and firmer, and again, then places his mouth over me and sucks. Another cry leaves my throat and I grip his hair harder. I don't know what is happening to me but I am burning hot, exactly where his mouth is, and it feels as though my entire body is focused on the sensations being created by Connor's lips and tongue. He then combines the two movements, licking me long and firm, then sucking on my clit until I am sweating and writhing about beneath him.

"Connor…" I whimper. I don't know what I need and I don't even know if he knows, but there must be some sort of end to this exquisite pain. He continues sucking as he presses a finger against my opening. My breath hitches. The last time something went up there that wasn't a tampon, it hurt bad.

But I am throbbing and my body is telling me I need more, whatever that is. I trust Connor. I part my legs without thinking and his finger slides inside. I don't know what it does in there but suddenly, every hair on my body stands up and I am in dire need of some sort of release. He slides his finger in and out, circling it softly, and increases the pressure of his mouth on my clit. I can feel his tongue pressing down, massaging the small bump. When I feel like I'm about to die, he releases a low moan that penetrates through my clit into my core and something inside me explodes. Everything goes dark. It's as though I'm looking down on myself, not recognizing what I see. My body is rising and arching like a wild animal and I'm dragging my hands through Connor's hair, pulling his mouth down harder onto me. I swear, ten seconds pass and I'm still spasming uncontrollably.

Connor slows his licking, which I'm thankful for, as sensitive doesn't even begin to explain how I'm feeling down there. I'm exhausted, and elated, and sedated. I feel Connor hover above me again and when I open my eyes, he's looking down at me with something resembling concern. I want to ask him what it is, but I can't speak.

"You're really tight down there, T. Are you a..." he pauses and I know what he's asking.

I shake my head and finally open my mouth. "I did it once, about six years ago."

He leans all his weight on one arm and he uses the other to wipe sweat from his brow and remnants of me from his lips.

"So, yeah, you're practically a virgin."

"Does it matter?"

Connor sits back on his heels and I immediately notice the giant bulge in his combat shorts. I can feel the ball of heat in my groin again and realize what it is. I want him inside me, the way his finger was. I've had a taste now; I've had the appetizer. I want to go straight to the main course.

"Look, T," he says, softly. "I don't know what this is—you and me. All I know is I want you in every way. I have since I first saw you climb out of that car and I don't have the strength to fight it anymore. But I can't promise you any more than this right now; I just can't."

I swallow, but I knew this already, and I don't care. I will take anything I can get.

"Those first sexual experiences... they should be with someone special. I'm not saying this can't be special—the sex, I mean—but I want you to be sure about this, before you give such a pure part of yourself to me."

"I want this," I say, breathless. "I don't expect anything else, but I want this Connor."

Right now, I don't care that he can't promise me anything. I don't care that we could do this and then he might not want anything to do with me again. I don't care that I'm giving a part of myself to him, a part I know I should reserve for someone who might one day be able to give me what I want. All I know is, I need to feel what I just felt again. I need to feel him inside me, to confirm what I think I know: that we fit perfectly together in every way. I need to have this just once, with him.

His eyes hold mine as his fingers reach down to his fly. He unbuttons it, more quickly this time and I can see the strain on his shorts vanishing with each pop. As his fly opens and his cock protrudes out behind his boxers, I swallow a gasp. What am I thinking? The guy who took my virginity had nothing on Connor. If it was painful that first time, this time is certain to be agony, but I need it. If anyone is going to hurt me doing something so natural, I want it to be Connor.

He reaches inside his boxers and pulls out his cock,

stroking his hand up and down its length. I gulp but my mouth has dried up.

"Can I?" I croak. I've never touched one before. The only time I came into contact with a cock, I just let the guy do all the work, I didn't get any closer or more familiar with it than I had to. It was a tool; a means to an end. But now, I need to know it, to feel it. It's a part of Connor. It is Connor.

He nods and his Adam's apple moves again. His eyes follow my hand as I reach out and touch my fingers to the crown. It jerks away and Connor chuckles softly, making my insides turn to mush.

I reach out again and grip it this time. Connor sucks in a breath. I'm surprised at how smooth it is and how solid. I wonder how guys walk around all day with these things between their legs. I get that they're not always this hard and heavy, but still. I move my hand up and down instinctively but I'm not really sure what I'm doing.

"Like this," Connor says, and folds his hand over my own. He guides my hand and curls my fingers, asserting more pressure around the shaft. He clears his throat and lets go, watching me move. I am absorbed and addicted to the look on his face. He drops his head back.

"Fuck, T," he breathes out.

"I can't believe how big you are," I marvel aloud, and I swear it grows another half inch beneath my palm. I glance down at his balls and they are red and swollen. Is that what they all look like? He raises his head again and he's almost gasping for breath. He puts a hand between my thighs and circles my entrance. Then he slips a finger inside, draws it back out and rims me again. It feels amazing.

"What are you doing?" I ask.

His eyes are like bullets when he answers.

"Preparing you."

In a beat, he's off the bed and shoving his combats and boxers down his legs, then in seconds, he's back between my thighs. He reaches across to a bedside table and pulls out a condom. He puts the foil between his teeth and rips it. It is one of the horniest things I've ever seen. I watch as he places the tip over his crown and rolls it down over his endless length.

"If you want to stop at any time, just tell me, ok?"

I nod and pull him closer, but he is tentative. He dips his hips, bringing his cock level with me, and holds himself up on one arm as he guides himself to my opening.

"Spread your legs a little wider."

I do as he says. In the corner of my eye, I can see the arm he's using to prop himself up, shaking. I push my fingers through his hair and pull his face upwards so I can look into it.

"I want this, Connor," I repeat.

He holds my gaze, his eyes dark and intense as he pushes into me an inch. I gasp and his brow furrows. Another inch.

"Relax, T. You're too tight."

I breathe out and consciously will my insides to stop clenching.

"That's it," he encourages, breathily.

Another inch. Surely that's as far as it's going to go. I take deep breaths and watch his eyes struggle to stay open. Another inch. That must be it. I don't think I can take anymore.

"Are you in?" I ask, cringing at my naivety.

He almost laughs. "Halfway."

"I don't think I can do it," I gasp.

Alarm infuses his face. "You can, T. Trust me."

"You need to do it fast."

"You sure? That might hurt."

"Like a Band-Aid," I say. "I think it's the only way."

"Ok," he replies, swallowing. "Ok."

"I…" I begin to speak again but all sound and air is knocked out of me as he thrusts in hard. His eyes close as though he doesn't want to see the pain he's caused, and a sound I've never heard before comes out of his gritted teeth. A searing pain courses through me and I swallow back a scream. Holy shit. Slowly, he opens his eyes and immediately searches my face for some reassurance that I'm ok.

"Fuck," I pant. "Ok. Ok, I'm ok."

"You're so freaking tight, I can hardly move," he whispers.

"I'm sorry." I feel like a failure.

"No, no, it's good," he replies quickly. "I just won't last very long."

"That's fine," I say. This is not what I was expecting and I'm pretty sure it was not what my body was expecting either. He moves slowly and the pain starts up again.

"Just tell me if you want me to stop."

I nod, keeping my lips tightly closed.

"You're so tense, baby. Please try to relax."

He bends down and touches his lips to mine, then pushes back in, slowly. A moan enters my mouth from his and I open up and let his tongue caress mine. It takes my mind off the pain. His movements are slow and gentle, and combined with the decadent exploration of my mouth again, my walls start to loosen and the pain lessens. I'm able to wrap my legs around his torso and even move in time with his hips.

"Jesus, this feels amazing," he whispers into my mouth, and I begin to agree. The pain has almost disappeared now and has been replaced by the heat I felt before when he was licking me. I rock into him, wordlessly explaining that I'm more than ok. He goes deeper and longer, sliding his cock in and out in long decadent strokes. He pulls his mouth away from mine and buries his face into my neck. I curl a hand around his neck and whisper into his ear.

"This is all I wanted Connor. It feels perfect."

He groans into me and quickens his thrusts. He then pushes up onto one arm again, anchoring it into the comforter and reaches a hand down between us. He finds my clit and massages my wetness into it. I am suddenly burning all over again.

"Connor," I gasp.

"Is this good?" His voice is unrecognizable. I nod, my breath coming out in reckless pants.

"Good."

He continues to thrust his hips, filling me and caressing some mysterious spot inside that is humming with need. His fingers press down harder and I can suddenly feel the rush again. It's like a ball of fire has ignited inside me and is coursing through my core, through my veins. My back arches again and my head snaps to one side, his name coming out of my mouth in a loud cry. He stills while I spasm around him, a string of curse words leaving his lips. The sensations drag me under and I'm barely aware of where I am, until I feel something else inside me. A pulse. Before I know it, Connor is driving back into me, faster this time. I open my eyes and his are closed in deep concentration. He's holding something back. With impeccable control, he thrusts in and out with short, sharp strokes, then his own body goes rigid and I feel fuller than ever as he empties himself into the condom.

He continues to move slowly, kissing me softly, as though he doesn't want it to end. I will happily do this for as long as he needs, but he eventually rolls off me and removes the condom, tying it into a knot.

"I'll be right back," he says, then I watch as he walks, naked and beautiful, into his bathroom.

I stretch out across his bed in a post-coital state of bliss and close my eyes. I've never been happier. The kisses before tonight gave a hint as to what sex would be like with Connor, but that was mind-blowing. My skin is still buzzing from the contact, however controlled and careful it was. I allow myself to relive it, then I remember what Connor had told me at the hospital—that I was the cause of his flashbacks. I look at the clock on his wall. He's been in the bathroom for ten minutes. I sit up, quickly.

"Connor? Are you ok?"

The door to the bathroom opens and Connor walks out.

"Yeah, I'm fine," he says. But his entire demeanor has changed. He doesn't look at me as he pulls on a pair of sweat-pants and climbs back on to the bed.

"Should I go?" I ask, nervously.

"Fuck, no," he says, pulling me into his chest so I can't see his face. "You're staying right here."

He doesn't say anything else but I can feel his heart beating rapidly against my ear. I know, in this moment, I owe it to him to put an end to this somehow. He can't fight it anymore, so I will have to. And that's the last thought I have as I drift into a deep sleep in Connor Johnson's arms.

# CHAPTER TWENTY-THREE

onnor

A BUZZING SOUND wakes me and I drag my eyelids open. The first thing I see is her hair. It's spread across my pillow and I'm half laid in it. It smells of salt air and coconut. My body is curved around her back and bottom, my left leg tucked possessively over both of hers, my left arm curled beneath hers, my fingers soft against her throat. I don't want to move but I have to, I should have been in the office two hours ago.

Memories of last night start flooding back. The drive home from the hospital, following Tawny up the stairs for what I thought was going to be the last time. I couldn't do it. Something snapped inside me. My physical need for her became far greater than the rational logic of my brain. For once, my training couldn't win. And it wasn't just my cock that overrode it; it was my heart. Ever since our fingers inter-laced across the table at Trey's Cafe, and I wrapped a towel around her shoulders that same night... ever since that fucking dynamite kiss on the beach where I came perilously close to succumbing entirely and taking things all the way... I've struggled to control this animal urge to wrap my body around hers, protect her with everything I have, and fuck her silly. And now I've given in to it, I'm scared. I'm scared of how this will end, of what it might do to her.

I fucked her as carefully as I possibly could, despite the fact holding back was killing me. I couldn't bring myself to fuck her the way I really wanted to. I was going to break her enough mentally; I didn't want to do anything that might hurt her physically. Control, control, control. Then I remember what happened when I went into the bathroom. Pretty much a repeat of the last time I orgasmed. Fortunately, I was half-expecting it, so I closed the bathroom door behind me and held onto the wall while the visions overtook me.

When I finally came round, I splashed my face with cold water and stared at my reflection in the mirror. I was no longer hurting only myself—I was hurting both of us and I hated myself for it. But she was there in my room and I was going to make the most of it while I had her, so I pushed the whole thing to the back of my mind and slid back into bed.

I carefully extract my arm and lean backwards to grab my phone. Swiping it unlocked I see it's a message from Carter. *Shit, Carter.* Now that starts coming back to me in horrid, vivid detail. Lucy. A baby. Carter. Hospital. The message is short. *Do you have a sec? I'm outside.*

I quickly type back. *Just give me one minute.*

I draw back my leg and Tawny moans sleepily. I nuzzle my face into her neck one more time, pull back her hair and let my lips linger against the soft skin between her neck and shoulder.

"I'll be right back," I whisper.

I open the door and Carter is standing there with his back

against the opposite wall. He looks a shadow of the guy I saw at the hospital.

"You ok, man?"

His eyes are red and I can tell he hasn't slept.

"She wants to leave, Connor. She wants to go home to her family."

I nod slowly. "Whatever she needs. Is she ok?"

He looks off to the side and shrugs. "She's as well as can be expected. They had to remove the fallopian tube, so one of her ovaries is effectively redundant now. The nurses said it shouldn't affect her fertility but it's really shaken her up. We had a talk…"

His voice breaks and he tugs at the end of his nose.

"What we have, me and her… it's not special enough."

I hold my breath and listen. He doesn't need answers or solutions. He needs to talk.

"That's what she said, not me. But I get it. We were playing around, you know?"

He looks back at me and I nod, not in agreement but to encourage him to continue.

"We were just having a laugh and a fuck. It had only been a few weeks, nothing serious." He wipes the back of his hand across his face and looks away again. "I guess she's right. I'm not the kind of guy a girl wants long term."

"That's not true."

He shrugs. "Not for her anyway. I'm not her future. She was brutally honest, but she had to be. She wants more. She wants a guy who can look after her, buy her a nice house, provide for her and their babies. I can't do that, can I? I have no fucking money, no house, no life outside this place."

"You have no money because you send it all home to your mom," I remind him. "Because she needs it. She needs to pay for rent, for meds. Your dad left you both with debts. You wouldn't be able to live with yourself if you didn't give her that money."

"But what does it leave me with, huh? Nothing. I have nothing to offer anyone. I never thought it would be an issue until now. But I came close to something with Lucy, you know? I saw further ahead than the next fuck. I didn't see marriage and kids, don't get me wrong, but when she got the test result, I started to think about things seriously for the first time in my life."

He sighs heavily and kicks at the ground. I can see his hands clenching and releasing inside his pockets.

"I feel like I was on the cusp of something pretty exciting. Fucking scary, but exciting. And now, not only has that been ripped away, but I feel like I've been beaten several feet into the ground. I feel fucking worthless, man."

He doesn't look up at me and I know this is the hardest thing he's probably ever had to say. I step forward and put my arms round him. This is something we don't do. Hug. Carter is not a hugger and I am definitely not a hugger, but I don't know what else to do. I know he needs something. To my surprise, he lets me hold him and I can feel dampness against my shirt. I thump his back.

"It's gonna be ok, man," I say, quietly. "It's going to be hard, the next few weeks, but it'll get better, I promise."

He nods against my shoulder, then pulls back and wipes an arm across his face.

"I feel like such a dick," he sighs. "Lucy is in the hospital, terrified about her fertility, and I'm here thinking about myself."

"You're not a dick. You just broke up. You care about her, but you've just been told you can't have her anymore. Don't be fucking hard on yourself."

He nods.

"Take a few days off, Carter."

He shakes his head. "I need to keep busy. Maybe just today, if that's ok?"

"Whatever you need, seriously."

He jerks his head towards the door to my room.

"Were you alone in there?" The tone of his voice is laden with suggestion. I can't lie to him.

"No."

"Good." He straightens and looks me head on. "Don't fuck it up Connor. She's a good girl, and you're a lucky guy. Don't do what I just did and realize exactly what you need when it's too damn late."

I don't say anything and he shakes his head again.

"Sorry. I don't mean to preach. It's none of my business."

"No, it's fine. You're hurting. But I can't promise anything. I'm as fucked up as you are; I don't know how this is going to end."

"Ok. But just remember this. It doesn't have to end, Connor, ok? It doesn't have to end."

---

EVERYONE SEEMS to be walking around like zombies. Even people who weren't close to Lucy have heard the news and are feeling it like they were her blood. That's what's so special about the Key. Regardless of how well or not we know each other, when push comes to shove, each of us is here for everyone else. We all found our way here, somehow. We all chose this because we needed something. And whatever that something is, Starling Key has it.

I don't see Tawny all day. She was out of my bed and dressed by the time I finished up with Carter. She stood on her tiptoes and kissed me on the cheek.

"I have to get to work," she said, apologetically. I held her face in my hands, Carter's words ringing in my ears, and kissed her long and slow on the mouth. I'd never felt so confused by my own thoughts. I was used to directing them a certain way, having total control over where they went, but something's changed. Tawny is in my head, and no matter how much I try to push her out, if only so I can focus on doing my damn job, she won't budge.

"I won't be around tonight," I told her, determined to put some distance between us, "but..." Despite every effort I made to not let the next words fall out of my mouth, they did. "I'll be wanting more of you soon."

Her face flushed, instantly, and she walked out of the room, mechanically, as though she was having to concentrate on putting one foot in front of the other.

---

MY BACK IS KILLING me from sleeping in the office. I somehow managed to stay up working until eleven, having had very little sleep the night before. I walk with Carter to the main entrance. Lucy's sisters have cleared her place and now she's waiting in the car to say goodbye to us all. Everyone is quiet, as though it's some sort of funeral, which I suppose it is in a way. A baby has been lost. I stay at Carter's side the whole way, even though the sight of Tawny in a tiny pair of white shorts and a bikini top hugging Lucy makes me want to bend her over right here, in front of everyone, and fuck my way through the sorrow. My senses are overwhelmed with all the emotions racing around my body. Grief and sadness for Carter and Lucy, mixed with burning lust for Tawny, and elation that we finally got over the line.

As we approach, Tawny steps back. Her eyes flicker over

me, then dart away, her cheeks flushing pink. It is beyond adorable. I discreetly take her hand as Carter steps towards Lucy. Everyone seems to get the same memo and the crowd around the car disperses, giving Lucy and Carter a small bit of privacy. I don't hear what is said, but I see Lucy wiping her eyes and holding Carter tightly. He rubs her back, reassuring her it's all ok. I feel Tawny sniff beside me and I squeeze her hand. Thoughts of the way she tastes beneath my tongue, the way she feels around my fingers, around my cock, threaten to cloud my vision, and I put all my focus onto Lucy and Carter.

I'm relieved when another presence appears beside me.

"Connor, do you have a sec?"

I turn and see Isaac.

"Everything ok?"

"You left the logbook on your desk," he says, quietly.

"Shit, really?" The logbook is a record of every side hustle deal we've been involved in and the amount of money we've made. If Starling happened to go looking for something in my office—which he has every right to do—and found the logbook, we would be screwed beyond belief. "Fuck, I need to get back to the office. Make sure nothing else is lying around."

"What about Carter?"

"Can you stay here? He's going to want to be alone, but… just in case."

"Sure Connor."

I bend down and kiss the top of Tawny's head. Her eyes are glazed when she looks up at me and I fight the urge to close my mouth on hers in an attempt to make it all ok again.

I leave them both and head back to the office, kicking myself. I can't believe I left the logbook out for anyone to see. It is cardinal sin number one. Keeping that thing hidden and secret is the most important fucking part of my job.

---

IT'S LATE AGAIN by the time I get back to the dorms. Everywhere is quiet, as though the entire staff is mourning Lucy's departure and Carter's loss. The sound is one of numbness. But I am feeling anything but numb. I am feeling need. Pure, untainted, unbridled need. And not just for anyone—for Tawny. I hate admitting it, especially knowing what the aftermath will bring, but right now, while all the feelings around me are so raw, I can't deny myself the one thing that is going to give me temporary relief. I don't even go back to my room first; I know exactly where I'm going.

She opens the door and steps aside. I press my lips against hers before she can say anything. I hold her as I walk her backwards to the bed, then I push her gently back onto it. She's still wearing those delicious tiny shorts that I cannot wait to get off her ass. But first things first—that bikini. I totally neglected her tits the other night. I owe them big time. She watches me curiously as I simply push the fabric upwards, revealing the soft mounds in all their pale perfection.

I waste no time in tasting them, dragging my tongue around the circumference and sucking the taut pink nipple into my mouth. I suck on it, gently, but relentlessly, my fingers toying with the other one, until she's wriggling beneath me.

"You're a genius with your mouth Connor," she says, breathily. I switch sides and suck on her other nipple, kneading the breast softly. "I might just come like this."

I don't respond; I just continue to lick and suck at the beautiful pink nubs.

"Can I taste you?" She asks. I look up and see her eyes wide and eager. I shove my pants down my legs and kick them onto the floor, then I crawl up, my knees either side of her, until my cock is level with her face. She licks her lips hungrily and I almost explode.

She runs her hands around the back of my ass and pulls my hips towards her, dipping the head of my cock into her mouth. The room spins and I have to put everything I've got into not coming straight down her throat. I need this to last. She swirls her tongue around the head and I grit my teeth. I can't stop myself from flexing my hips and sending my length deeper into her mouth. She responds with a moan and I ache with the need to control myself. She wets her lips and clasps around my girth, then she pulls me into her, gagging as I touch the back of her throat. I feel blind with the effort of holding back, so I let myself go. She pulls and pushes my hips, letting me fuck her mouth, and I relish the feeling of her hot wet lips sucking me in, letting me withdraw, then flicking her tongue around the crown. I am almost delirious when I pull out of her.

Without asking, I pop open the buttons on her shorts and pull them down her legs. Then, in one quick, easy movement, I flip her onto her stomach and pull her up onto her knees. Her breath quickens and I can already see the dampness between her legs. Sucking me off turned her on. Or it could have been the attention I gave her breasts. Either way, I am painfully hard and need to sink myself into her, bury my bad self in her goodness. I am half off the bed when I bring my mouth to her ass. I feed my tongue through her legs to her clit and drag it backwards, all the way.

She gasps, her arms collapse and her forehead hits the

comforter. I guess she likes that. I do it again and again and feel more wetness on my tongue. She was so freaking tight last night, I need to make sure she's ready. I keep going until she's panting my name. I crawl up behind her, roll on the condom I had tucked into the pockets of my shorts, and put the head of my cock to her entrance, asking for permission.

"Fuck me, Connor. Do whatever it is you need to do."

I hesitate but she doesn't. Without warning, she presses backwards, half filling herself with me. My name tumbles from her lips when she hesitates, and I bury myself the rest of the way. I reach the hilt then hold still, giving her time to relax around me. Staying deep inside, I press her stomach down to the mattress and spread her legs wider, then I fold myself on top of her, being careful not to crush her with my weight. I want a slow, lazy fuck. I want to feel it all.

I run my hands along her arms until our fingers meet and I push mine through hers, entwining them. Her face is turned to one side and I suck her earlobe between my lips, my breath making her shiver. I love this about her. Every single little thing I do elicits such a strong, beautiful reaction. I breathe in the scent of coconut again and let myself sink into her. I use my knees and toes to control the flex of my hips, pulling almost all the way out, then pushing myself back in smoothly. She lets out small moans of surrender, one after the other and she's becoming wetter with every thrust; I know she's close.

I stop moving in an attempt to slow us both down, but neither of us can take it. Her hips push backwards, greedily, and my hips flex forwards, giving her what she needs. Another moan.

"I will never get enough of this," she whispers. "God help me."

I feel exactly the same but I won't admit it. I kiss the side of her neck, eliciting louder moans from her lips. I will never get enough of that sound. I drag the edge of my teeth along the back of her shoulders and her skin breaks out in little goose bumps. I bring back a hand and push it beneath her, feeling for her hot little nub.

"Fuck, Connor..." she buries her face into the comforter. She's so impossibly wet it's hard for me to focus my fingers on the hard clit but I persist, massaging over it, back and forth. I continue to slide myself in and out of her. It's becoming easier the softer and wetter she gets but she's still tight enough that it's testing every ounce of control I have.

"Connor!" She cries out and presses her hips down on my fingers and I feel her orgasm in every possible place. She throbs against my palm, clamps around my cock, sucking me deeper and deeper, and spasms against my chest. My orgasm shoots out of me abruptly and loudly. Her name leaves my mouth as I drive into her as deep as I can possibly go. We are glued together as we both come hard. Her spasms draw out my own, and mine reignite hers.

After the longest climax I've ever experienced, I roll onto my side to avoid hurting her and lay with an arm across her back. She turns to face me and I kiss the tip of her nose. She studies me without saying a word, then after several minutes have passed, she speaks.

"I meant what I said," she whispers. "How am I ever going to get enough of this?"

I don't answer because I'm scared of what will come out of my mouth.

"I didn't think it could get any better than last night, but that... God Connor, that just took my breath away. I've never taken drugs, but I imagine that's the sort of high that keeps an addict coming back for more."

I close my eyes and roll onto my back.

"Connor? You haven't said a word since you walked in.

Was it the same for you? Or am I just so inexperienced I don't know that all sex is that good?"

I take a deep breath. "No, Tawny. Not all sex is that good. In fact, sex is very rarely that good."

I can sense her smiling. Part of me wants to get up and leave in case another wave of memory threatens to drown me, but a greater part of me doesn't want to leave. It's a part that weighs me down to the bed, makes it almost impossible to move. She rolls onto her side and perches on one elbow.

"You might be a man of not so many words this evening, but they're all the right ones," she grins and bends forward to kiss me. I'm tempted to stop her so that I can make sure it's right. But I'm paralyzed, so I let her. Only after I've made her come again with my fingers, do I get up and head to the bath-room, and let the swelling tide drag me under.

# CHAPTER TWENTY-FOUR

onnor

"CONNOR, I think we might have a problem."

Words I am never fond of hearing. We're standing in the main casino space which is now fully decorated, and the tables and slots are starting to be erected, making everything seem real.

"What is it, Isaac?"

"I just checked inside one of the packages we got last week—the roulette table."

"Yeah?"

"It's really damaged. I don't think we can use it."

"What?" I run a hand through my hair, impatiently. "Why wasn't it checked on arrival?" We'd started to split the delivery checks between us because with the casino opening now only a week away, they are coming in thick and fast. Isaac coughs; he looks uncomfortable.

"It was one of yours," he says. "You'd assigned yourself

to check that batch of deliveries. I thought you had. Did you notice any breakages? Maybe the damage has happened in the last few days while we stored it."

I think back to the day the delivery came in. It was early in the morning, straight from one of the ports upstate. I hadn't had any sleep; I'd been up all night fucking Tawny. It's been two weeks since I gave into my desire and we haven't slowed down since. If anything, my need for her has only grown; nothing seems to sate it. While we've managed to keep a semblance of dignity during working hours, as soon as we're out of sight of guests and staff, my hands and lips are all over her.

I can hardly even remember what the inside of my room looks like as I've slept in Tawny's every night since Lucy left. The only thing I've had any control over is the way we fuck. I'm so scared of breaking her, of hurting her, I keep my touch light and my words scarce. I know she wants more; she wants it rougher, but I simply can't give her that. I'm hurting her enough by letting things get this far, I will not put her at any further risk by forcing the true nature of my desire onto her. I want to throw her around the room, put my hand around her throat while I fuck her hard into the bed, torment her until she's begging me to give her release. I want to pound her hard and fast, I want to make her open her throat and take all of me in her mouth. But all these things could not only hurt her, they could increase the severity of my flashbacks.

The flashbacks. They come and go sporadically. Sometimes, they're passing washes of white that cause me to stop and have to hold onto something. Sometimes, they're all-consuming and debilitating. And as for what causes them, there seems to be no rhyme or reason. They don't always happen right after I climax—which is what I'd been most afraid of—

but they're happening with increasing regularity. The only definite link I've made is that the more I lose control with Tawny, the more severe the flashback seems to be. If I'm measured in what I do with her, gentle with my touch, slow with my movements, if I do suffer a flashback afterwards or later, it tends not to be as severe. If I find myself getting carried away, thrusting a little harder, biting down with my teeth or pinning her so she can't move until I've come, the flashbacks are worse.

"I don't remember checking it, Isaac," I admit.

"Ok. We need to order a new one, and fast."

"That one took twelve weeks to get here, by boat," I reply, feeling the weight of guilt land heavily and square on my shoulders.

"Ok, so we just get one from the States and we pay the extra for it."

"Do you have any idea what these things cost?" I scrape my hand through my hair again.

"Yes, Connor, I file the expenses, don't I? And I'm not stupid."

"Ok, ok, I'm sorry. I just... I can't believe I let that slip. If I'd checked the delivery last week, the supplier could have flown one in at his cost but I think it's too late for that now. Fuck."

"Don't worry, Connor. You get onto the supplier, give him your particular personal brand of shit. I'll look into roulette tables we can get our hands on quickly and I'll bring you some costs."

"Ok, thanks Isaac."

I turn to head back to the offices when Isaac puts a hand on my arm.

"Is everything ok, Connor? You never normally miss anything, but you left out the logbook the other week, and now this. I know the Lucy thing has shaken everyone. Is that it?"

"I'm fine," I insist. "I feel bad for Lucy and Carter, I really do. But I can't blame anyone or anything else for this. I guess there's a lot going on."

"So, delegate it."

"I'm fine Isaac, honestly. I'm right back on top of things."

I could punch myself. I've dropped the ball twice now in two weeks—that never happens. It has nothing to do with what happened to Lucy, although I was telling the truth—I do feel incredibly bad for them both. But my failure to lock away the logbook and check through the deliveries I said I would, is down to one thing and one thing only. Tawny. Or rather, my inability to think of anything else.

"Ok, well, if you're sure."

"I am. But thanks for saying something Isaac."

"No problem. Where you heading to?"

"I'm going to give that supplier hell, then pummel myself in the gym."

"Good idea. Might see you in there."

I head straight to the office and close the door, then pick up my phone and do exactly what I said I would. I give that supplier a quick trip to hell and back.

When I'm done, I sit back in my chair and look out the window. We unfortunately don't get a sea view from our offices, but I can see most of the manicured gardens in which our standard—but still incredibly luxurious—villas are peppered. And even indoors, I can still smell the sea breeze and sun-warmed grasses. There's a base note of coconut from where I fucked Tawny this morning and didn't shower after-wards. I wanted to feel her on me all day.

My breath catches in my throat. What's happened to me? I'm doing exactly what I promised myself I wouldn't do. I'm getting in deep with someone, and it's affecting my game. I'm not on the ball anymore; there are cracks in my work. If Isaac hadn't spotted the damaged roulette table, we would be way more fucked than we already are. No one opens a world class casino with no fucking roulette table. I drag my fingers through my hair. And the logbook. Christ. That contains everything the cops would need to stick us all behind bars.

I hear the sound of a helicopter overhead, reminding me of the arrival of our latest VIP guest, a male soap star and his social influencer fiancée. Jaxon's on daytime detail, Hud is on nights. I make a mental note to check they have everything they need. The whirring gets louder as the helicopter approaches the landing pad up on the roof. Suddenly, I feel my blood run cold, and panic flood into my bones. It's happening again.

I'm lying on the ground, my ears numb from the sound of the explosion, the air white with dust. As the sky clears, the sun is blinding. I roll onto my side. Everything hurts. Pulling my knees up, I crawl along the hard, dry ground. I don't know where I'm going. I think I'm crawling away from the noise but I can't hear anything anymore. Textures begin to form in front of my eyes. Mounds. Khaki-colored shapes. Black leather. Steel bars and struts. Panels. Heavy cloths. Metal shards. Blood. I look down and my hands are ripped to shreds, either from the explosion or from attempting to claw my way across the debris-filled ground—I don't know. I hear the sound of someone's voice, far off in the distance, someone groaning loudly. I rotate my neck trying to look all the way around me, but it hurts so bad. Behind my left shoulder I see a blood-covered face. It's mouth opens and there's the sound again. It's coming from right behind me but it sounds like it's miles away.

I turn around, shaking, and wipe some of the blood off his

face with my hand. It's fruitless. I merely wipe my own blood onto him.

"Sullivan," I croak.

"Help…" His voice is broken. "Get… help."

I scan my eyes down his body then they stop at his thighs. Because there's nothing else there. I spin away so he can't see me throw up.

Out of nowhere comes another deafening crash.

I open my eyes and I'm on my hands and knees back in my office on Starling Key, staring at a pool of vomit. I am soaking from head to toe in cold sweat, shaking like a leaf, and panting like a rabid dog.

The whirring of the helicopter has stopped and I can hear voices several stories above which tells me our guests have disembarked safely. I envy them. Not because they have fame, money, each other, and a luxury two-week-long vacation ahead of them. But because they were able to get off that helicopter. I was one of only three survivors that day. I will never be able to get off.

I slowly crawl to my feet even though everything seems to ache. My body takes on the physical sensations as much as my mind takes on the mental recollection. I may as well still have six broken ribs, severe muscle tears, and second degree burns. I grip my desk and pull myself up, then I set about cleaning up the mess I made on the floor.

# CHAPTER TWENTY-FIVE

awny

"This is delicious," I mumble, as I attack another slice of Fitz's apple walnut pie.

"It really is," Esme agrees. "Even though you shouldn't be baking in your state right now."

Barbie waves her hand, sending drops of her Pink Lady cocktail flying onto Connor's leg. "No one can stop Fitz from cooking when he sets his mind to it."

She places her other hand on Fitz's knee and he looks up at her with so much love in his eyes I'm rendered momentarily speechless. I'm thankful my mouth is full of pie and I have an excuse not to speak. Connor tightens his arm around me as I lean back into his torso. Since Barbie's birthday booze cruise ended abruptly with Fitz's fall, we decided a more risk averse celebration for Barbie's belated 'actual' birthday—which coincided with Fitz returning from hospital —would be a simple, small gathering on the beach outside

Reef Street. Connor and I are sitting on a blanket, me between his legs, with Esme and Shell sitting opposite us, and Barbie and Fitz are perched higher up on their 'thrones,' as Barbie calls them.

"You're looking so much better, Fitz," Esme says.

"You are," Connor adds. "You had us all quite worried there."

Fitz grins. "I was always going to be fine, it was just a little break. You can't keep me away from this place for long."

"Especially with the casino opening next week," Barbie says. "I'm so excited, and I need a date, don't I, Fitz?"

"You don't need anyone, Barbie. You're just fine on your own."

"Ok then. I don't *need* a date, but I'd *like* one." She smiles at him and I swear I can hear his heart thumping from six feet away. "I think it's going to be a very special night. In fact..." Barbie turns to look at Shell. "I don't suppose you would do my makeup for me, Shell? It would be such a treat to not have to do it myself for a change."

"Of course, Barbie," Shell replies. "As long as I'm not on shift." She looks over at Connor.

"I'm sure we can arrange it so you're not," he smiles, his voice carrying past my ear, making my pulse rocket.

"I still don't know how you came to be a makeup artist," I remind her. "You never told me your story."

"Oh, it's a goodie," Barbie says, taking a long sip of her cocktail.

Shell sighs and Esme claps her hands together. "Come on, Shell, I never tire of hearing this."

I finish the last mouthful of pie and try to give Shell my full attention, even though the feel of Connor's fingers as he gently strokes my thigh, is immensely distracting.

"Ok, so I was in high school, flunking everything—I'm not what you would call an academic," she begins. "I used to spend my weekends sitting on the streets around our neighborhood, sketching pictures onto the sidewalk with chalk and crayons. People used to pay me because they thought the pictures were pretty good, so I made a bit of pocket money. One weekend I decided to go up to Sunset and try my luck doing some drawings there... After a while I started to get a little attention, and people were travelling across Hollywood to look at my drawings. I used to do portraits of actors and actresses—I loved all the detail of their faces and would spend hours at home trying to perfect the lines and the contours. There was this one woman who came every week. She wouldn't say anything; she would simply stand and watch me draw, sometimes for about an hour. Unfortunately, things at home were pretty bad."

Esme puts a hand to Shell's back, as if she knows this part of the story is hard for Shell to recall.

"My dad was an alcoholic and used to beat my mom. It was around this time he beat her so bad she ended up in hospital. Until that point, he'd never laid a hand on me, but when Mom wasn't there, he had no one else to vent his drunken anger on. So he beat me."

"Oh my, Shell..," I say, lost for any other words.

"I left. I packed my bags right there and then and left. I had nowhere to go. If I'd stayed with friends, Dad would've tracked me down. He would have been sorry, I know. He would have apologized and said it would never happen again, just like he did with my mom, but it would still happen. So I went by the hospital, say goodbye to my mom and went straight up to Sunset. I used the money I made with my drawings to pay for hostels, but I didn't always make enough, you know? So I often slept on the street."

I stiffen and Connor's fingers stop stroking my leg as he curls his hand around me instead.

"I must have started to look like a homeless person because one morning, this woman came back to see my drawings and offered me a job. She was a makeup artist working for the movies. She was getting offered more work than she could physically do and wanted an apprentice. She was real good to me. Put me up in a one bedroom place, made sure I had a salary to pay for it, and she trained me up."

"Who was she?" I asked.

"Well, this was the thing. I never knew at the time. I only knew her name—Ida Pinks. She never told me anything about herself. All we ever talked about was makeup and art and pigments and brushes. She taught me everything I know about makeup artistry and I will be forever grateful to her."

"Ida was a legend," Barbie muses. "She did my makeup once. I hardly felt a thing—she had such a light hand. And when she'd finished, I looked like I wasn't wearing any makeup—I was simply a much more beautiful version of myself."

"Ida always said we don't create beauty; we enhance what's already there," Shell replies.

"What happened to her?" I ask.

"After I'd worked with Ida for about a year, she was accused of theft by one of the studios. One of the actresses reported some jewelry missing, and all the fingers pointed at Ida. I wasn't there that day, but I didn't believe the accusations—Ida would never have stolen from a client, she was always too focused on the work she was doing. I think it broke her heart to have her reputation dented in that way. She took her own life soon after."

"That's so sad," I whisper.

"Yeah. No one wanted to work with me either. I mean,

even though Ida had taught me so much, I was still technically an apprentice, but with no one training me anymore. I asked around some of the other artists to see if I could work with them, but no one wanted to know. So I decided to go somewhere totally different, earn a few bucks and send myself to beauty school. That's why I came here. It's as far away from LA as I can get, but I still have the beach and the sunshine."

"Do you still plan to study?"

"Yeah, I've almost saved enough and there's a course at one of the local colleges, so I might be able to work here and study."

"Maybe you could offer makeup classes or services here," I suggest.

"I can't see why not," Connor adds, squeezing my thigh. "We can always tell guests it's an option, then see if its popular."

"I would love that," Shell grins.

"I'm sorry such tragedy brought you here," I say, looking at both Shell and Esme.

"It's ok," Shell replies. "Our tragedies have had a happy ending. We found a place where no one judges us, and we can be whatever and whoever we want. This place has been a godsend for us both." The two of them hug and I can see they've found such strength in each other.

"Don't you have to head off soon, Shell?" Esme says as they release each other.

"Of course," Barbie says. "Big date!"

"Who with?" Connor asks.

Shell looks sheepish. "Oh, nobody."

"Oh come on," Esme laughs. "Everybody knows who it is, you've been drooling over him for months."

Connor laughs. "Eddie, right?"

We all collapse laughing.

"That obvious, is it?"

"I'm saying nothing else," Esme laughs.

"Good, because you're next."

"What's that supposed to mean?"

Shell stands and pulls her jacket around her. "Eddie has lots of buddies. I'm keeping my eye out just for you," she grins.

We say our goodbyes as Shell leaves, then I get up to help Esme carry the plates back into Barbie's villa.

"You two look so good together," she says as we load the plates into the dishwasher. I feel a blush creeping up my cheeks. "I knew something would happen once he got over himself. And he's smitten, everyone can see it."

I stand and look back at her, warily. "Do you think? I'm such a novice at relationships, I've no idea if something is going well or not."

"Believe me. The man hasn't been able to leave you alone since you got here. He can't hold you any tighter. And when I see you and him during the day, when you're both working, he looks over at you constantly, as though he needs to know where you are every second. I'd say it's going well. Now that he's finally got over whatever issue he had in the beginning."

"Mmm," I nod. I'm not so sure she's right about that. Connor does seem to have got over the fact I look like his ex, but I'm pretty sure he's still having flashbacks and nightmares; he just isn't telling me about them. I need to talk to him about it, try to get him to reconsider getting help. I'm falling for him hard, and I don't want there to always be this dark cloud hanging over us all the time.

But the idea of bringing it up fills me with dread. I don't know how long I can continue to be the source of his pain. If he is still having the flashbacks, or if they're getting worse, I know the kindest thing I can do, if he won't get help, is to leave. And I can't even entertain that thought—it hurts too much. Maybe with the casino opening next week, and Connor being so occupied with that, things will straighten out. He's already prepared me for the fact he won't be around the next few days as he really needs to focus. There's so much riding on this opening—Connor's reputation, Starling's reputation, money... Maybe it will be a good thing for both of us to have some distance, as much as I don't want it.

We head back out to the beach to say our goodbyes and I wrap my arms around Connor, holding onto him for as long as I can.

# CHAPTER TWENTY-SIX

onnor

"HEY MAN, are you going to come up for air?"

Isaac is hovering above me as I run through the plan for this evening's opening night for the fiftieth time.

"Do we have enough champagne behind the VIP bar?" I ask, ignoring his question.

"Yes. I checked a half hour ago when you asked me then. Don't worry about it. Ché has everything under control."

"Do the marketing and PR guys have everything they need for the red carpet?"

"Yes, again, I checked earlier."

"And the contracted security guys. Every single one has been briefed? They know where the safety bunks are if they need them? We've done thorough background checks?"

"Yes, yes, and yes. Connor, you need to breathe, and you need to eat something. I know you're a perfectionist and all, and we love you for it, but I haven't seen you this… *obsessed* before."

I stop reading through the words. They're all blurring into one anyway.

"Isaac," I say, looking up. "This is a huge deal. Opening a brand new, premium casino puts us in a whole different league to other resorts. We've got TV crews and reporters from all across America coming—half of them are already here. We cannot put a step wrong. I'm taking this seriously, and you should, too."

"I am, Connor. We all are."

He looks at me despairingly.

"I know you've been struggling a little, you know, with the flashbacks and everything. Carter told me. I think you're throwing yourself deep into this to avoid facing the fact you need help."

I grit my teeth and glare at him. I don't appreciate advice about my mental state at the best of times, least of all on the most important day in the history of this resort.

"Are you here to help or just nag?" I snap.

He holds his hands up. "I just care about you, man. I don't want to see you burn out. We need you."

I sigh, watching him.

"Have you seen Tawny at all in the last week? I ran into her. She's worried about you."

Something tightens in my chest at the sound of her name. I've managed to keep her out of my head for the most part, but not without a great deal of effort. She's blurred my vision. She's invaded my thoughts. I've become single-mindedly focused on the way she feels beneath my fingers and around my cock. I've become sloppy; I've been making mistakes. My flashbacks have been getting worse and all because I've

been losing control. I'm falling for her fast, and sliding down
the slippery slope towards insanity.

"No, I haven't seen her. I've been busy."

I've had to be. I've had to find a way to make this work.
As it turns out, for me there's no such thing as work/life
balance. It's either sanity or insanity. For the sake of the
resort that I built, almost single-handedly, and the livelihoods
of everyone on the island, I've had to choose sanity. And
that's why I told Tawny I needed space to get through this
week. I turn back to the screen, signaling the end of the
conversation.

I sense Isaac shrug. "Fine. I'll let you do whatever you
need to do, Connor. See you at the huddle." Then he walks
away.

THE GUYS ARE WAITING for me when I finally emerge from
the back office in the casino. The dealers are ready and
waiting by their tables, the hosts and waitstaff are poised with
trays of champagne and canapes. The photographers and
camera crews are in position at the main gates and the doors
to the casino itself, as well as being lined along the red carpet,
prepared to capture the brave and the beautiful as they enter.
Eric and Maria are on their way to the front doors along with
their daughters who've flown back from England especially
for the big night. The marina is full, the villas are full.
Everyone who's anyone is here for the opening of Starling
Lights, the most luxurious casino in the Keys.

"Hey," I nod. The guys are suited and booted in their
smartest Starling Key Security uniforms, earpieces in,
weapons at their sides. They look overpowering and fucking

mean, just as they should. Even Luca looks fierce beyond his years, despite his baby blues glinting under the strip lights.

I walk up to them and see nothing but respect in their faces. At some point in the last few days, every one of them has pulled me up on my seemingly self-sabotaging, unwavering focus, yet they've put their pithy concerns to one side for this moment. They know who's made this night what it is, and they know who's boss.

"I'm going to start by saying thanks to you all. You're not only incredible colleagues and talented security professionals, but you're my brothers. I know you have concerns about the way I've been in the last few weeks, and I appreciate that. But this is it. This is what it was all for. Tonight is going to be a night we'll all remember for a long time. We made this happen. We designed and almost built this casino with our bare hands. Every single one of you has put your stamp on it, and you should be proud. Tonight, we're going to make sure each of our guests and visitors feel fortunate, special, and most importantly, safe. We're dealing with more money than we've ever had on this resort. Our focus needs to be all over the place, all the time. There are going to be some pretty ladies out there tonight—no wandering eyes..." I grin, knowing my boys wouldn't even look twice. When they're working, they're working. End of.

"Just to recap, Carter, you're on the door with me. Isaac, you're at the front gates. Luca, you're inside. Jax, you're on the cameras, and Hud, you're on patrol. Everyone clear?"

"Yes, boss."

"Let's do this." I slap each of them on the back and make a move towards the door leading out to the main casino.

"Connor," Jax says behind me and I turn. "I just want to say, on behalf of all of us, thanks. This was your vision, you've made it happen, and it's only going to solidify our future here—our livelihoods."

"Yeah," Hudson adds. "Whatever you need, we're here for you."

Luca thumps me on the back. "Let's have a great night."

Isaac and Carter don't say anything and I know what they're thinking. *We'll give you this night, then we're gonna talk.*

I nod, then walk through the door.

The floor staff are beaming with anticipation as we walk through. I notice a team of hostesses waiting by the tables of champagne and feel their eyes follow all of us as we stalk past them. Most of our wait staff are permanent and used to seeing us around, but tonight we're in all our security gear and traveling in a pack. I can almost smell the lust radiating from them.

We reach the lobby where some of our other teams have been dispatched for this evening to help with cloakroom duties, to support the media and the publicists, and to generally be available for any eventuality. I made sure Tawny was one of those people. I need her close where I can make sure she's safe.

As though my eyes are programmed, they shift sideways and land on her standing to the side of the main door, dressed in her Starling Key uniform with her hair pulled up into a tidy bun. My throat is dry. She sees me and her mouth drops open slightly. Only then do I realize she's never seen me in my security gear. I know I look half-cop, half-billionaire boss. My heart thumps against the wall of my chest as I fight the urge to run over there, sweep her up and carry her to the cellars to do filthy things to her. I turn to Carter.

"I need to be outside. You stay inside the door... and can you keep an eye on Tawny?"

"Sure thing," he replies, then turns to head in Tawny's direction. I head out of the door and survey the scene.

"Three VIPs heading your way." I hear Isaac say through my earpiece.

"Roger that." I nod to two of the agency guys and they discreetly position themselves where the cars are to be directed. A steady stream of island guests are now entering. Some of the photographers generously make a big deal of them, even though they're not famous.

I notice Barbie and Fitz making their way slowly along the red carpet. Esme is pushing Fitz in a wheelchair and he's smiling so broadly it looks as though his face might burst. One of the photographers recognizes him and within seconds, he's being interviewed about his new life here on Starling Key. I return my eyes to the crowd, always watching. When I look back at Fitz, he gives me a giant smile.

Barbie is in her element, dressed in some flowing gold number, decorated seemingly all over with feathers. They're even sprouting out of her hair. When I catch her eye, I get a flirtatious wink. A publicist whispers something to one of the cameramen, and suddenly, they all erupt.

"Jay-Z! Jay-Z!"

Flashbulbs pop and the security guys sidle up to the car, forming a human shield around our first guest. He gallantly pauses to answer questions and pose for pictures, then makes his way inside. If I was a gambling man—which, fortunately I'm not, otherwise this casino would be the death of me—I'd put money on Barbie attempting to drape herself across the poor guy right about now.

Another car pulls up spitting out another A-list celebrity, then another. I train my eyes on the people immediately around them and beyond. I watch for darting glances, unnatural movements, shadows. Only one guest diverts my attention, and that's more out of surprise than anything else. A nondescript car pulls up and out steps a man I recognize. I quickly try to place him while continuing to scan the crowd. Then I remember. His was the face that opened the door of 84 Manaqua Drive, the first house Tawny and I delivered money to on our road trip to Miami. I recognize his long, sharp nose. He's one of Bianchi's mob. I don't remember inviting him. He walks up the red carpet and spots me at the top. He smiles, discreetly, and I hear the words "Good evening", as he passes.

I update Carter through my mouthpiece. "Can you keep an eye on him?"

"Is he alone?"

"Looks like it."

"Probably just wants to throw some mob money around," Carter says.

"Then he can be our guest," I reply. My gaze turns back to the train of VIPs still arriving, one after the other. I'm thankful for the need to focus. I need to think of something—anything—except the woman standing at the other side of the door.

# CHAPTER TWENTY-SEVEN

awny

I'M STILL GASPING for breath when Carter comes to stand a few feet away from me. The sight of Connor with his hair slicked back, wearing his security uniform—the pristine tuxedo, the headset, the guns at his side—has sent my stomach into a spin. He's always smart and wearing some shirt or suit, when he's not in mouthwatering combat shorts, but to see him looking so elegant in his tux, yet so… dangerous, with the guns and the earpiece, has triggered feelings in me I'd temporarily buried.

Now, seeing him this evening, watching his blue eyes flicker towards me the second he entered the lobby, then his body stalk towards the door in all that gear, has weakened me all over again. I'm grateful when guests and VIPs start arriving because it gives me something to do. Rhonda asks me to be a 'runner' for general supplies and VIP requests because I know my way around now more than some of the

others. I run to the kitchen to request more canapes, I run to
the back offices to get more chips, I run to the dry cleaner to
get tomato sauce off of a VIP's shirt. I run a lot.

"Tawny, honey, we need more napkins for the dining
room," Rhonda calls out to me as I return from the cellar with
two magnums of Krug champagne. She takes them from me.
"They're in the storage unit behind the wall. You ok to run
over there?"

"Sure, I'll go now."

"You're an angel. Two packs should do it."

I turn to head out through the kitchen exit—it will be less
crowded and I won't have to tiptoe around celebrities navi-
gating the red carpet. Arnaud and his team are moving around
seamlessly, as though they're in a ballet. Their focus is unwavering but their spirits are high—I can feel the buzz and
adrenalin hanging in the air. I creep through the exit and
breathe in a lungful of fresh, slightly warm sea air. We'd be
surrounded by snowdrifts six feet high by now in New Jersey,
but down here the air is still balmy after the sun has blazed
through the day.

I hear the crunch of footsteps on the gravel about fifteen
feet away and it makes me jump. I slowly turn my head to see
a man dressed in black with his back to me, talking quietly on
a phone. It doesn't occur to me in the moment that it's strange
for a guest to be round the back of the giant casino on
opening night. Instead, I think nothing of it and go to walk
past him towards the northeast wall. As I pass, I hear his
voice and it's familiar. I only know it's familiar because every
single hair on my body has stood on end and I feel freezing
cold and light-headed. I force my steps to slow as I carefully
bend my head. It can't be him. On Starling Key, of all places.
It can't be.

My gaze travels along the gravel towards his feet. They

are dressed in shiny, black, expensive shoes. His dark suit pants are fitted along the thickness of his thighs, and the suit jacket hangs open, revealing a half-buttoned white shirt and a thick circular tattoo across his chest. I don't need to see his face, because I know. I flick my head forward and keep walking, forcing my gait to remain steady. My heart is beating out of my chest as it dawns on me: I can never get away. I will never be free of this. No matter how effectively I live, breathe and believe the life story I've been trotting out, no matter how many times I change my identity, there will always be one of them out there, waiting. Waiting to skin me alive.

As soon as I reach the wall, I break into a sprint, following it around to the goods entrance which at least is lit up. I unlock the storage unit, slip inside and slide down the wall. My mind has shut down, completely overtaken by the whole body tremors that now rack me throughout. I can't feel my breath anymore, and I can't see anything but the man standing outside the casino.

Even when the door bursts open and someone grips my shoulders, I don't come around. I can feel myself being shaken—my spine is hitting the wall behind me. I can hear a voice far away but I don't know who it belongs to or what it's saying.

"Tawny! Say something. Tawny, what the fuck is going on? What just happened?"

It seems as though a whole hour has passed before a figure begins to form in front of me. The shaking has stopped and in its place is pure adrenaline. I flash my eyes up at the person kneeling before me. I almost don't recognize him behind all the security gear.

"Connor," I whisper.

He sighs, sounding relieved. "Tawny, what happened? Why were you running here so fast?"

I need my brain to work. If one thing has been drilled into me since all of this began, it's to never tell a soul. I need to remember that. The voice and words are still as clear as crystal. Even if you fall in love, don't ever tell.

"What?" Connor says, quietly.

"Even if you fall in love, don't ever tell," I whisper, unsure of which world I'm in. The real one, or the one of my nightmares.

"Don't ever tell, what?"

He watches as the glaze across my eyes clears and I slowly become present in my own body again. "Tawny, what can't you tell anyone?"

I feel as though the blood in my veins has frozen, because I can't move. I can't even open my mouth to speak. I've fucked up.

Connor waits, patiently, and I know it's too late. I've fallen for him, and he now knows there's more to me than meets the eye. And knowing Connor and how he likes to be across everything, so he can control it, he won't let this lie for as long as I'm on this island. I either have to leave, for good, or tell him the truth. Both options scare the life out of me. But the idea of leaving this man behind, after everything we've both been through, after everything we're trying to conquer together, isn't tolerable.

"I'm not who you think I am," I whisper.

His eyes narrow. "What do you mean?"

"My name isn't Tawny Graham."

He sits back on his heels, the air leaving his lungs in a rush. "Ok. So what is it?"

"Natalie Grey."

He takes a minute to process what I'm saying. "Why would you lie?"

I hesitate. I haven't actually thought through what I would tell someone, because I never thought I would.

"Because I have to."

"What did you see back there?"

"Someone who wants me dead." The words sound foreign to me but I can see the cogs turning behind Connor's eyes.

"Bianchi's guy? You were running from him?"

I nod, slowly.

"Why?"

"Think about it, Connor, why would I be running from him? What could possibly have happened to make me so afraid of him?"

He frowns as he thinks and my heart pounds with the hope that I can trust him.

"Are you in witness protection?"

I nod, slowly.

He rubs his face. "Fuck. What did you see, Tawny?"

I picture the exact scene—the same scene I relayed to an untold number of detectives as they scribbled notes, made recordings, muttered between themselves, and eyed me with concern.

"I'd been out, for the first time since Mom died, to organize flowers for her funeral. My head was all over the place and I got lost in my own damn neighborhood. Before I knew it, I was down some back street and I heard voices at the other end. It was the middle of the afternoon so I wasn't afraid. I was actually hoping to ask for directions. But as I got closer, I realized I was seeing something I shouldn't. There was your guy, from the opening…"

"He's not *my guy*…"

"He was just standing back, watching the whole thing. And another guy who was bent over something, growling like a dog." I shudder at the memory and bile starts to rise up my chest.

"I started to back away because it was clear something bad was going on, and I didn't want any part of it. Then I saw the guy who was bending over pull another man up off the floor. I hadn't seen his body, but his head had been shoved down into an old bathtub. He came up coughing and spluttering. Then it all happened real fast. Your guy…"

"*Not* my guy…"

"Threw the other guy a lighter. He struck it and set the third guy up in flames. They'd been soaking his head in gasoline."

I wretch into my hand. It's an image I will never forget for as long as I live.

"Jesus." Connor pulls me towards him. Only once his thick arms are wrapped around me do I realize I'm soaking wet—from sweat and tears. "Is anyone behind bars?"

"The guy who struck the lighter. He just got life."

"Has the guy here seen you?"

I pull back but he keeps a hold of my arms. "I don't know. I don't think so. How would he know I'm here?"

Connor falls still and doesn't answer me.

"I need to get rid of him," he states. "But he's one of Bianchi's guys. I'll need to think carefully about how we handle this."

"Wouldn't it just be easier if I left the island?"

His grip on me tightens and his eyes flash. "No. You can't keep running from this. We'll fix it, I promise."

My body floods with sensations of relief and fear. I can't seem to think for myself so I'm beyond grateful when Connor takes control of the situation.

"You need to stay here, ok? I'm going to go out there and

personally see that he's gone. Lock the door behind you and don't come out until I say so. I'll send one of the guys over."

I nod. He lets go of my arms and stands. With his hand on the doorknob he turns back.

"Jesus, Tawny. Why did you let me take you to all those drops in Miami?"

"I had no idea that's what you were going to do, and I could hardly say no. You'd have asked why, and I find it hard to lie to you."

"You've done a pretty good job," he says, his face serious. "Your parents… you being an orphan. That all true?"

"Yes, it is. Everything I've told you has been the truth. I just didn't tell you *everything*. I couldn't even tell it to myself; I've had to live and think as though nothing ever happened—it's the only way I know to keep from giving myself away. That is, until I saw the very person I'm hiding from."

He sighs, bracing himself for something.

"Wait right here. Lock the door."

# CHAPTER TWENTY-EIGHT

onnor

MY HEART IS HAMMERING as I close the door on Tawny and wait for the lock to click. She's in witness protection. She's vulnerable. She needs me. She represents everything I've been fucking running away from, and everything I've been born to do. But I'm the very person who's put her at risk, by taking her to Miami. I stop myself slamming a fist into the wall. How could I have been so fucking stupid? And selfish. I dragged her up to the city so I could punish her when she hadn't done anything wrong. Bianchi's guy must have seen her in the car when he looked past me. Fuck.

I have to get that man off the island. I have to make sure he doesn't come back, without telling anyone why. Even with the anger and adrenalin coursing through my veins, my logical mind knows that isn't possible. That the only way I can truly know he will never come back is if he's killed. And I don't kill.

I protect people. My job is to protect. My calling is to protect. It's in my blood, in my bones, and I can't run away from it anymore. My calling doesn't care if I failed to protect the twenty-seven who lost their lives that day in Iraq. My calling doesn't care if it can't protect my heart from the reckless abandon of someone I thought I loved and trusted. My calling doesn't care that my mental health is suffering the consequences of my failed attempts at protecting others. My calling only cares that there's woman locked in the room behind me, a woman I've fallen for despite every effort not to, who's in danger. And every cell in my body is gearing up to fight for her.

It doesn't matter that she isn't who she said she was. From the little I now know, she's exactly the same person, but with a different name. I didn't fall for her name.

I force myself to walk at a normal pace out of the goods bay and back towards the casino. I can't talk about this through the mouthpiece, it's too risky. I need to find one of the guys in person, get them over here, then track down Bianchi's guy. *Fuck.* That's one connection I can't afford to lose. The casino entrance is still buzzing with people standing outside getting air, having a smoke. I can't see any of my guys anywhere. I realize I've turned my headset off. I must have done it as soon as I'd seen Tawny break into a sprint.

I switch it back on and hear multiple voices—Carter, Luca and Hudson all speaking at once.

"Hey," I start.

"Connor, where the fuck you been?" Luca sounds panicked, which is highly unusual for him.

"What's going on?"

"Carter and Hud are on the beach. A boat's come in."

"To the beach?" My blood runs cold for the second time

this evening. There's only one reason a boat sidles up to the beach as opposed to the marina. Illegal immigrants.

"No one's got out yet, Connor." Carter says. "Can you get down here?"

"I need someone to stay with Tawny."

"C'mon man, she'll be fine…"

"Carter, listen to me. I can't get into it now, but trust me when I say I need someone to stay with her."

"I'll go. Where is she?"

"Thanks Luca. She's in the storage unit by the goods entrance. Do not let her come out until I get there, do you understand?"

"Absolutely."

"Ok, I'm on my way, Carter."

This is a fucking nightmare. And one hell of a coincidence. We've managed to keep our shores free of rafters for four whole years. It seems weird we get one on the night of the casino opening—when we're all distracted.

I break into a run, keeping to the shadows so as not to alarm any guests who might be walking the grounds. It's almost two am, but the casino is still swinging. As soon as I reach the edge of the beach, I see it.

A large fishing boat is perched on the sand, bobbing gently as the foam from the waves crawls up and down the shoreline. Hudson and Carter stand about twenty feet up the beach, their guns pointed at it. There are no lights, no safety gear, no inflatables. Nothing. Nothing to suggest it's equipped to sail three-hundred miles or more. But then again, these kinds of boats, used for this purpose, never are. We all edge closer to the boat, me with my back to the mangroves. It's better to allow whomever is in it to emerge of their own accord, rather than us having to break our way in and drag out whatever bodies might be crammed inside. Hopefully alive. We have to be patient, and we will be. Because this is what we've been trained for.

# CHAPTER TWENTY-NINE

awny

I'M STILL TREMBLING, despite the heat. The storage unit is like a pizza oven—I'm surrounded by thick slabs of wall and barely any airflow. I'm also shitting myself. Every time a car leaves the resort, I jump out of my skin. Every time I hear a creature rummaging through the bins, my heart leaps into my mouth. I'm petrified. I'm also convinced I'm the reason Bianchi's guy is here. He must have seen me when I accompanied Connor to drop off the money. He came for me. And if he's that committed, he's not going to stop searching until he's turned over every stone.

A soft knock at the door sends the blood rushing to my feet.

"Tawny, It's Luca. Can you let me in?"

I don't move. I know Luca is built like a truck, just like the others—he could protect me. But he's young, he's still impressionable. I can't be certain he's alone.

"Connor sent me," he whispers. "He asked me to stay with you 'til he can get back."

I reach up and click the lock. Luca pushes the door ajar and squeezes through. As his eyes become accustomed to the darkness and he takes me in properly, he takes a breath.

"Are you ok?"

I don't know what Connor has told him. Nothing, I hope. I can't risk more people finding out the truth about me.

"I'm fine," I lie, blatantly. "I just saw someone I know from way back and need to wait until they're gone."

Luca could ask me a million different questions but he doesn't ask one. Instead, he sits down beside me and takes my hand. I've noticed this about all the people who work here. There's a quiet acceptance that each and every one of us has history. Apart from the occasional playful gossip, there's a genuine respect for peoples' pasts, and an understanding it doesn't all need to be aired like dirty laundry.

"What's happening at the beach?" I ask, after several minutes have passed.

"We've got a rafter."

"A what?"

"A stray boat—one we think is carrying immigrants, illegal immigrants."

"How do you know that's what it is?"

"They're pretty common on the Keys. We've kept our shores pretty clean, worked with the coast guard to make sure anyone who does bypass the border by coming here is processed appropriately. We don't get involved. Our main concern is that they're alive. They're not always, and... well, it's hard. To think those people were so desperate they were prepared to risk their lives sailing hundreds of miles in a crappy boat, only to lose their battle with the sea."

Luca goes quiet and I can hear a muffled voice through his earpiece.

"You're kidding me. How old?"

He goes quiet again. And pale. And for someone with a tan to rival one of our sun-worshipping guests, that's saying something. When it's clear he's no longer part of a conversation happening on the beach, I ask, "Is it children?"

He nods, then is suddenly distracted again. I can hear another muffled voice through his earpiece.

"Isaac. Hold on. Say that again." Luca presses a finger to his ear as though he's trying to make out what Isaac is saying. "It's going on now? In the casino?" Luca flicks his eyes towards me. "I can't leave here. Connor's orders. They're all on the beach. Isaac, man…"

The muffled voice stops and Luca looks back at me.

"Fuck. Tawny, I have to go to the casino. A fight broke out and we're down three guys. Jax can't get involved and Isaac's on his own. Can I trust you to stay here and not move? Not even an inch?"

"Yes," I say, but already, all I can think of is there are children getting out of that boat.

"Lock the door again. Stay here. I'll be back as soon as I can, ok?"

I nod. "I'll be fine Luca. You go."

He shoots me a concerned look before sliding out of the door and closing it silently behind him. I wait sixty seconds for him to run out of the goods yard onto the main drive, then I clamber to my feet. I have to get to that beach. And I have to get there without being seen.

I decide to head back through the accommodation blocks, the same way Connor carried me after the cactus incident, and out onto the northeast beach, as far as possible from the casino. From there, I jog down to the retirement village, stopping at each cluster of palms to catch my breath. Once I get past Reef Street, I sprint through the gardens, keeping to the dark patches between the villas, until I reach the mangroves on the other side. I'm about a hundred yards from the main beach but the space is more open on the shoreline, so I crouch down amongst the mangroves and crawl as best I can through the roots and tendrils, until I hear voices. As I peer through the gaps in the undergrowth, I can see the boat. I shift slightly, holding my breath, trying to soundlessly move each muscle, until I can see the figures forming around it. I see Hudson, his long hair now flowing behind him, his arms raised holding a gun. Then I see Carter. His hair is still slicked back but he's also brandishing a gun between his hands, his arms outstretched. Then I see the children.

There are four of them, all huddled together in front of the boat. They can't be more than six years old. I'm not close to them but I can see them trembling, their faces overwhelmed with fear. Something takes over me. I forget why I'm even hiding. It's only Hudson, Carter and four children.

Before I can question what I'm doing, I'm bursting out of the mangroves and flying down the beach towards them, pulling my jacket off as I go.

"Tawny! No!" I hear Connor's voice yell, but I ignore him. I need to get to those children. I can sense someone running at me, but I keep going. The sand makes it hard to pick up any speed, but I need to get to those children before Connor gets to me. Then I'm suddenly swept up into the air. I can see the faces of the children. They're petrified. Then I hear a gun cock near my ear and I'm set down on the sand, facing up the beach. An arm reaches around my neck and I see Hudson and Carter staring at me and whoever is holding a gun to my head. Then I hear the man speak, and my worst fear is confirmed. It's Bianchi's guy. The guy I need to run away from.

"I knew it was you," he hisses. "They thought you'd be safe down here, right? You're not safe anywhere my love."

Carter's eyes narrow as he tries to understand what's going on.

"You tried to put me behind bars, you little bitch." Saliva hits my face where he's towering over me and the steel of the gun presses cold against my face.

"What the fuck is going on?" Hudson demands.

"Let go of her. Now." I hardly recognize Connor's voice. I can't see him but he sounds about ready to kill someone. I hear his footsteps coming towards us but the man's arm stays around my throat, pinning me, steadfast. A sound comes from the boat and Carter and Hudson both turn to see what caused it. I'm spun to the left as the man holding me also turns to look, and I can see the shadow of a slim, lithe figure stepping out of the boat. It's a young woman, olive-skinned, with long jet black hair flowing down her back. I'm too far away to tell just how beautiful she is, but I can tell from the looks on Carter and Hudson's faces, they're fighting intrigue. She steps slowly through the water, apparently unfazed by the fact her tight black jeans are now knee-deep in the sea. She walks past the children, stroking her hand across the shoulder of one, and stops within a few feet of Carter.

I hear another gun cock to my right and crane my neck to see whose gun is responsible. Out of the corner of my eye, I see Connor's form standing next to the man behind me, his gun to the man's skull.

"I wouldn't do that if I were you," the man sneers.

A third gun cocks and I'm spun again to face Carter who now has the barrel of his gun up against the girl's forehead. I gasp before I realize she is still completely unfazed. The man behind me speaks again.

"And I *really* wouldn't do that."

"Why? Who is she?" Hudson spits.

The man restraining me takes a breath to speak but the girl beats him to it.

"We are all relatives and acquaintances of Mario Bianchi. He's expecting us in Miami in five hours. If we don't arrive there by eight am, he will send people down here. He knows where we were docking; it has all been planned."

"What does Mario want with children?" Connor asks, failing to hide his disgust.

The girl turns to face him, despite the steel rod aimed at her head. "Mario? You use his first name? You must be acquainted with him yourself."

Connor doesn't answer.

"These are the children of people who have helped the family. They have worked hard for Mario and this is how he repays them. He brings their children here so they can be reunited with their parents."

"You mean their children are put on a floating death trap?" Carter says.

"It has survived the journey more than once," the girl says, giving the boat a cursory glance.

"I can't let you go through the island," Connor says, his tone absolute.

"Then I will have to put the children back on the boat," she replies, straightening her back. I don't know what it is about this girl, but I believe every word that comes out of her mouth.

"And what about you? Who the fuck are you?" Carter snaps again.

She turns her head slowly to face him then broadens her

lips into a seductive smile. "I'm Seleste Ortiz, soon to be Seleste Rodriguez, wife of Antonio."

I feel Connor stiffen, even though he's several steps away.

"Well, congratulations. Lucky fucking you," Carter says, then he looks back to Connor. "What do you want to do, man?"

"Oh, so you're not the boss guy?" Seleste says to Carter, her smile taking on a wicked slant.

Suddenly, a gun goes off right next to my ear and I fall to the ground, pulled down on top of the man who'd been restraining me. His arm loosens and I'm dragged away. I look back to see the guy I'd been running from. Connor has him face down in the sand, blood pouring out of his right thigh. Hudson lifts me to my feet as though I'm as light as a feather. The children watch, aghast, silent tears rolling down their cheeks.

"Block their view," Connor shouts to Carter, who steps between the children and their view of Connor while still holding Seleste at gunpoint.

In the split second that Connor's face is turned away, the man strikes out, landing a kick to Connor's knee. Connor buckles. The man clambers quickly to his knees and pulls his gun upwards.

"Give me the fucking girl," he spits, "and I'll be out of your hair."

"What do you want with Tawny?" Carter asks, still pressing his gun to Seleste's head.

"She owes me. Life for a life."

"What's that supposed to mean?"

"She's a snitch, gentlemen," he says with a sneer. "This little witch sent my brother down after she saw us having a chat with an errant supplier. She told the police everything."

My blood almost erupted. "You were not having a chat," I

yell. "You tried to drown him in gasoline, then you set him alight."

I hear one of the children let out a sob.

"Mind what you tell this one," he continues, looking up at Connor. "She might have won you over with those pretty little eyes of hers, but she will rat. Let me take her off your hands. I'll deal with it."

"Deal with it?" Hudson snarls. I'm shaking like a leaf. I'm pretty sure Carter and Hudson have caught on to why I'm here. Whether or not they'll think it's safe for me to stay, knowing I've talked to cops in the past, is another question.

"Yeah." He speaks slowly. "Dispose of the issue."

Connor throws himself forward, smacking the gun out of the man's hand and knocking him back to the sand. I see the man bringing his hands up and around Connor's neck.

"Hud!" I cry, grabbing his arm.

Hudson lunges forward but it turns out he isn't needed. Connor pulls an arm back and punches the man in the jaw. I see splatters of blood land on the gleaming white sand, then Connor does it again, and again.

"Connor, stop!" I shout. I can't take any more violence. Even if the guy wants me dead, I can't watch Connor kill him. Connor stops moving, then climbs off the man's body as it lays still below him. He turns to face me, his jaw firm, his eyes black.

"Search him," he instructs Hudson.

Hudson feels around in every pocket and pulls out a wallet, a second gun and two phones. Hudson slips the gun into his uniform and throws Connor the one the man had held to my head.

"What do you want me to do with these?" Hud asks, holding up the wallet and phones.

"Get rid of the phones. Give him back the wallet."

Hudson opens the wallet. "Stefano Morelli," he says, simply. Then he pulls the cell phones apart, crushing pieces between his fingers, before hurling them into the sea.

One of the children yelps with fright at the unexpected splash.

"Let them go," I plead. I'm not even sure who I'm saying it to. "It's not their fault. They're not to blame for whatever it is their parents have done. It's not our place to keep them apart. Please… They need to be with their families."

Connor straightens and sets his eyes on me.

"Hudson. Make sure he doesn't move," he says, nodding to the guy on the floor.

"I don't think he's in any hurry," Hudson smirks.

Then Connor strides towards me, grabs my arm and pulls me up the beach. It hurts but I can hardly complain; he's probably just saved my life.

"Where are we going?"

"Out of earshot," Connor says, pulling a phone out of his pocket with his free hand. He continues pulling me as he waits for the other person to pick up. I can hear the words clear as day.

"Ah, Connor, I thought it might be you."

"What the fuck is going on, Mario? I've got four kids, a feisty woman and an unconscious dumbass on my beach. It's an important night for me; I'm sure that factored into your thinking. What the hell do you want me to do?"

The voice is tinny but I can make out the words.

"I need you to get Seleste and the children to a car. It's waiting right now outside the goods entrance. It will bring them to Miami and no one need be any the wiser. You were never meant to see the boat, Connor. I didn't want to get you involved—I know how queasy you are about… people."

"Do you realize I've got every fucking A-lister and their

entourages on the island tonight? And you want me to escort four bedraggled children across the island to a blacked out vehicle without being seen?"

"Well, I had hoped the boat would arrive sooner and all your visitors would be safely inside your casino, but the ocean doesn't always play ball."

"Fuck this, Mario. This is not part of our agreement."

"You're right, Connor. I owe you a favor. Just get the kids in the car will you?"

"I have another problem."

I hear a sigh through the phone, but Connor continues, undeterred.

"One of your guys is here…"

"Stefano. He's not one of mine. He's just an associate. I needed someone to create a distraction, make sure the delivery changed hands, as it were."

"The fight in the casino…"

"Oh dear. A fight was not a part of my brief."

"Well, he's a problem. I need him gone."

"Gone from the island, or gone from the earth?"

"Earth."

"Why is that, Connor?"

"It's personal."

"Personal?"

"Look, do I ever ask you about your business? No. He's a threat to someone very important to me. Like I said, it's personal."

"So, get rid of him."

I suck in a breath. Bianchi wants Connor to kill the guy?

"No, Mario. I don't 'get rid' of people. None of us do."

Connor turns his head slightly and I can no longer hear what Bianchi is saying.

"Fine," Connor says. "We'll hold up our side of the

bargain—we'll get those kids in the car. Then you hold up yours."

Connor doesn't wait for an answer before he hangs up and slides his phone back into his pocket. I look up at him and his eyes are almost black.

"You didn't hear any of that," he says, his voice grave.

"What if they let him go?" I whisper.

"They won't. Hudson will make sure of it. He's going to follow in a truck. Go to your dorm right now. Do not stop. Do not speak to anyone. Do not even think about doing anything other than what I'm telling you. Take the main road and walk fast. If you're not there when I'm done here, I swear to God, Tawny, I might have to kill you myself."

# CHAPTER THIRTY

onnor

THE SCENE HASN'T CHANGED. Carter is still holding the girl at gunpoint, four terrified children cowering at her feet, and Hudson has his giant foot across Morelli's stomach, pressing him down into the sand.

"Let's go," I say.

"We're taking them to the entrance?" Carter asks, not taking his eyes off the girl, who I swear is taunting him with her feline eyes.

"Yes. Follow me. And make sure those kids stay quiet," I glance over my shoulder at the girl. Hudson hoists Morelli over his shoulder. I take the lead. The kids come next, followed by the girl, with Carter right behind her, the barrel of his gun pressed into her back. Hudson brings up the rear.

I ask Jax to check the cameras round the back of the northeast wall, to confirm the exact location of the car, then I brief Luca to go stand outside my dorm in case Tawny decides to go on yet another excursion of her own free will. It turns out the fight had calmed down as soon as Luca had arrived on the scene, pretty much at the same time as Morelli snuck out of the casino and made his way to the beach, funnily enough.

"We'll have to go through the mangroves. There are too many people wandering around. It's the best chance we have at getting to the exit without being seen."

I am livid. I know exactly why Mario Bianchi planned for this cargo to land on our beach tonight of all nights. He figured we'd be too preoccupied to notice. But if word ever got out that we—the staff of Starling Key—helped some immigrants get ashore without reporting them, we could not only lose our jobs but we'd have to serve time behind bars. Even with our connections and, for many of us, our military or public service accolades, if this finding made its way into the wrong hands, we'd be screwed. Sure, we could talk. We could give up what we know about the Bianchi's or any of our other not-quite-straight-and-narrow 'friends', but then our lives either side of the bars would not be worth living.

I lead them into the first set of mangroves. It's too dark to see all the roots but I can't switch on my torch, it's too risky.

"Take it easy here," I say. "Try not to trip over these things."

I can just imagine the sound of children wailing, bringing the few guests who opted to stay indoors tonight out onto their balconies. If villas four and five did just that right now, they'd see us, no problem. I grit my teeth when I hear one of the children come thudding to the ground.

"It's ok, it's ok," Seleste whispers. "You're doing so well, and we don't have much further to go."

We manage to get through the first set of mangroves, then we have to run across the most southern garden to the next set. I look behind me and see Carter trailing the girl closely. For a second I think he's checking out her ass in those tight black pants. If he is, I will kick his ass later. Now is not the time, and knowing what I know of Mario Bianchi and Antonio Rodriguez, that girl is not the girl.

"How much further?" Seleste whispers.

"Five more minutes, then we'll be on the northeast beach."

I hear her reassuring the kids again. As soon as we're out of the mangroves and on slightly safer ground, I stop to let them all catch up.

"You don't need to get so close to me you know," Seleste says to Carter, dragging her eyes over him, lazily. "I'm going the exact same way as you."

Carter looks surprised while I swallow a small grin. It's not often a girl calls him out.

"You should feel damn lucky we're helping you," he snaps in a stage whisper.

"You didn't really have much of a choice there though, did ya, boss man?"

I turn to face them both, about to tell them to shut it, but decide against it. I need to focus on getting them out of here. Carter doesn't reply; I think he's a little lost for words.

"Yeah, keep rolling your eyes," she continues. "You never know, you might find a brain back there."

"Oh, so you're a smart ass?" Carter bites back, blithely ignorant to the fact there are children present.

"It's better to be a smart ass than just an ass."

"Jesus," Carters mumbles. "Does Rodriguez know what he's getting himself into?"

"No," she quips. "I don't think he does, actually."

I lead them through the storage units, eventually coming out at the top end of the northeast wall, right by the goods entrance. The door opens and Isaac appears at the other side.

"What the hell is going on?" he hisses.

"Bianchi's people," I reply, knowing he won't ask any further questions.

We walk through the door and across the loading bay.

"Anyone leaving the resort now will be able to see us, ok? You need to stay close until we get to the road." I look at the girl, Seleste. "This car... it's definitely there?"

"I couldn't see anything on the cameras," Isaac adds, and part of my stomach drops. If there's no car there, I'll need to figure out a plan B and fast.

"It's there," she replies, confidently. "Its lights won't be on."

"Of course," Carter chips in. "That seems to be how you guys roll."

She turns to face him and flicks her long jet black hair back over her slender shoulders. "I'm surprised someone like you, all big and dressed up in your good cop finery with a loaded gun in your hand, hasn't figured that's a given. We're illegal immigrants if you hadn't already worked it out. Of course we're not going to broadcast our whereabouts with *lights*."

"Will you two keep it down?" I hiss.

Isaac smirks then coughs in an attempt to cover it up and show some sort of brotherly support. Carter steps right up to Seleste, earning himself a small gasp from the two children holding her hands.

"If there weren't kids present, I'd be giving you the double finger right now."

She tilts her face up to Carter's and brings her lips so close they are almost touching his.

"Is that a promise?" She says, silkily. She lets out a small, wicked giggle, then flicks her head away and guides the children towards the loading bay exit.

"Let's go," she commands with an unnerving authority that reminds me distinctly of the family she's sailed here to join.

# CHAPTER THIRTY-ONE

 awny

I DID WHAT CONNOR SAID, and came straight back to my dorm. Even though Connor has knocked Morelli out cold, and a shot in his leg probably rendering him incapable of walking far on his own, I am so on edge I'm about to fall over it. My head is spinning. I've told Connor the truth, and Carter and Hudson both know. I'm in a witness protection program. The words still sound alien to me and have done ever since Millie entered the room and told me.

Millie is not my aunt; she's my protection officer, tasked with ensuring I settle into my new home, undiscovered. In the last few days of the investigation, she and I formed as close a bond as we could, considering we were complete strangers to each other, thrown together by the criminal act of one man setting another man on fire right in front of my eyes. I didn't think things like that happened in my neighborhood, but I guess a lot had changed while I was holed up behind closed doors taking care of my mom. It was useful that I didn't have any friends or other relatives to speak of; it made the move a lot easier. I had no one to lie to, no one to leave behind. No one at all.

I can hear voices outside my dorm and I freeze. It's going to take a long time for the nerves to settle, knowing he's still out there, that he has a connection to this resort of all places. I only heard parts of Connor's conversation with Bianchi. I know something's going to happen to Morelli, but I don't know exactly what, and I'm not sure I want to. Watching that poor man die right before my eyes was enough; I don't need to be responsible for the death of another, no matter how worthy of it he might be.

I recognize Connor's voice and let out a long breath. He knocks at the door and I go to unlock it. I see Luca's back disappearing down the corridor before Connor hustles me back into the room.

"He's gone?" I ask him, unable to conceal the fear in my voice.

"Yeah, he's gone." Connor strides past me to the window and yanks the curtains closed. I hadn't even thought to do that.

"What's going to happen to him?"

When he turns back to face me, I notice his jaw is set firm, and his whole body is braced as though ready for an attack.

"You don't need to know. Let's just say, he won't be coming back here again."

His chest is heaving up and down, as though he's trying to contain something.

"Are you mad at me?" I whisper.

"Yes, Tawny. I am." The words come out in a low growl.

"Why?"

"You should have stayed in the fucking storage unit like I told you to."

"There were children on the beach," I reply, my own anger rising to the surface. It feels as though all my emotions are colliding and need to be released somehow. "*Children*. Who'd sailed hundreds of miles to get here."

"It doesn't matter. Your life was in danger."

"In no more danger than theirs."

"You have no idea what you're talking about."

"Don't I?" I snap. "I'm the one in witness protection, Connor. You don't think I know when I'm in danger?"

"Oh, I think you do, but I don't think you know what Stefano Morelli was capable of. If I hadn't been there when he found you, you wouldn't be alive right now. You should have stayed where you were."

"Tell me Connor, are you more angry that I had a close brush with a guy who wants me dead, or that I disobeyed you? Because I'm afraid it might be the latter."

"Are you kidding me?" His boots land heavily on the floor as he stomps across the room, stopping only feet away from me. "You scared the crap out of me back there. I had no idea what was going to happen to you. All I knew was I had to protect you. You'd told me what was really going on and I needed to keep you safe. You have no idea how it felt to see you come running out of the fucking mangroves like that. If you don't do what I say, I can't protect you."

"What if I don't need protecting, Connor?" I shout.

"You could have fooled me. You were a wreck when I found you in the unit."

"I don't only mean tonight," I snap, taking a step towards him.

He glares at me, his jaw clenched.

"You can't protect me all the time, Connor."

"Yes, I can protect you, Tawny," he replies, his voice eerie with conviction. "And I will."

"I don't need it, Connor. I'm a grown woman. You have to stop treating me like a porcelain doll. I can look after myself."

His nostrils are flaring and I'm bunching my own shirt with my fists out of anger and frustration.

"When have I ever treated you like a porcelain doll?"

It's too late to feel embarrassed now.

"When you fuck me, Connor. That's when. You hardly touch me. It's as though you're not even there. I want to feel you. I want you to smother me. I don't want gentle; I want hard. I don't want you to control every touch and every move. I want you lose control. Completely. Just once. Just…"

I don't get to finish my speech because my back is on the floor, the air knocked out of my lungs as he comes crashing down onto me, his hands ripping at my shirt and skirt, his mouth attached to mine like some wild animal. I can't move, I can't think. I hear the rip of his fly, feel his hands push through my hair, pulling at the roots, pinning me down. His knees kick mine apart and I can feel him right there. He gives me no warning as he barrels into me, bare, with a loud cry. I'm full and searing but the feeling of lust and triumph overrides everything else. He's not being gentle, he's not afraid to break me, and he's going to damn well try.

He stills, panting into my ear, as though he too needs to recover from the sudden togetherness.

"Thank you," I whisper into his neck.

"You're not going to thank me for this," he growls.

A surge of lust ripples right through my core.

"You want me to lose control? This is it."

He pulls back and in the corner of my eye I can see every

muscle in his thighs engage, then *bam*. He embeds himself even deeper and I gasp his name.

He reaches around his neck to grab my hand and pins it above my head, then does the same with the other. My arms are outstretched above me and held fast, my two small hands inside one of his, then he reaches down to my ass and pulls it up off the floor. I can see the veins popping out of his biceps with the strain, then he powers forward into me, flexing his hips at an angle to reach every sensitive spot I own. With each grind he gasps and curses through gritted teeth. I am burning up as the flat of his perfect stomach grazes across my clit with each thrust. Our eyes are locked—his determined, mine triumphant. We challenge each other to go the furthest, but I can't move; he has me pinned and lifted while he fucks me with absolutely no control at all.

"Connor!" I gasp. I can't stop the ball of fire rolling. He drops my ass to the floor and fingers my clit, slants his mouth across the soft skin around my jaw and bites. I explode into a million pieces while he rocks into me rhythmically, drawing out my climax, and drags his teeth down my throat. Before I can gather my senses, I feel emptied, then turned onto my left side then filled again. Connor lifts my right leg up high and hooks it over his arm as he drives into me. His fingers reach up to my breasts and he kneads them, not gently. When he finds my nipples, he pinches them sharply and I jump under his touch.

"Is this hard enough for you?" He growls into my ear.

I can hardly speak but I manage a moan.

"This is nothing," he promises, and a ripple of lust runs through me again. His hand strokes down my breasts, down to my belly and then to my pelvis where he pushes me backwards into his thrusts, reaching depths of me I haven't felt before. He curls a leg over mine, pinning me in place while he fucks me with short, sharp strokes. He's completely bare and I can feel all of him.

"Then give me everything," I say, in a low voice.

He growls again and deepens his thrusts. Then I hear "fuck" and I'm rolled onto my front and pulled up onto my forearms and knees. Each thrust now hits my very edge, causing the pleasure to mingle with pain. He drives into me relentlessly, as I battle to stay upright.

"This is me," he says, panting. "Is this what you wanted?"

"Yes," I gasp. I'm flung over again so I'm on my back facing him. His knees push mine apart and he slides inside, my opening stretched and ready. I reach up and take his face in my hands, watching his jaw clench and unclench with each hard thrust. I can feel the orgasm balling in my core. "Don't stop, Connor."

"Are you going to come like this?"

I can hardly speak.

"Answer me."

"Yes! Oh God, Connor."

"That's it, sweetheart. I want to feel you come while I fuck you properly."

He yanks one of my legs up and over his shoulder, the new angle propelling him into an even deeper place. I yelp with the sudden sharp sensation. He reaches a thumb down to rub my clit as I buck beneath him, trying to find some comfort in the sudden ache.

"Connor…" I don't know what I need to say. The combination of sharp pain and urgent need is overwhelming. Before I know what's going on, my back arches and I cry out. Connor continues rubbing me and driving himself forward, hard and relentless, the sensations barreling through me like a flooding tunnel. I arch again and this time he brings both hands to my waist pulling my stomach up towards him, finding yet another new angle. He continues to fuck me hard while I hang limp below him.

Then, he's coming. He's coming and he isn't pulling out. A roar comes from deep within as he fills me completely, my back still arched, my head and shoulders resting on the bed. He continues to move as he lowers my back, making me more comfortable, and he brings his lips down to mine. He kisses me soft and slow, a complete contrast to the aggression he just spent the last fifteen minutes displaying. I know he's come and he's spent but he keeps moving inside me, as we slowly kiss the life out of each other.

When he eventually stops and reluctantly pulls his lips from mine, he looks like a different person. His brow is tense, his eyes almost black and his cheeks are hollowed.

"Connor?"

He doesn't say anything. In fact, I get the haunting feeling he hasn't even heard me. His eyes are staring right through me to the bed sheets.

"Connor, are you ok?"

He pulls out of me and sits back, staring not at me anymore but square ahead, at the wall. His breath is harsh as it drags through his lungs, in and out. His chest is rigid and his fists are clenched so tightly they're as white as the sandy beach.

I am frozen to the spot. I don't know what this is. Is he having an extreme reaction to what we've just done? Or is this… is he having a flashback?

I push myself backwards slowly until I'm at the head of the bed, a safe distance from him. He's still staring at the wall but he's shaking now. I knew my heart would break if he decided he couldn't do this with me anymore, but I can feel it falling apart right now, just watching him going through something so far away I can't reach him.

I have a dreaded feeling something is about to happen, so I gently lower my legs to the floor. I accidentally knock my cell to the floor. It makes a sound which turns out to be a lot louder than I expected against the unnerving silence in the room. I don't even get a chance to turn back to face Connor when I hear him roar behind me. I leap off the bed but I'm too late. His arms are around me, dragging me back along the bed towards him. This is not the rough, untethered touch I wanted from him earlier; this is something else. He's crying now and pawing his hands over me. My eyes fill with tears at the sight of this man. He's like a broken vase whose paint has worn away, in this instant showing every single one of his cracks.

"Connor, it's ok. Connor…"

I grip his shoulders in a bid to shake him out of this trance but he's immovable. He's still gripping me hard and swiping at my face, his eyes erratic and wild.

The serenity of fullness I felt only minutes ago has gone and the man who'd fucked me the way I wanted it, finally, is gone too. It dawns on me, this is my fault. I made him lose control and it's caused this.

Tears roll down my cheeks as I put my palms to his cheeks.

"I'm sorry…" I hiccup. "Connor, I'm so sorry."

He continues to moan like an injured animal, his mouth forming words that don't see the light of day, then he drops his head to my chest, his hands firm on my shoulders.

I'm scared and rigid. I know he's not in control of himself right now, but the tears are coming fast and I can't stop them. Slowly, he moves his head up to my neck and buries it there. He's still, apart from the tell-tale rocking of a man crying. I realize whatever it was that just happened to him, it's over. I wrap my arms around him tightly because I know the minute he pulls away he's never going to come back.

We lay like this for what seems like an eternity and I will every second to slow. He is heavy and hot and cold. His sweat is drenching me but I wouldn't change anything in this moment—I want it to last forever. It want it to always be 'now' not 'then'.

"I love you."

The words have been on the edge of my lips for weeks, and I let them fall out now because I have absolutely nothing left to lose; he's already gone.

I sense him wiping his eyes, then he slides off me, turning immediately towards the window, then he sits on the edge of the bed facing away. This view, the sight of his back, coated in sweat but alive with the beautiful prey bird spreading its wings across him—I don't even remember him removing his shirt—send me hurtling back to the first day I met him. He'd insisted on making me stand and watch while he rebuilt that damn wall. And knowing what I now know about Connor and his role in this resort, I am confident he didn't need to do that. Pretty much anyone would have dropped what they were doing for him, to help. It hits me. He was fighting this then, and I've been chipping away at him selfishly ever since. And now look at what I've done. I feel like the devil himself for what I've made him do, so when he utters the words, "this can't happen again," with unwavering conviction, I simply nod.

He bends down and picks up his torn clothes, then walks to the door. I expect him to turn around and look at me at least once, but he doesn't. He just walks out.

# CHAPTER THIRTY-TWO

onnor

"Connor, you in there?"

Carter's voice wrenches itself through the door frame.

"I'll see you in the office," I say, my voice straining after the tears it has shed.

"Everything ok?"

"Yeah. I won't be long."

"Ok, man."

I hear his footsteps as he walks away down the corridor to the stairs and I look down at the envelope nestled between my fingers.

I feel empty, finally. I've just spent the last two hours pouring everything I've got into this letter because I can't face her after that.

I love her too. It's a different kind of love to the love I've felt before. With Clarisse it felt more like security, like the familiarity of home. With Tawny it's raw. Before I lost control and found myself back in Iraq on my hands and knees, trying to wipe the blood and sand out of Sullivan's face, it was whole body need. It was as though I needed to immerse every single part of myself inside her, around her, within her.

When I came around after seeing again only the upper part of Sullivan's body intact, and found myself sobbing into her skin, I felt as though a limb of my own had been removed, and the pain was searing. This limb was located right in the center of my chest, and it was bleeding. It is still bleeding now.

The letter is me in black and white. My past, my present, my future, as I have meticulously crafted it. It is my why. Why I can never be hers. Why I have nothing to give anyone, because I gave it all up when I lost my friends, my colleagues, my family that day. Why I need to keep my promise to stay away from her for good. In the letter I beg. I'm not beneath it now—she's seen me at my worst and I know she understands. I beg for her to stay away. I've already demonstrated to myself, to her and to everyone around us that I can't keep away from Tawny Graham—I have no control when it comes to her. I need her to be strong for both our sakes.

I also tell her I'm sorry, for everything. She's already been to hell and back with the loss of her parents and the trauma of witnessing a murder on her own doorstep, and last night I gave her a complimentary trip down that memory lane, on the house.

What I can't tell her and what I can't ever think about again is that I have never felt as close to anyone as I did last night when I was fucking her exactly as I'd always wanted to —urgently, fully, uninhibited. Our bodies moved together like they'd been molded that way. Instead of holding back and barely grazing her skin with my fingers and lips, I truly felt her. I buried my hands into the soft skin of her ass, I felt her hair whip across my shoulders when I flipped her over, I felt her nails leave delectable tracks down my back when she came. And when she came... and when I came... we were raw and together, with nothing else between us. I felt her heart and I felt her soul. And that was when it happened.

I'm not stupid. I know that moment when I became closer to Tawny than I've gotten to anyone in a long time, opened up a small window I've managed to keep closed ever since I landed on this island. It let in light, along with a stream of demons that just won't let go of me.

I've never felt such intensity as I felt there in that room with her. Both from the sex and the elation that followed, and from the flashback to that fateful day in Iraq.

It was the most exquisite experience and yet the most terrifying. I can't go through it again. I know she understands now why I can't, but I owe it to her to give her a chance to understand me. And to understand why she never stood a chance herself.

I push myself up to standing, grab my jacket and head out the door. As I pass Tawny's, I slip the letter under it. It will be the last time I am so close to her, even with a door between us. My chest tightens and I shut it down, push it away, take a deep breath, and keep walking.

---

TWO DAYS HAVE PASSED since that horrifying night. Tawny must have read my letter because I haven't seen her since. I don't know if she's been deliberately avoiding me, like I asked her to, or if she's taken time off, or if she's sick. I can't ask anyone either. I told Carter to make it explicitly clear to the guys that no one is to mention her name, and no one is to ask any fucking questions. So, I can hardly break my own rule and start asking them how she is, even though she's all I can think about.

I tunnel my vision into the steps I'm taking towards the Grand House. Eric is already waiting on the porch with a whiskey in his hand. It isn't even five o'clock. But I guess, when you're that rich and you have a team of security guards running your show for you, you can drink whatever you want, whenever you want.

"Mr. Starling," I say, mounting the wooden steps towards him.

"Ah, Connor, good afternoon my son."

I cringe inwardly and take the seat he's gesturing to, then he turns and gives me his full attention.

"I haven't seen you properly since the night of the opening." His face is serious, more serious than I've ever seen it, and it's unusual and unnerving.

"Did you have a good time?" I'm hoping my sudden nerves don't show. "It certainly looked as though you, and Maria and the girls were enjoying yourselves."

"Oh, yes," he says, waving a hand but still not smiling. "They had a wonderful time, we all did. But that's not what I want to talk to you about."

My chest freezes. Has he seen something? The logbook? One of our shipments? Maybe someone saw the boat and told him we'd chaperoned a bunch of immigrants across the island. That would mean a certain end to this life for me and the guys. "Is something bothering you?"

He rests a chubby chin on a chubby hand. "Yes, Connor, there is."

I take a deep, controlled breath and swallow. "What is it?"

"I'm feeling a little, um… shall we say… anxious."

"What about? It was a roaring success. Have you seen the latest press reports? And Vanity Fair is running a piece online later day, so I heard."

"Well, yes, exactly. It was a roaring success. That's what I'm afraid of."

I'm confused. Did he think the event was too successful?

"I'm afraid that we can't follow it up."

I concentrate hard on not letting the sigh of relief escape my mouth, so I laugh lightly instead.

"Is that what you're worried about? Mr. Starling, you have nothing to worry about. The whole point of this casino is to put Starling Key on the map, take it up a level. We're the only luxury resort on the Keys with a casino to rival Bellagio. We don't have to top that. We're done—at least for a few years, anyway. Our focus now should be on maintaining the experience that guests are already queuing up for. We don't need to break our backs trying to outdo ourselves. We're the best, and no one else is anywhere close, so you can relax."

He does, visibly, and I allow myself to also. I'm on edge and I know why. But I just need time. Time to get her out of my head. Time to focus on the things that matter. Time to get my sanity back and my form on track. Then everything will be ok.

"Ok, Connor. I trust you."

He leans back in his chair and stretches his arms and his whiskey overhead.

"Maybe I need a vacation. I've been thinking about it."

*A vacation? The man already lives in paradise.*

"Where were you thinking of going?

"Well, I haven't been home in a while and I know the girls would love to see their mother and father during term time. And I haven't seen Europe for an absolute age. Maybe I'll treat the Mrs."

"We have had a lot going on these last few months, and you know we have everything under control here."

"Yes, I know. Ok, well maybe we'll head back to the UK for a traditional white Christmas, not that it *ever* snows in England at Christmas—that's a total myth."

Christmas on the Key without Starling looking over my shoulder. No Tawny distracting me. Freedom to run the place uninterrupted, exactly as I want to.

"Sounds like it could be just the break you need."

After a short debrief, I leave Starling contemplating his forthcoming voyage and head back to the office. I'm about to walk through reception to the office when Carter stands in front of me, blocking my path.

"What's up?" I sigh.

"You're coming with me," he replies, his eyes deadly serious.

"Is everything ok?"

"No, Connor, it's not."

He turns and I follow him back out of the main reception into the café where the rest of the guys are sitting, waiting, apparently for me.

"Did I miss something?"

"Yeah," he says, without turning back. "A fucking trick." He pulls out a seat. "Sit."

I'm about to pull rank and tell him to screw himself, but then I see the faces on Isaac, Luca, Hud and Jax. They're serious too.

"Has someone died?"

"Might as well have," Carter says, cryptically.

"Ok, I don't have a lot of time for this." I sit anyway.

When they have my attention, Isaac is the first to speak.

"Tawny's leaving."

My chest constricts so tightly I can barely breathe, but I hold myself together.

"None of us know what the hell happened the night of the opening but the two of you are broken, and we can't sit by and watch it anymore."

Carter picks up. "I know you asked us not to mention her name because you need to get over her, but we can't stand by any longer and watch the two of you slope about, shadows of your former selves, not eating, not talking, looking pale as dust. It's no way to live."

"You can stop her going," Luca says, hopefully. "She won't be out of here until tomorrow. She's staying tonight, you can still talk her out of it."

I'm still holding my breath because I don't know how to tell them to back off in a way they'll respect and accept. All I can do is be honest. And that doesn't come easily to a guy who's been their leader, their rock, for five years—a guy hardened by the military, a guy bold enough to funnel money from the resort owner to help other people get by. I'm not the guy who breaks down in tears on top of a woman. I'm not the guy who shoots his load into the woman he wants more than anything, then falls apart. I look around at their faces. They're not mocking me, or accusing me; they're genuinely concerned.

Fuck it.

I breathe out slowly, then reply.

"I can't stop her. I want her to leave. I need her to leave."

"Why?" Hudson says, genuinely perplexed. "Don't you like her?"

"Yes, I do." I train my eyes on my interlaced fingers resting on the table. "That's the problem. I like her too much. The night of the opening, after she ran down to the beach and got held up at gunpoint, I flipped. I couldn't bear the thought

I didn't know where she was, she might not be safe, I couldn't protect her. She really stood up to me, told me she didn't want to be protected. I got the impression I was being a bit too 'delicate' with her."

I don't need to explain to my boys what that means. They know.

"Anyway, we… you know."

Nods around the table.

"Right after I… you know… Well, right after that, I had the worst flashback I've had in four years. And she saw all of it."

I finally look up and see their faces again. This time there's genuine sadness in them. They know what happens to me when I have flashbacks. They saw what those memories did to me before I learned how to control them. Carter keeps his mouth shut, because he knows more than the others. He knows that exactly four years ago, I tried to end it after a particularly traumatic episode. He found me prepping a boat, a loaded gun in the pocket of my shorts.

"She isn't going to judge you, man," Isaac says. "She'll understand."

"That's irrelevant," I continue. "I get them nearly every time we're together, ok? I don't even have to sleep with her, I can just be getting my rocks off thinking about her and it happens."

Their faces freeze as they tried to process the horror of what I've been going through.

"She can't be in my life. It's as simple as that."

None of them speak. Carter tips his chair back and drags his hands across his face and up through his hair, with a frustrated moan.

"We had no idea," Isaac says, quietly.

I sigh and shake my head. "I know you all want the best

for me. This is it. I can only function when I'm alone, when I have no distractions. I've said it all along. Part of me knew something like this would happen."

"So, you've told yourself so," Carter says, looking at me sideways.

"What's that supposed to mean?"

"Well, you conveniently proved yourself right," he shrugs. "You knew you wouldn't be able to handle falling for her, so now these episodes have started back up, you know for sure, so that's that."

"Carter…" Isaac warns. He can probably warm his hands on the blood that's boiling in my veins.

"What the fuck are you getting at?" I demand.

Carter slams his fist on the table and faces me. "It's a fucking excuse, Connor. You're using these flashbacks as an excuse to push her away and not be happy. If I could have the chance you've got, I'd be grabbing it with both hands…"

"Oh, that's what this is about, is it?" I growl, getting to my feet. "You couldn't have Lucy, so you're trying to live your life through me?"

Carter springs to his feet too, knocking over his chair. Isaac stands up, his hands poised to keep us apart.

"Do not bring Lucy into this," he snarls. "This has nothing to do with her and everything to do with you and your fucking obsession with everything being perfect, and this ridiculous need to control everything. You have a problem, man, and it has nothing to do with Tawny Graham. You need to fix it."

"Don't fucking tell me what my problem is, Carter. Right now, my problem is you. I need you to get out of my face."

"Because you can't face up to what I'm saying, right? You know you need help. You've always known it. But you're too proud to get it and stick at it."

My fingers flex at my sides and Isaac's arms widen.

I keep my voice level. "I already got help, and everything has been fine until she showed up, and you know it. The problem is fixable and that's how: she needs to leave."

Carter sighs and his shoulders relax.

"You didn't get help, Connor. I called your therapist to see how it was going because I was worried about you. She said, after the first time, you never showed up."

If I wasn't already steaming, the fact Carter had been spying on me, tips me over the edge.

"It's none of your business whether I went or not. I don't fucking need help. I know exactly how to stop the episodes, as you call them, and if, as you say, the cause of them is leaving the island tomorrow, you can bet your ass I'll be fucking fine."

I kick my own chair and turn to walk away, but I spin back around and face them all.

"I appreciate your concern but it isn't warranted. Now, you should all get back to work. We've just wasted twenty minutes."

Then I storm out of the café feeling the eyes of every staff member as I go.

# CHAPTER THIRTY-THREE

 awny

"DRINK UP, darling, the champagne isn't getting any fizzier," Barbie says, holding a bottle of Veuve Cliquot over my glass.

"I can't get drunk," I protest. "I have a long drive ahead of me tomorrow."

"I think that's her plan," Esme says through the corner of her mouth at me. "It's a delaying tactic—she doesn't want you to go. None of us do."

I do as I'm told and down the last bit of champagne before allowing Barbie to top me up.

"But I'm serious, no more after this. I can't be crashing into any more walls."

Barbie sniffs. "Ah, the infamous collision. I knew then you were going to be a special lady." She wipes a finger under her eye. "I still don't understand why you want to leave all this behind. This is paradise. And you love your job; everyone can see it. And you have a family here now. Why are you moving all the way to California where you don't know anyone? You'll be so lonely."

I only decided on California a couple of days ago. I knew I had to go somewhere and I knew I didn't want that somewhere to be New Jersey. So, I thought, if I could go anywhere in the States I wanted, where would it be? The answer came immediately. San Francisco. I've been fascinated with the place for as long as I can remember and now there's nothing holding me back—I can go anywhere I like. So, I'm going there. The sale of Mom's house left me with enough money to lease a small place while I find a job, and the road trip will do me good. I'm not planning to drive all the way. Maybe to Atlanta, then fly the rest of the way. It's not like I have a life's worth of stuff to haul along with me.

Carter broke the news to me that Morelli won't ever be a problem now. According to Hudson, the guy didn't even get out of the trunk before Mario put a gun to his forehead and pulled the trigger. Even so, I still think moving to the other side of the country might help me feel safer. As far away from the Bianchi's as I can get. If I don't have Connor protecting me, I need to be able to protect myself.

"I'll be lonely wherever I go, at first. But I'll meet people. I won't love them as much as I love you guys, but I'll make friends eventually."

"Well, ok, I wasn't going to say anything because I was hoping we might talk you out of it, but seeing as you're determined to go, let me at least help you get set up in California."

Esme and I both look at Barbie. "What do you mean?"

"I have friends there. Friends with apartments going spare. I'm sure someone will let you stay a few months for free while you find your feet."

"Barbie, no, I couldn't possibly…"

I'm silenced when Barbie takes my hands in hers and

holds my gaze. I'm reminded of what a formidable woman she is, a trait apparently not dimmed by her advancing years.

"Listen to me. You have brought life to this island. It was fun before, but… Fitz and I have never had so much fun as we had during all those trips you arranged for my birthday week. You really took the time to get to know us, to ask what we think and what we want—you'd be amazed at how many people assume that when you hit a certain age, you're incapable of deciding anything for yourself. But not you. You see us as the bright young things we still feel we are, and that's so rare. I want to repay you by helping you get set up in San Francisco. Let me do that for you."

I can barely speak, and not just because Barbie's offer is so generous, but because I had no idea I'd made such a big impact on their lives. I figured all I'd done was organize a few boat trips. All of a sudden, I feel incredibly sad to be leaving them.

"That's so kind of you and I really appreciate it. What would I do without you guys?"

"You'll be just fine," Barbie replies. "You'll get a nice place, you'll make a new life for yourself, just like you did here. Don't underestimate what you are capable of."

"I don't know…" I shake my head.

Barbie gave me a look. "You know, Eleanor Roosevelt once said, 'a woman is like a tea bag. You never know how strong she is until she finds herself in hot water.' You're gonna show the world what you're made of."

"What will you do when you're there?" Esme asks.

I lean back against my hands and let my toes curl and uncurl in the sun. I'll miss this heat. Sometimes it's been intoxicating and claustrophobic, challenging, but it's forced me to acclimate to a place I'll remember for the rest of my life.

"I'll get a job, find my feet, then I might look around at some of the local colleges, see if anything interests me. I've enjoyed arranging events for you guys. Maybe I could train up properly to do something like that."

"Will you keep in touch?" Fitz asks, hopefully.

"Of course!" I sit up and pull him into a hug, remembering how frail he's become since his fall. "I'll write lots of letters. Stay in touch the old-fashioned way."

"That would be wonderful."

"Is anyone going to mention the elephant in the room?" Esme asks, cautiously.

Damn. I was hoping I wouldn't have to talk about Connor.

"What about him?" Barbie spits.

"Please don't be mad at him," I say. "This was my decision. I was the one who came along and trampled all over his life. He always said he wasn't the relationship type; it's my own fault for getting in deep. And it was my decision to leave."

"Not the relationship type. I don't believe that for a second," Barbie says, taking a long drag of her cigarette.

I should have known Barbie would cling on to that part and I wish I hadn't said that, because now she's going to think badly of Connor. I haven't told them the half of it. I haven't told them about the boat with the children, I haven't told them the real reason I'm here, I haven't told them about Connor's flashbacks. I haven't told them about the way he held me so tightly I could barely breathe.

"Well, if you care about me at all, you'll be nice to him, ok?"

"Civil," Esme says.

I sigh and shake my head.

"Don't worry, Tawny," Fitz says. "I'll make sure no one takes this out on Connor."

"Thanks Fitz," I smile. "Now, I don't want to spend my last hour moping about. Is anyone going to open that picnic basket, because I am starving, and I need to mop up some of these bubbles."

Barbie's face softens. "Of course, darling. I made extra so you can take some with you on your road trip." She opens the basket and takes out her famous crab quiche. I smile, remembering the first time she'd made it, for a beach picnic she and Fitz invited me to when I first arrived.

"Ooh," I say, rubbing my hands together. "Delicious."

"Well, it's enough that you're moving away. I can't have you wasting away too."

———

I INSIST on saying goodbye to them this evening, because I want to make a quick getaway in the morning. Also, goodbyes make me extremely emotional and I don't want to be driving back up the highway with tears streaming down my cheeks. After we've dropped Barbie and Fitz back at Reef Street and exchanged salty tears and not-so-airborne air kisses, I stand outside block 8 with Esme's arms clamped around me.

"Shell is going to be so pissed she didn't get to say 'bye,'" she sobs into my shoulder.

"I'll write her," I say. "I'll write you both. And you can come visit me."

She finally releases me and takes my face in her hands.

"Will you ever come back here?"

I swallow and shake my head slowly. "I doubt it."

She drops her voice.

"What really happened, Tawny? There has to be more to it than you just deciding to end it. I saw the way you two were around each other. It wasn't just some fling; you guys were in love. It doesn't make sense that you could both let that go so easily."

I take a breath and think for a moment.

"You're right, Esme. There is more to it, but I can't tell you. I can't tell anyone. You just have to trust me, and know that I'm doing the right thing."

"For him…"

"No, for both of us. He really can't be with me—I know that for a fact, and I'm ok with it. But I can't be reminded of it every waking hour of every day. I'm just really glad I met him, and all of you. Especially you." I pull her into another hug and this time it's my turn to squeeze the air out of her. "Thank you for making it so easy for me to settle in. You've been such a special friend to me."

We finally part and say our goodbyes, then I go back to my dorm, have one final shower and lay down in the bed I will always remember as the one I shared so many times with Connor Johnson, my first ever love, and I go to sleep.

---

I WAKE at six am before my alarm goes off, pull on a pair of jeans and a t-shirt, and tie my hair up in a bun. I don't even run a brush through it; I just want to get going before I have a chance to run into anyone. I throw the last few items into my bag—toothbrush, face cloth, towel, deodorant—then zip it up and carry it to the door. I tug my jacket down from the hook and take one last look around. I will never forget this place. It's where I found sanctuary and safety when I needed it; it's where I passed out after long, tiring but rewarding days at work; it's where I discovered all the secrets my body had long hidden from me, as Connor kissed every inch, devoured my mouth and penetrated my core; and it's where I finally discovered the truth about me, about him, about us. I've only lived within the walls of this room for three months, but they've been the best three months of my life, even if the ending isn't what I'd hoped for.

I drag my eyes back to the door, open it and walk through, hearing it close softly as I leave it all behind.

onnor

I WATCH as she heaves her bag into the trunk and closes it before getting into the driver's seat. There's no sound on the CCTV so I can't hear the engine grumble to life, but I watch as the archaic black Chevy backs out of its parking space and ambles towards the exit, carrying Tawny Graham back to the very place I first laid eyes on her. The gate opens automatically, letting her drive through. The Chevy hesitates for a few seconds, then ploughs forward, up the ramp and off towards the highway, out of sight of the camera. I stare at the empty view for a good twenty minutes, half hoping the Chevy makes a U turn somewhere and comes back down the ramp, but even as I think that, I know it wouldn't make any difference. Tawny is doing the kindest and most compassionate thing anyone has ever done for me; she's leaving. She's putting my cold, lifeless heart before her own warm, loving, broken one. In this long, excruciating moment, I hate myself more than I've ever hated anyone in my life.

---

THREE HOURS HAVE PASSED since she left and I haven't moved. I'm still sitting in my office staring blankly into space. Only when someone bangs at the door do I make a conscious effort to snap out of the self-inflicted trance.

"Yeah."

The door opens and Carter hovers there.

"You ok?"

"Yeah, fine," I lie.

He studies my face, looking for a small sign of weakness, of vulnerability. "It's not too late to go after her."

"No, Carter," I say, firmly. "It's over. It's for the best. I don't want to hear her name mentioned again, ok?"

He grinds his teeth. "Fine. I won't mention it, but I can't promise every other fucker on the resort will comply. Tawny made friends here. There are a lot of people who didn't want to see her go. Only you."

"I didn't want her to go."

"Oh, so you wanted her to stay, so you could get your kicks out of seeing her around while she had to endure the fact you wanted nothing to do with her? That's even worse, Connor."

Carter…" I warn. He's really pushing it. As a friend and as an employee.

"No," he snaps, stepping into the room. "I respect you. You know I do. I respect you as a boss, as a friend, as a brother. But I'm disappointed in you, man. I'm disappointed that you despise yourself so much, you're prepared to let someone like that go. And you can't fool me, Connor. I know you fell for her."

"I don't despise myself," I say, quietly.

"Why else would you let her go? Don't give me that baggage bullshit. Baggage can be fixed any time. Life isn't a game of poker. You can't just keep getting dealt a fresh hand every time the last one let you down. You get one hand to find your soulmate, and you just folded."

*Soulmate?* I look at him and see the disappointment clearly in his face.

"What do you expect me to do?"

"See someone. Get therapy. Get meds. Do whatever you have to do so you can hold it together and be with her at the same time."

"I don't know, man." I look down at the floor. I feel empty. And despite everything I've achieved for this resort, even the casino opening that, even though it wasn't without drama, was still a resounding success, I feel like a complete failure.

"I need some space, ok?" I glance up at him and hope he knows I'm spent. I can't argue with him right now. I just need to be alone.

He sighs, knowing there's no more he can say. "Fine. Whatever you need."

———

I CONTINUE to sit and stare into space for probably another hour when another knock comes at the door, this time it's a tentative one.

"Yeah?"

The door opens a crack and a small eye pokes through the gap. I sigh, inwardly. I don't want to deal with anyone today.

"Can I come in?" The door opens a little more and I realize it's Fitz Bellamy.

"Sure." I suppress another heavy sigh as I gesture to the chair opposite.

He hobbles across the room and sits down. I notice he's looking much older after his fall, and I make a mental note to make sure the Reef Street team keep an eye on him, that he gets enough good food and vitamins.

"How can I help you?" I force a smile.

"Oh, I didn't come here for help, son," he says, and I baulk at the word. It doesn't particularly register when Starling calls me 'son' but when Fitz does, it feels more authentic. He's closer to my dad's age, for a start. And he gives me that look that says he's lived a longer life than I have and is ten times wiser for it. I brace myself for whatever is coming next and hope it's not a lecture.

"I came to give you something," he says, surprising me. He reaches inside his jacket, pulls out a small envelope and pushes it towards me. He watches as I pick it up and cautiously tip the contents onto the desk. I draw in a breath as the pain in my heart intensifies. Tawny Graham is staring up at me.

"I hope you don't think I'm overstepping the mark by giving you these," he says, watching as I pick up each of the three photographs and look at them in turn. "I took them not long after she first got here. The sun was setting, the light was perfect and her face was just so vibrant and full of love. We never stopped laughing that evening, and Barbie and I remember it as the first time in a long time we didn't feel like the old people we are."

I study the contours of her face. Her eyes are creased as she laughs open-mouthed and the breeze flips her long hair across her face, glinting with warmth. My heart aches.

"She was a credit to this island, Mr. Johnson. You did a good thing in hiring her…"

"I didn't hire her…"

"Well then, her arrival here was even more serendipitous, don't you think? Look, I'm not here to judge, and I know there's a lot more to why she's gone than she will ever reveal…"

I'm suddenly overwhelmed with gratitude—she doesn't need to keep my secret safe. Even though her departure could reflect badly on her, she's still chosen not to reveal why she's decided to leave.

"…but I will say this. I have spent the last fifty years trying to convince the woman of my dreams to love me back. I would give anything for her to feel the same way I do, even for one day. But I've learned to live with it. I've learned to accept that I will be alone for the rest of my life. Even though she's only next door, she isn't in my arms. It's caused me physical pain and I've learned to live with it, but I would never wish it on anyone else.

"Son…" He waits until I look up at him before he continues. "I don't know what it is you've been through, but it must have been pure hell for you to give up someone like Tawny, just so you can fight it or live with it on your own. But believe me when I say this, living through hell is a lot easier with someone you love at your side, than it is without."

I don't speak. I can't. I look back down at the photographs and realize my fingers are white where I've been gripping them so hard the blood flow to my fingers has stopped. I glance up and Fitz has noticed too.

"You do so much here to make other people happy," he says softly. "Don't you think it's about time you did that for yourself?"

A thick hard lump has formed in my throat. Then, before I can stop him, he gets to his feet, grabs my face and pulls it towards him. He kisses the top of my head and releases it. A tear falls down my cheek from nowhere.

"No one's judging you, Connor. Not even your best buddy out there. Everyone wants you to be happy. The only person who doesn't, it seems, is you."

Then Fitz hobbles back to the door, holds it open and turns to look over his shoulder.

"I know you'll make the right decision, son. Just don't leave it too late."

Then he's gone.

I put the pictures down on the desk and drop my face into my hands. What the fuck have I done? Everyone else has been able to see it but me. And now, what's replacing the debilitating sense of loss is embarrassment. I am such a fucking idiot. I'm also scared—petrified. I'm slowly realizing I've sent away the one person I need more than anyone, yet I don't know how I can handle the ramifications of having her back. And that's if she'll even take me. I'm suddenly over-whelmed into paralysis. I raise my head again and look at the wall, then I'm suddenly reminded of an F Scott Fitzgerald quote that is frighteningly apt: *The loneliest moment in someone's life is when they are watching their whole world fall apart, and all they can do is stare blankly.*

I'm relieved when my phone rings. It's an unknown number but I don't care. I'm grateful for the distraction.

"Connor Johnson."

"Just the person."

"Ange?"

"Yes, it's me."

"Hey, how are you doing?"

"I was doing fine until about a half hour ago, but now I'd say I'm not totally fine. If anything, I'm confused."

"What are you talking about?"

"There's a beautiful woman sitting in my restaurant who looks like a shadow of the one you brought here several weeks ago."

"Tawny? Tawny's at the diner?" I don't know why but my heart is doing somersaults and my fingers are scratching about for my keys.

"What the hell did you do to her, Connor?" She has her voice lowered, and I suspect it's so Tawny can't hear.

"I've been an ass," I say, taking two strides to the door and flinging it open.

"Um, I'll say," she continues. "She said you two had a thing. I was not surprised. When I saw you two in here it was obvious. The chemistry coming off you guys kept our damn ovens alight. But she said you're finished now, even though it's obvious she's completely in love with you, and I'm really not sure she should be driving in the state she's in. She's defending you, Connor. She won't have a bad word said against you, but no one gets this upset of their own volition. What did you do?"

"I let her go," I say, reaching the main exit and shoving my way through. I break into a run.

"You know I love you, Connor, even though you hardly ever come to see us anymore…"

"Do me a favor," I interrupt, climbing into my car. "Can you keep her there for a few hours?"

"What? How? What do want me to say?"

"Nothing. Don't tell her anything. Ask her to help with the open mic night or something. She loves all that."

"Are you going to make it worth her while, Connor? Because if you're not…"

"Trust me, Ange. Just keep her there please. I gotta go." I hang up, start the engine, grab the steering wheel and spin the car, sending gravel flying into the air behind me.

# CHAPTER THIRTY-FIVE

awny

IT WAS a relief when Ange asked me to stay the night. After she disappeared for some team huddle or something, she came back out and told me one of her staff members had called in sick and could I help out with the open mic event. Truth be told, I couldn't face the drive to Miami. I'd cried so much on the way here, I could barely see the road ahead, and I'm so tired I could curl up into a ball right here in the diner and fall straight to sleep. Instead, I force myself to stay awake as I copy out the Specials menu onto sheets of card and chalkboards while listening to the different acts coming onto the stage behind me.

I'm particularly enjoying the latest act, a young teenage girl with the voice of an angel. I've managed to lose myself in her beautiful, melancholic songs for the last fifteen minutes and I'm sorry when I hear Ange's voice thanking her at the end of her set.

"Now, I'd like to introduce the next act," she says, while I focus on writing out *Trey's Cheddar Grits* with as steady a hand as possible despite my blurred vision. "I've known this person a long time and I know that while he's been in way more challenging environments than this, standing on a stage at an open mic night is possibly his biggest fear. So please kindly welcome my good friend, Connor Johnson."

My heart stops and my hand falls off the edge of the board trailing a long, messy line of chalk right through my tidy efforts. I turn around slowly, my eyes passing Ange as she looks at me anxiously from the side of the stage, until they land on the man standing in the center of it. He holds my gaze for several seconds then looks down at the paper in his hands. I notice they're shaking.

He looks up again and casts his gaze across the small audience.

"Someone extremely important to me came here once," he begins. "She told me about a poem she heard being read out on stage one time that meant a lot to her. So, for what it's worth, I'm going to read it now. There's a murmur of appreciation amongst some of the tables and I'm rooted to the seat. I don't know what's going on. Why is he here? Why is he reading my favorite F Scott Fitzgerald poem? I hold my breath as he begins.

*"For what it's worth:*
*it's never too late or, in my case,*
*too early to be whoever you want to be.*
*There's no time limit,*
*stop whenever you want.*
*You can change or stay the same,*
*there are no rules to this thing."*

He pauses and glances up at me. I simply stare, open-mouthed. He drops his eyes again to the piece of paper and continues to read.

*"We can make the best or the worst of it.*
*I hope you make the best of it.*
*And I hope you see things that startle you.*
*I hope you feel things you never felt before.*
*I hope you meet people with a different point of view.*
*I hope you live a life you're proud of."*

He raises his eyes again and looks right into my soul.

*"If you find that you're not,*
*I hope you have the courage to start all over again."*

He pauses, then folds the piece of paper and slides it into the back pocket of his jeans. Then he brings his mouth to the microphone again.

"Tawny Graham." My heart bangs against my ribcage. "I know now who I want to be and I'm choosing to change. You startle me. You've made me feel things I've never felt before. You make me want a life I'm proud of. But more than all of this, I want you to feel proud. I know I've hurt you badly, so if moving on and starting over is what will make you feel proud, I will turn away and let you go."

The audience follows his gaze to the back of the room, to me, and I can't move. Has Connor Johnson just stated, on an open mic stage no less, that he does actually want to be with me? That he's prepared to deal with the demons that still haunt him so we can be together? Those questions are still unanswered.

I'm grateful when Ange starts clapping at the side of the

stage and ushers on the next act. Connor walks forward and jumps off the small stage, not taking his eyes off me. It strikes me again just how beautiful he is, even more so now I think I'm seeing the real Connor Johnson—the one he's been hiding for the last five years. He threads himself through the few tables scattered between me and the stage, then walks up to me, stopping only a foot away, thankfully blocking out the stares of anyone who might want the next instalment.

He reaches out and takes hold of my hands, looking down at me as his hair flops over one eye. "I don't want to lose you," he says, softly. "I know I have to get help. I'm going to do it. I'm sick of running away from it, I'm sick of shutting everyone out. I want to be with you, more than anything in the world."

"Connor," I whisper. "You tried getting help before, remember?"

"I'll stick with it this time, I promise." He pulls me up to my feet and takes my face in his hands. "I promise." He kisses me softly on the lips and I inhale him until I'm dizzy. "I know what I've got to lose, and you're everything to me."

He kisses me again and I sink into him, oblivious to everyone around us. My hands hold the back of his neck and slide up into his hair, while he grips me tightly around the waist, holding me close. When I think I'm about to pass out from pleasure, he moves his lips down to my ear where he nuzzles against my neck.

"I know you don't need protecting, especially now you're out of harm's way" he whispers. "But the truth is, I want to protect you. I want to make sure you're safe and happy and you have everything you want."

I close my eyes letting his words flitter through my ears.

"Ok, but... I'm not going to break, Connor," I say, quietly.

He brings his lips back to mine and speaks as he presses against them. "Oh, I know you're not. I won't protect you in the bedroom, T."

His tongue sneaks between my lips and flicks against mine, then he pulls back again.

"In fact, I won't be held responsible for what I'm going to do to you in the bedroom. I haven't done half the things I want to do to you."

I pull back and look at him seriously. "I don't want you to suffer again, like last time."

"I won't. I promise. If you can wait a little while, I'm going to overcome this, ok?"

I nod, but before I can reply, his mouth has eclipsed mine and he's taken total control. And I can sense that this time it's not because he needs to. It's because he wants to.

# EPILOGUE

 onnor

TWO WEEKS HAVE PASSED since I brought Tawny back to Starling Key. It was eleven at night when we walked hand-in-hand to the bar behind the northeast wall, and I was surprised even the retirees didn't hear the claps and cheers we received when everyone realized we'd arrived. We've been pretty inseparable since then. We've somehow managed to resist having sex, and I've abstained completely from climaxing until I can sort myself out. But that doesn't mean I can't please Tawny, so that's what I've been doing every night, for hours on end, until she begs me to stop so she can sleep.

I've started an intensive therapy program supported by medication in the short term. My therapist told me to give it two weeks before resuming any sort of a sex life. I've been counting the days.

I walk past Tawny's desk and give her a wink as I head to

my office. I don't realize she's got up from her desk and followed me until I go to close the door.

"How can I help you?" I grin down at her.

"Oh, I just came to give you a preview," she says, sidling past me to my desk.

"A preview of what?" I follow her, greedily, with my eyes.

She turns around and shoots me a look of feigned innocence, then she knocks a bunch of paper to the floor. "Oops!"

"What are you doing?"

Instead of replying, she turns on the ball of her foot and bends over, her skirt rising so far up the back of her legs, I can see her ass. *Her ass.* I gulp.

"Are you not wearing underwear?" I'm amazed I still have a voice.

"No, Sir, I'm not. Is that bad?" She stands again and looks at me with her eyebrows raised.

"Jesus," I breathe out, checking my watch. "And I have to go another four hours knowing this." We both wanted it to be perfect, and safe. We'd planned on sleeping together in my dorm—it's familiar and I have everything I need there in case the worse happens and I do have another flashback.

"Not necessarily," she says, sauntering the couple of steps towards me.

"You're making this very difficult," I murmur.

Her face falls and she's suddenly serious.

"I'll respect if you don't want to do anything now, but Connor... I'm dying here. I feel like a freaking bitch on heat. Feel this," she takes my hand and places it between her legs. She's soaking.

I sink my fingers into her and her eyes roll backwards.

"Please, Connor."

She's begging me to fuck her.

"Oh hell," I gasp, withdrawing my hand and turning her to face the desk. I step back and flick the lock on the door, using the other to pop open my fly. I don't even need to maneuver myself towards her; my cock knows exactly where it's going. I reach around to finger her clit as I inch my way inside, both of us groaning with relief. It's like I belong here; like I've come home.

I move slowly at first, in and out, in and out. But it isn't long before she's thrusting herself backwards onto me, forcing me deeper, faster. I take hold of her hips and slow her down.

"I love you," she says, turning her head so I can hear. A moan leaves my throat because I have no words. The feeling of being inside her again is too much to contend with.

"I'm going to come already," she gasps. I press down on her clit and stroke her insides with my cock and she turns her head back towards the table in an attempt to muffle any sound. She tightens around me, drawing out my own orgasm. I forget everything as I empty myself into her warmth, still moving because I don't want to stop.

Before I pull out, I stroke my hands down her back.

"Thank you," I whisper.

"For what?"

"For being patient with me."

"I hardly call this being patient. I needed you Connor; I couldn't wait anymore."

"I don't mean right now," I almost chuckle. "I mean since we met. Thank you for persisting, for being convinced that this could work when I couldn't see past my fear."

She reaches behind her and takes my hand, pulling it to her lips where she kisses it softly.

"I love you," I say, feeling a flood of emotion surge up through my chest.

"I love you too," she whispers.

---

WE CLEAN ourselves up and I follow Tawny out of my office, watching as she sits back at her desk, shifting slightly against the sensation of having been fucked over mine. I'm cautiously optimistic that a flashback isn't coming my way, and I silently thank God I've been attending all those sessions, despite them being the most painful periods of time I've experienced since I returned home from Iraq.

I make my way down to the beach where the boys are having a quick break. I need to talk to them. There's a specific conversation we need to have—all six of us—and it's well overdue.

"Hey man," Carter passes me a soda and a plate of nachos. "How's it going?"

"Good," I smile. "Really good."

The faces on the rest of them are noticeably relaxed—more relaxed than I've seen them in a long time. I understand now that my behavior weighed on them more than I'd ever realized. Now that I'm getting help, the Starlings are off on vacation, things have quietened down and Christmas is around the corner, everyone seems lighter, happier.

"We need to talk," I begin. "There's one update from you all that I haven't yet received, and I haven't updated you all either. And it's about time."

"What are you talking about?" Isaac says, confused.

"The chat. We missed the pre-season chat with all of us together. I think we should have it now."

Grins appear on their faces as it becomes clear what I'm asking.

"Ok. I'll go first. Get it over with," Carter says. We all

turn to face him, not feeling too optimistic. "I'm going to give the General a bit of a break this season. He's been working hard, you know? Needs a rest." And with that, he shovels a handful of chips into his mouth and whips out his phone. I know he isn't swearing off women because his cock is tired. He's had his ego whacked. Lucy didn't want him because he couldn't provide, and now he thinks no woman is going to want him for the exact same reason. I give him a few seconds but he doesn't elaborate; for him, the conversation's over. As happy as I am for my own situation, I can't help but feel devastated for Carter. He always wanted the best for me and I want the same for him.

"Ok, bro'," I say. "Isaac?"

"Well, I have my eye on a couple of MILFs. Mrs. Carmichael in Villa twelve has made it clear she's interested."

"The wife of the guy who's off diving every day?" Luca chips in.

"That's the one. I get the impression they live completely separate lives."

"Yeah, he spends all day drooling over Autumn," Luca frowns. "I don't blame his wife for looking elsewhere."

"So, nothing happening with you and Autumn?" I ask him.

"Hey, I told you. We're just friends." His narrow and we all keep our mouths shut. "I've been hanging out with one of the temps anyway, if you must know."

"Which one?" I ask.

"Britney. Works in the restaurant."

That earns him a few impressed nods.

"Nice. Hudson?" I nod in his direction.

"I'm wide open this season, gentlemen."

Isaac laughs. "Maybe one of the Christmas guests will fancy a little Hudson-shaped present this year."

"Here's hoping," he grins, cocking his soda towards us then downing it in one.

"Ok, Connor," Carter says, and everyone goes quiet. "Your turn."

"C'mon guys, you know it wouldn't be fair to you if I threw my hat in the ring…" I start, and Carter punches me in the ribs. "Ok, ok…" I hold my hands up, then rest them on my knees. I take a deep breath and look around at their faces. They each look back at me, holding back smiles. In this moment I am consumed with gratitude for each of them— Carter, Isaac, Luca, Jax and Hud. They're my team, my family. They've stuck by me through thick and thin and I owe them everything. I can't hold back the words anymore. "I'm officially off the market…"

I don't get to say the rest of my spiel because I'm suddenly pushed to the ground, the guys landing on top of me, their arms flying everywhere in hugs and playful punches. After several minutes of almost-suffocation, they finally get off me and I brush the sand out of my face.

"It's about fucking time," they all say in unison.

We sit for another twenty minutes, chatting idly about girls, poker games, the holidays, and I feel—for the first time in all the years I've worked on this island—wholly and completely myself again.

When my phone rings and I recognize the number, even though I would never store the name in my phone, I get to my feet and nod to Carter who follows.

"Connor Johnson."

"It's Mario."

"I know. What can I do for you?"

There's a heavy sigh at the other end of the phone. "Connor, I need a favor."

"Another favor?" I raise my eyebrow at Carter.

"If I remember correctly, I repaid the last one, saving you from getting your hands dirty."

He's talking about his agreement to 'get rid' of Stefano Morelli, so I didn't have to.

"Ok, fine," I sigh. "What do you need?"

I listen as he relays his request and Carter watches me for some reaction.

"She can definitely dance?"

Carter looks at me, questioning.

"When will she get here?"

Mario gives me a few more details, then we hang up.

"What was that about?"

I take a deep breath. This could go one of two ways. I actually don't mind which—either one would justify popcorn.

"Remember the girl who arrived by boat with the children? Seleste?"

Carter doesn't flinch but I know he's working hard not to. "Yeah."

"Apparently her husband-to-be is a little… shall we say, tied up at the moment. Wedding's on hold. Bianchi wants us to keep her busy for six months."

"What?"

"Apparently she's a dancer. We could provide dance classes for guests, or she could do shows, depending on how good she is."

"Are you serious? She's coming here?" Carter appears shocked but I know my friend. His pulse is racketing beneath all those tats. I know the two of them gave each other hell when we escorted her and the children across the island, but the back and forth brought Carter back to life. And after everything that's happened with Lucy, he could use a little excitement.

"Yes. Tomorrow."

"You're kidding me."

"Nope."

"She's going to be a freaking nightmare," he warns.

"Your freaking nightmare, Carter. I would like you to be her boss."

# EXTENDED EPILOGUE

arter

I STARE AT CONNOR, open mouthed.

"You're kidding me," I repeat.

"About which part?" he asks, with a look of mock innocence that I want to wipe clean off his face.

"Both. The fact she's coming here at all, and the fact you want me to be her damn boss. I've no idea how to manage a dancer, for Christ's sake, and did you hear the woman when she got out of that boat? She's got a mouth like a dumpster and she's one of Bianchi's people. I mean, do you need any more reasons why this is a mistake? It is such a bad idea."

But even as I say the words, I know they are purely for show; my heart isn't in them. Because although I only had a brief window in which to make my acquaintance with Seleste Ortiz, I felt a whole bunch of feelings I'd never felt before, and a large part of me wants them back.

I remember the moment like it was yesterday.

While we stood at the shore watching the kids walk out of the sea, my eyes went back to the boat. It was as though they were drawn like a magnet. Even when I heard Tawny come running down the beach, being chased by Stefano Morelli, one of Bianchi's crew, my eyes didn't waver. I heard a gun cock and Connor growl but the sounds all merged into one when the door swung open again and a long, slim leg reached out like a cat uncurling after a long sleep. A hand came next, gripping the edge of the doorframe with tapered nails, then a sheath of long, ebony hair.

A vision emerged from the small doorway and unfolded slowly, taking a little bit more of my breath with each second. When she finally straightened up, my eyes took on a life of their own and scanned from the crown of her head, down past her feline eyes, sharp nose, perfect, pouting lips and delicately pointed chin, to the slim peaks of her shoulders, rounded, womanly hips and skyscraper legs. *Fuck me.*

She stepped seamlessly out of the boat and walked through the water, past the children and directly towards me. She stopped just feet away, undeterred by the fact I was aiming the barrel of my gun at her head. She didn't even blink. Somehow I knew it wasn't the first time she'd been held up at gunpoint; she exhibited a fearlessness that came only from placing very little importance on the value of life.

I stepped forward and brought the cold steel to her skin. Her eyes locked with mine and it felt for a second as though we were the only two people on the beach. I remember asking her who the fuck she was.

She turned her face slowly back to mine and almost broke me with a seductive smile. Her voice was brimming with smug satisfaction when she replied.

"I'm Seleste Ortiz, soon to be Seleste Rodriguez, wife of Antonio."

Those words ignited pure anger in my belly. I'd never had the pleasure of meeting Antonio Rodriguez, but I'd heard of him. Everyone in our line of work had heard of him. Mario Bianchi might have been the poster boy for his self-styled mob, but Rodriguez was the devil in the detail. He was pure venom. No one crossed him. He had the conscience of a caged animal and more blood on his hands than Ted freaking Bundy. If this woman was lined up to be his wife, she was probably no innocent.

When we finally got them to the car, I got the shock of my life. After one put-down too many, I stepped right up to her. I needed to intimidate her, or at least *affect* her. I can hardly remember what was said as my head was suddenly filled with her scent. After days spent on the ocean, it was pure her, pure intoxication. There was talk of fingers and promises, I remember that much, and although my sleepless nights are still filled with Lucy and her parting words that I would never be the one, my scant moments of sleep send me Seleste and the feel of her skin, the graze of her breath.

I became aware that although I'd never met Rodriguez, I hated him with an intensity that scared me. I knew she was joking that night; she was playing with me. But she knew exactly what she was doing. She was showing me exactly what *he* was going to get—those eyes, those lips, those legs, that attitude. She held my gaze as she flicked her hair and walked towards the car. Everyone else's eyes were on Morelli being stuffed into the trunk, but mine were on her, and hers were on me. I knew in those few seconds I'd be seeing her again. I just had no idea it would be so soon.

And now, she's coming here, to taunt me.

To show me more of what I can't have.

And I know, no matter what happens, I can't have her.

Because she's his.

The end.

Thank you for reading *The Brain! Go to*
**https://bit.ly/TheBrainXtra** to join my mailing list and
download the ***Deleted Scenes***, for FREE!

If you enjoyed Connor's story, go to
**https://www.januaryjamesauthor.com/the-brawn** for links
to read Carter's story, ***The Brawn.***

## THANK YOU

Thank you for reading *The Brain*, the first book in the Starling Key series. If you are happy to take a few seconds to give this book a star rating or leave a short review wherever you purchased this book, it would help me immensely!

If you enjoyed *The Brain*, you can also pre-order the second book in the series, The Brawn. Read the blurb overleaf.

Thank you so much for reading my words. Your support means the world. X

# THE BRAWN

**Seleste – F – Spanish origin – meaning:** *celestial, heavenly*

There's a joke if ever I heard one. Seleste Ortiz is my idea of hell.

Feisty, cocky, and out of my league, and the new star of Starling Key.

The most beautiful woman I've ever seen.

The most infuriating woman I've ever met.

But there's more to Seleste than meets the eye.

Behind that tough exterior is a scared little girl.

When her arranged marriage is put on hold, she comes back to Starling Key, to kill me slowly.

When her flirting goes too far and I give in after just one night, we wake a beast that won't go back to sleep.

Just six months.

Then we have to stop.

Then I have to watch her return to her drug lord fiancé.

And there's one small problem.

I don't want to let her go.

# ACKNOWLEDGMENTS

This book took me on quite a journey so there are some people I owe huge thanks to for supporting me through it and helping me make it the best it can be. First of all, Chris. You are always open to my ideas and so extremely generous with your support. I honestly don't think I would be six books down—or all the other things I am today—without you. And our little girl, for giving me even more of a reason to do this.

A huge thanks to my besties Sarah and Seema for the cover input and critique. Apologies for the random deluges of man chests. It was so important I got the right cover for this book and I think we nailed it. And to that end, a massive thank you to Michelle for the incredible image, and to Tommy for letting me immortalise you as Connor Johnson.

Next, my betas, Michelle, Kristen, Elke and Sara. I gave you quite the task with this one and you stepped up like the amazing humans you are. Thank you for the time you invested in helping me make this book what it now is. Thanks again to my Boss Grrrls—you've been with me since book one and I'm running out of ways to tell you how grateful I am for your support. And to my wonderful readers who make this so worthwhile. In the beginning I wrote for myself, but hearing about your connection with the characters I create spurs me on to write more and write better.

And finally, to all the authors who've shared their own journeys and experiences this year, from whom I've learned so much. You've each inspired me in different ways and I hope one day I'm privileged enough to be able to meet you in person, because you're all just so cool. Melanie Harlow, Elle Thorpe, Ines Johnson, Kandi Steiner, Skye Warren, Willow Winters and Ivy Smoak, thanks for your wise words—and the TikToks.

Forever grateful x

# ABOUT THE AUTHOR

January James lives in the smallest cottage in East Sussex with her husband, daughter and imaginary cockapoo (she will get one, one day!) Until recently, she inhabited the fast-paced, adrenalin-fuelled workplaces she writes about, as a communications professional. Now she spends her days dreaming up new characters and stories and trying her best to avoid indoor soft play.

[instagram icon] instagram.com/thejanuaryjames
[facebook icon] facebook.com/januaryjamesauthor
[goodreads icon] goodreads.com/januaryjames
[bookbub icon] bookbub.com/authors/january-james

# ALSO BY JANUARY JAMES

**Square Mile series**

A Class Act

He Turned

Chasing Flames

**Fémmes Féroces series**

Man Eater

Dirty Diana

**Starling Bay series**

The Brain

The Brawn

Ingram Content Group UK Ltd.
Milton Keynes UK
UKHW040806240723
425668UK00003B/192